Crocodile Soup

Julia Darling was a novelist, poet and playwright. Born in Winchester in 1956 in the house that Jane Austen died which partially inspired her first novel *Crocodile Soup* (1988); it was long listed for the Orange Prize for fiction. Her second novel *The Taxi Drivers Daughter* (Penguin 2003) was set in Newcastle upon Tyne where she moved to in 1980; it was long listed for the Man Booker Prize and short listed for the Encore Award. She wrote many plays for stage and radio, including *Manifesto for the New City* for Northern Stage and *Appointments* and *Personal Belongings* for Live Theatre. An anthology of her plays *Eating the Elephant and other Plays* was published by New Writing North in 2005. The title play was about breast cancer which Julia was diagnosed with in 1994.

Through her poetry collections *Sudden Collapses in Public Places* (2003), and *Apology for Absence* (2004), she sought to open up the language around illness and healthcare, particularly breast cancer. Julia's on-line weblog was adapted by Jackie Kay into *The Waiting Room* and was dramatised on Radio 4 in 2007. Julia was Fellow in Literature and Health at Newcastle University and edited *The Poetry Cure* (Bloodaxe, 2004) with Cynthia Fuller. In 2003 Julia was awarded the Northern Rock Writers Award and in 2014 was honoured by the Newcastle Gateshead Initiative with a Local Heroes bronze plaque in the city. She had made Newcastle her home since 1980 until she died in 2005. To find out more about h

Crocodile Soup

Julia Darling

This edition published by Mayfly Press, 2015

Mayfly Press
Chase House
4 Mandarin Road
Rainton Bridge
Houghton le Spring
DH4 5Ra

First published in Great Britain by Anchor, a division of Transworld Publishers Ltd, 1998

Paperback ISBN 9781909486157

Ebok ISBN 9781909486164

Printed by Martins, cover design by courage.

Acknowledgements

I would like to thank the following people for their support during the writing of this book: Bob White and Jane Whitely for hosting the writing of the first draft in Fremantle, Australia; Bernard and Mary Loughlin at the Tyrone Guthrie Centre in Co Monaghan, Ireland where two subsequent drafts were written; John Murray of Panurge Books for believing in me; Jenny Attala and Chrissie Glazebrook from the literature department at Northern Arts for their continual help and support. Tom Shakespeare, Nicy Rushton, Wendy Robertson, Graeme Rigby, Josephine Darling, Karin Young and Charlie Hardwick for their constructive comments. Debbie Taylor, Andrea Badenoch, Jane Harris, Penny Smith and Kitty Fitzgerald for sharing the agony; Gillian Allnut and Margaret Wilkinson for their inspirational sessions 'Writing From Inside Out'; Sean O'Brien for being there; Bridget O'Connor for her inspiration; Wendy McEvoy and Dave Eadington at Siren Films for their encouragement.

Jane Bradish-Ellames at Curtis Brown for her sound advice. Also, my mother, Vicky Darling, for her love of words, and my friend Jan Johannes for listening. I also gratefully acknowledge the support from the Arts Council of England, who gave me the financial space to finish the novel.

For Bev, Scarlet, and Florrie.

The First Letter

Dear Gert,

I know I haven't been in touch for some time, but then neither have you. Cameron died last week, of a brain haemorrhage. He collapsed in the middle of playing my favourite tune, 'Making the Waves Sleep', at the local club. We used to go there every Saturday night. I'm not sure what to do now. We've been living in a small flat near Waterloo Station, but the landlord wants me out and I've got nowhere to go.

I was wondering if I could stay with you. Please get in touch soon, as I'm already in arrears.

With love
Your mother, Jean

A Vision In The Stuffed Bird Room

The day that I got my mother's letter it was autumn and the air was thick with the fumes of sparklers and the breath of nervous dogs. I stuffed the letter behind the radiator, along with various questionnaires and memos. Upstairs, the museum was closed. I was looking into the caverns of an Egyptian pot, lost in a hieroglyphic daydream, when I heard a tapping sound coming from the stuffed bird collection which was right above my room. For a moment I thought the frozen birds had stepped down from their perches and were pecking the long oak floor with their beaks. I put down the fragment and wiped my spectacles. I frowned. The sound had a rhythm.

I walked nervously up the wide stone steps; past the fossilized turtle and the depressed newts, and into the bird room. I peered through a glass panel containing a golden eagle. I blinked. There in the half darkness was a figure. She was dancing a tango on the empty floor to an audience of perplexed birds. She tapped and circled, concentrating with the most extraordinary poise. She was holding an invisible partner, I watched her, mesmerized. Then, just as she pivoted and turned, she raised her head and saw me. She stopped dancing. I recognized her. She was the new girl who worked in the canteen. We stared at each other in shock. Then she disappeared.

The next day, my colleague Theobald, who worked with insects, told me the girl serving coffee was called Eva. When he said her name a light went on somewhere inside me. Suddenly everything was illuminated. I noticed the dust everywhere; and the fact that at night fine specks drifted from old exhibits onto my papers, so that when I drew my hands across them in the morning, they left a path. I realized that as I sat there, dust was gathering on the crown of my head.

I was in the middle of labelling a vast collection of ancient artefacts. It had taken me years to reach this position. I had burrowed my way down; from lofty university campuses, to archaeological digs, to the reading rooms of basement archives, and finally to a comfortable underworld, an archaeological institute in the centre of a Northern city, beneath a municipal museum. Not far from where I sat there were bridges and council estates, shops selling mops for seventy-five pence, shopping malls teeming with Northern people carrying plastic bags full of consumer goods that would be eaten or played with, and then discarded, and buried beneath the ground. This was the kind of thing I thought about, and which sometimes could make me have panic attacks the size of Egypt.

But other days I wondered if anyone actually read my well-researched labels. It could take six months to trace the exact origin of a cup, or a brooch. I rarely saw the public, although I heard them sometimes, rattling through the tannoy system, dropping coins and munching mints.

I liked my work. It was intricate and elaborate. It absorbed me into long trances when I forgot everything. It was a passion.

Eva looked ordinary in the canteen. She was in her twenties; she wore an overall. She had strong eyes, short modern hair and a high forehead. She reminded me of a figurehead of a ship. She ignored me. I sat, drinking her coffee, which was strong and frothy, watching her.

I felt as if I had discovered a totally intact early Egyptian scroll and that I should handle the find with care.

But I was also not myself; romantically or professionally. I was not used to emotion. The institute was not generally an emotive place. It was good for shelving and filing, and storing, and that's why I liked it.

But after the day when I first saw Eva it occurred to me that I may as well be an exhibit myself, and that maybe lunch was more interesting than history.

My Mother Told Me Not To Speak To Strangers

When I was six, our kitchen was very cool and quiet, with a red waxy floor. There was always a bee struggling against the window pane. I could do anything I wanted. Our cake tins were full of Victoria sponges. We had butter on everything.

I opened the back door and stepped into a side street. Outside it was a sleepy afternoon, and wood pigeons were cooing. My twin brother Frank was playing his violin, and it made this carping sound that spoilt the peace of everything, but Frank was like that. My father, George, had gone to post a letter. My mother was having her afternoon rest. I had some bread in my pocket and a threepenny bit from the toby jug in my father's parlour. I believed that I could go anywhere that I wanted. So I walked along a bit, until I came to an area I didn't really know. There was a lily pond with mammoth goldfish that were too cramped to swim and bumped into each other. I stood on some grey steps and threw my bread at them. Some of the crumbs landed on the water lilies so that a few birds flew down and ate them. I hung about, watching, for some time.

The stranger was long and green, like a bottle. His neck was a stalk and his eyes closed upwards. He appeared to have grown from behind a bush. He came up very close, smelling of dead birds trapped in a shed. He looked down at me with his great cowlike eyes and I knew he was afraid of me. Then he opened his mouldy coat and showed me his penis, as if it was all he had to offer. I stared at it without blinking. It was like a version of Frank's new telescope. It had rings round it that were similar to the tube that ran from the back of our washing machine. I nodded, and he gratefully folded it away into the rusty linen of his old trousers. There was nothing more to say so I slipped from the tow of his shadow and ran, looking back for a second to see him shrug and gulp as if he was out of breath.

When I got home everyone had woken up. The kitchen was full of appliances whirring and bubbling and my mother, Jean, was smoking a Dunhill cigarette. The packet was blue and white and smoke filled the room. I hadn't realized she smoked. I was quite surprised.

She asked me where I'd been and I said, 'To look at a pond.'

She said, 'That's too far, you might have been accosted by strangers or something.'

Then she stubbed out the cigarette in a matchbox and stuffed it into the bin, while I scampered to the toby jug to replace the threepenny bit.

Origins

Jean had two babies altogether, who found themselves transplanted from her relatively safe cave into an uncertain environment. We dived from water to air, one after another, landing in an embroidered basket that stayed for months by our mother's bed. I was the first and then there was Frank.

Apparently I was beautiful, with diamond eyes and waving victorious arms, while my twin Frank was limp and runtish, with a streak of pimples and a flattened nose. He was grey and I was pink. He lay stomach down, examining the whiteness of his pillow, while I gazed angrily at the ceiling, kicking my legs, as if I was trying to climb back up an impossible staircase. They called me Gertrude, apparently in memory of my dead grandmother, but I think they did it to counteract my looks. I was obviously not a Gertrude, and the name quickly got shortened to Gert, which was even worse. I grew into my name unwillingly, and I often wonder what would have happened if they had called me Emily or Lucretia, or some other name with an aura of dignity. Because of my name my legs are now short and my hair is heavy and flat. I also have my grandmother's thick ankles and slow jaw.

Jean was only twenty-two. A year before she had been learning how to dance. I was one of the things she wanted then.

You see, I was born in the wrong place. I should have emerged on the west coast of Scotland, or in some wild borderland, or near a crashing ocean, but instead I was dragged by my head into a room in a market town in a southern English valley, surrounded by sharp flint walls. It sounds safe but it wasn't. Rocks circled hungrily above its spires, and a river named the Cut, filled with fine green hairy weeds, razored through it. Odd gargoyles peered down from the edges of church roofs with swelling eyes and leering tongues. Old ladies carried rat poison in their shopping bags. Disintegrating drunks urinated in the public fountain, rolling their plastered eyes at church men and choirboys.

I found myself in a lopsided Georgian house with beady windows and faulty guttering. The house was elegant but nervous. It sat tremulously at the bottom of a winding hill, wrapped in a shawl of ivy, fearing subsidence from above.

My mother never spoke of her childhood, and if her parents phoned up she would hide in the downstairs toilet.

I imagine she materialized at a ball. At least there was little evidence of her before then. She had been encased in a strict and starched childhood and made to eat cabbage disguised as tomato.

She wore a hushed cream dress with gloves to her elbows. She had made the dress sitting under a forty-watt light bulb in a back room wallpapered with thorny pink roses. Downstairs her own mother straightened the antimacassars and hummed, marvelling at her daughter's eyes which had recently mutated from childish grey to blue. She had also developed thigh muscles. Jean was a filly on the make; looking for a home with non-stick saucepans and an account at a department store. She had studied the manuals, and this was how you got one; by smiling, by dancing, by being a girl with broad hips and plucked eyebrows.

Lines of men and women faced each other on the grilling dance floor. The women wanted to be picked and were afraid of being left behind like abandoned gas masks. They craned towards the men like flowers to an unreliable sun, offering their looks and naked shoulders; their domestic muscle and wartime childhoods. Everyone was out to forget.

Yet Jean was distressed. She had an inappropriate imagination. Her personality wriggled uncomfortably under her girdle. Her friend Mabel had floated off with a man who had brackish teeth. She wanted to take off her red patent shoes and throw them at the next man who proffered his fat hand. She was tired of terse, trivial conversation. She concentrated on a vision of an array of modern domestic appliances, from automatic dishwashers to car hoovers. When George clumsily pushed her onto the dance floor she thought of Kenwood mixers.

There was not a trace of bright colour on the dance floor, apart from Jean's shining shoes. It was predominantly black and white; a flurry of swirling opposites, magnetically pulling forwards and away.

When the band broke the women gathered in the toilet to swear and stuff their brassieres with pads, and to pluck unruly eyebrows into flirtatious arcs. They dabbed away their sweat with powder puffs and revitalized their smiles for the next hunt. They rubbed their armpits vigorously with sweet scents to hide the smell of their unfeminine opinions. They rummaged in dirty handbags for the ends of lipsticks, and topped up the thick foundation that covered the ironic lines around their mouths.

Once alone they stopped trying to be women and became loose and funny, as if their bodies were clothes released from their hangers. They lounged lewdly over the edges of the washbasins. They calculated the bank accounts and backgrounds of potential partners. They wanted servants and patios, leisure and rose gardens, and bedrooms to rest in. They didn't know then, these clever women, how those floral, middle-class rooms would become prisons and how they would end up bewildered, standing at dawn in the garden in a pair of old trousers trying to work out what went wrong.

And the war girls who conspired with Jean in the toilet, lending her sanitary protection and heaving the pedals and handles of the ghastly incinerator, were the same women who pioneered premenstrual tension in post-war suburbs. They made it into soufflés; they polished floors with it, and they pushed prams on its onerous power.

Jean did the best she could on this occasion with the blood that seeped out from under her creamy gown. She plugged herself up with bandage and pad, which made her too heavy below and increased her sense of mastlessness. She returned to the punishing dance floor and engaged herself in the Dashing White Sergeant. She knew that George would propose. He had a glazed, dysfunctional look and his big hands were caught on the hooks of her bodice. Their steps collided as they always would, and with horror she realized that blood was running down her new stockings, dripping into the net of her underskirt, and finally cascading in clots onto the parquet flooring. She tried to pull away, her heel skidding in a glutinous red drop, but it was their turn to skip under the arches. No one noticed, apart from a black trumpet player, called Cameron Drinkwater, whose eyes rolled in his head and who fixed on Jean for one long sympathetic note. He was the man she should have married. When she could she ran to the toilet. Three friends galloped after her, seeing the whites of her eyes as she fled. They gathered around her in a life belt and escorted her back to the coven of toilet bowls and basins, to swab her down and lend her corsetry and courage.

I sometimes think of the men who danced briefly alone after those women had gone, standing puzzled on the dance floor, holding invisible partners for a second, before turning and walking back to their table.

I feel sorry for them. Those men.

Incidental Thought

Perhaps it will be all right, I thought. Perhaps, when I go to work, there will be peace, and Theobald will stop jumping from foot to foot, and Eva will no longer be beautiful. Perhaps they will realize that the lottery grant was a big mistake. The Head Curator will go on a sabbatical, and things will stay as they were. We will all slide back into our lamplit rooms and watch history from a safe distance. We will be able to keep it behind glass, where it can fascinate but not hurt us.

Family Life

Can I tell you how much I loved my mother? I loved her like a dog loves an old bone. Then, when I was just a comma in the kink of her arm, I gazed at her perfect blond face, her reticent eyebrows, her heavy eyelashes, her scarlet Bombay lips. She smelt of crisp meringue and she said words like, 'Miraculous'. She was very pale. I heard people commenting on her tubercular, romantic complexion.

My brother and I competed for her elegant smiles, her coochy-coos, her naked body. We knew every mark on her. We knew her like a weatherman knows his isobars, like a beaver knows its twigs. When George walked into the room we clung on to Jean as if she was a ship and George was a storm. Poor George. He had started to smoke a pipe and sucked his way through our first year.

*   *   *

As soon as each child could walk we were handed a bottle and sent from our mother's bedroom to a room at the end of an immense corridor. The room was called the Furthest Nursery. The journey took several hours. I remember stumbling into cupboards and dangling from crooked banisters trying to find my way. When I eventually got there Frank was waiting. The room was large and white with expectant toys sitting on painted shelves.

Once the door was closed we were sealed off from the rest of the house. It was in this room that Frank bent my pliant limbs, and it was here that I coached my army of one-legged, shaven dolls. It might as well have been a forest outside the door, as we rarely went out. Sometimes Jean brought us meals on a tray, or appeared with clean clothes and ushered us downstairs to meet a relative or a neighbour before sending us back up again.

At moments like these I clung to her legs and screamed for mercy. I even bit her long white fingers. She never smacked me. I remember long hours in a playpen. I think some grandparents were there. I saw a wrinkled tongue and some creased up eyes shaking a rattle in front of me. When you're wailing everything else is very quiet. I grew to like the sound of hoovers.

The house was complicated and difficult to clean. It was full of unnecessary space; box rooms and ante-rooms and sheds, sculleries and parlours. It was designed by Georgian midgets. Jean, defeated by its nooks, hired a cleaner called Carmen who wielded a dangerous brush and had horsy black hair. Her arms bulged out from the sleeves of her blouse, and she had large and potent breasts that Frank and I tried to recreate with cushions. She brought us treats wrapped in newspaper that looked like sweets swept up from a factory floor. Then she would put on a pinafore with flaming summer flowers printed all over it, and strap cricket pads to both her knees. After that we left her alone. Carmen did not like to be spoken to while she was cleaning. If we crept past, backs pressed to the wall to avoid her damp, heaving back, she scowled at us, and even swiped at our ankles with her yellow chamois leather. George lurked around her with interest, but I never saw her speak to him. She sang operatically into her bucket, and polished everything until it gasped with exhaustion and gleamed with fear. Her rumbling arms could be heard from the bilious depths of the house. When she had gone her presence continued to resound throughout the hallways.

We grew steadily on iron tablets and spoonfuls of cod liver oil. We were difficult to catch and wouldn't come downstairs to have our photographs taken. We were busy frightening each other; making poisonous pastes from Vim and mustard, or playing unhappy families with the one-legged dolls. Frank lit Bunsen burners and fried crystals with my dolls' cookery set. The room was acrid with burnt plastic, and tortured teddies. Downstairs Jean was redecorating the dining room, or folding pale green napkins into doves' tails. Meanwhile, George gravitated to the only room in the house with a high ceiling, which was a tall parlour with small anxious windows, where he looked down ruefully at sheets of blotting paper, or drew diagrams of tiny vermicelli wires on graph paper. If we cascaded down the stairs in search of string or sharp needles, toasting forks or live wood lice, Jean put her thin finger to her soft lips and told us that he was busy. I would peek through the keyhole and see him sitting by a fire, looking helplessly at lengths of rope in his hands, and twisting them into knots, his big forehead wincing and furrowing with the effort, his pitted cheeks lit up by the fire. He looked like an exhibit in a waxwork museum.

We only saw him at breakfast.

Each morning George boiled an egg with scientific precision, as if he were conducting an experiment. First he punctured the egg with a sterilized needle, then he lowered it slowly into boiling water on a silver spoon. He turned the egg-timer upside down and watched it intently as the water bubbled. Then when the egg was cooked he placed it in a heavy china egg cup and sliced its top off with one blow of his Egg Knife, spooning the contents into his mouth in less than three shovels. Then, when the egg was scraped clean we would squeak, 'Daddy, look at the bird on the fence!' and obediently he would look up with exaggerated surprise, while one of us turned the eggshell upside down in the egg cup.

'Daddy, here's your second egg!' we chorused.

He guffawed then, and roared 'A second egg! How kind you are!' and crashed his shining teaspoon down on the empty shell that shattered into tiny fragments.

Then he pretended to cry in desperate, grieving sobs, and we watched him, horrified and open-mouthed.

The theatrical nature of our lives was enhanced by a mysterious line of people that drifted past the front door, looking vaguely confused, watching our house as if it was under glass. I thought perhaps they had heard about my beautiful mother, and had come to see for themselves, but one day George took me outside and lifted me high up on his bony shoulders and showed me the plaque that was fixed above our front door: IN THIS HOUSE HARRIET SMILES LIVED AND DIED 1821-1870.

'She wrote poetry books,' he said, turning to nod at a group of Japanese scholars, who stared back at us through photographic lenses.

Our lives were acted out in front of this perpetual audience who peered through the windows holding heavy cameras and binoculars, pressing their faces to the glass with their hands cupping out the light.

They saw George, bent over strands of rope, knotting the days away, and if they stepped back and craned to see into higher windows they might catch a mirror reflection of Jean, dabbing her ears with Tweed, lying on her wide bed, mentally calculating the worth of her silver knives and forks, ignoring the faint stench of burning plastic drifting up the stairs, fearing that all the money would be spent and she must eat cabbage and brown paper again.

Like monkeys in a zoo we became accustomed to being stared at, but their stares did not really see us. We were just shadows flitting behind the thick glass windows. My shadow inhabits photograph albums all over the world. I still worry about that; that bits of me are caught behind cellophane in other people's living rooms.

Someone To Look After Me

My last relationship was with a linguist called Barbara. I met her in Paradise, a women's bar behind the bus station. She was wearing a low-cut dress with several straps that left indented marks on her clavicles. Her lipstick was smudged, and her eyebrows were plucked into an expression of continual shock. She looked out of place in Paradise because everyone else had short barber's haircuts and wore denim shirts, or vests, or jackets with the collars turned up (apart from the occasional huddled group in the corner wearing bobble hats, stripy scarves and donkey jackets who had come from an animal rights meeting). Barbara was very feminine and had no idea how to swagger.

I bought her a gin and tonic. We were both alone and reading novels, which initially made conversation easy. After we had looked at each other's books, however, we were both plunged into bleak embarrassment, unable to return to our reading or look one another in the eye. I looked at my hands, which are both wide and bony and Barbara said, 'That's a nice ring. Is it an antique?'

'It was my aunt's,' I said, then, 'are you meeting somebody?'

'No,' said Barbara. 'I'm new.'

New to what, I thought.

'I haven't told my mother. How do you really know that you're...?' Barbara leant towards me, her dress gaping.

'Ages. Since I first saw Dusty Springfield.'

We looked around the bar room together. There were PE teachers and headmistresses and lawyers and beach guards. There were shopgirls and window cleaners and hairdressers and actors. I started to tell Barbara about another bar that had closed now that was down by the river, but the jukebox drowned me out and all the women were singing along with Tina Turner. I suddenly imagined we are all on a great cruise ship, voyaging together, the boat rocking from side to side, the jukebox playing and playing until it squeaked and gasped with the effort. I shouted over at Barbara.

'This is all we've got!' even though it made no sense. Barbara burst into tears. I put my arm round her and my bare skin stuck to her neck. I kept thinking about primitive vessels with pieces missing, leaving unmendable, echoing holes, and how all those women would disappear into the daylight, dissolving like soluble aspirin. Barbara's face was smeared with gin. She looked like the type who cried if you showed her affection... I did and she cried for weeks. Sleeping together was always wet, but not in the erotic sense. Her straps got in the way and she ground her teeth at night which drove me crazy.

That's the general course of things. I take off my spectacles, put on hair gel and a leather jacket and meet women in bars and take them home. I look after them. In the end I stop listening to them, and they leave and go somewhere else. They write to me, and tell me how their lives have changed and how they have found themselves in Blackpool or the Gambia. I am always part of their former lives, an incidental step in their struggle for identification and self-awareness. That's how it was with Barbara, who went to Marseille. We left the bar together and tottered home. I showed her my collection of Egyptian nick-nacks. She fell asleep, her dress crumpled.

It would not be like this with Eva, I thought. Eva would be consistent. She was not the type that needed to be held up with scaffolding. She had no special scent that she kept in a bottle until the dark hours when it was safe to splash it on her wrists and smell out others with the same pong. All right, she was probably straight, but people change, and underneath her overall she had a significant swagger. I would change her, I thought. Then she could look after me.

The Ruination Of Jean's Legs

The first spell in the nursery was really very happy. There was some physical discomfort, but most of the time I was lost in some other landscape, not in a house at all, protected by the mess of my imagination. Things started to deteriorate one day when Frank and I reached a terrible stalemate in a furious night-long battle between the men of Lego and the strange doll army. By morning both sides lay massacred on the floor, and there was nothing left to kill. The atmosphere was so bad that I escaped down the narrow corridor looking for somewhere to examine my bruises, leaving Frank pulling the last hairs from an innocent doll's bewildered head.

At the top of a landing I smelt roasting dinner and heard tinkling voices, the colour of confetti. Guests, I thought.

When guests came to the house Jean often pretended that she had no children, and put on airs that were made of brandy and aspic, and demanded sophisticated conversation. I carried on upstairs, and went into Jean's bedroom.

I went straight to the cupboard. I was completely naked as Frank had thrown all my clothes out of the window. The cupboard was as large as a room and was filled with feathery dresses and sulky coats, huddling together in the dark. I crouched among a row of viciously spiked shoes. I could hear Frank prowling through the upper corridors holding a flaming torch, with a plastic bag pulled over his head.

I climbed further in, over hat boxes and shoe horns, and that's when I saw the pair of red shoes, wrapped in a fragile cloud of white tissue paper.

They stood brightly beneath Jean's wedding veil, which was made of garlic skins and silver fish. I touched the shoes. They smelt warm, as if they had recently been on someone's feet. I put them to my ear, and heard a distant trumpet playing jazz, and then I put them on. I pulled Mother's veil from the peg and hung it over my face. I felt airy and diaphanous. I wondered if I might be invisible.

I stepped out of the cupboard. It must have been Sunday because the stairs stank of gravy. I tiptoed down to the first landing, glancing down a long corridor to see Frank at the top of a winding staircase preparing a lethal and complex trap for me with drawing pins and a pair of sock suspenders. He didn't see me as I glided past in my splendour. I navigated the lower landings and the uneven stairs, leaving imprints in the carpets with my high heels. In the dining room they were clinking, purring and giggling. I pushed open the door and smiled proudly.

The room was filled with bulky suburbians, and a grandmother with wired teeth. They turned to me fiercely and put their sherry glasses down. I started to whirl around, with my arms outstretched, in a giddy circle. My body seemed to take on its own momentum and, spinning, I crashed into one of the guests, spilling brown-coloured drink down his white shirt. Jean was shrieking. George was guffawing. In the oven a lamb was just beginning to burn. I fell backwards onto the floor, banging my head on someone's pointed shoe.

There was a long, baking pause.

'Someone has been where they shouldn't!' lipped a man with poodle whiskers.

Jean snatched the veil from my head. My body was immediately cold. The grandmother made a slurping sound. Jean caught my wrist and ankle, and scooped me up. The last red shoe dangled from my toe as if it hung from the tip of a tongue.

She carried me up the stairs, snarling, and stormed down the long corridor to the Furthest Nursery and tripped on the sock suspender, dropping me as she tumbled.

It should have ended there, the small domestic accident during Sunday dinner, but instead it expanded into a full-length feature. Frank and I stared with wide-open dolly eyes as Jean began to fall down the chasm of spiky stairs, banging her fragile head over and over again. She slumped into unconsciousness around a potted plant. Her feet seemed to be pointing the wrong way.

I think that Frank disappeared. George phoned an ambulance.

I thought I'd killed her.

Downstairs the guests sat in ecclesiastical silence.

And I opened my eyes and saw the red shoes walking back up the stairs, by themselves.

I suppose that was the start of it; the hallucinations, if that's what they were.

The incident of the Red Shoes permanently injured Jean. She spent some time in hospital, and her ankles were never as fluid again. (One was broken, the other badly sprained. She also had three stitches in her head.) She was less connected, and her whole being became more glassy.

Jean never mentioned this incident, but I think of it every day. I wonder, if she had retained the agility of her legs, if she would have been a happier person. On the other hand, if her legs had been stronger then she might have run off. Frank was never punished for his part in Jean's accident. George observed him as if he was an enigma, or a trick question that they couldn't work out the answer to. Frank, on the other hand, had an answer for everything. He never even looked guilty.

Eva

On firework night I saw Eva meeting another woman under a lamp post. Eva had taken off her overall and was standing dreamily in a pool of ochre light opposite the institute, when a fierce woman appeared with arms outstretched, apologizing for her lateness. She kissed Eva on both cheeks, and Eva smiled calmly. The two of them were like night and day. Eva was pale with moon-coloured skin, and her friend was hot and summery with bright clothes and curling ginger hair. As the woman spoke I saw her reach up to Eva's face and wipe away a smudge of lipstick left by the kisses. I could hear her voice rising and falling from across the road. They linked arms and walked away, and I stood there watching as Eva chattered into the other one's ear.

They disappeared behind a wall of double decker buses, and I was left standing in the dark, twiddling my fingers in my pockets, wondering if I was jealous. In the distance I could hear fireworks screaming and exploding. As I walked home I thought about George on firework nights, lighting the blue touch paper and retiring, while Frank and I stood dumbly watching a Catherine wheel reeling, then spluttering to a cindery halt. That's the bit I remember most about fireworks. The way they died.

The Attic

While Jean was in hospital I was given a new two-legged doll with luscious blond hair and eggshell eyelids that gurgled with despair when I held her upside down, and who wetted herself continually, and a pyjama case in the form of a sleeping lion. At first I thought it was my birthday, but then I realized that the gifts were heralds of terrible news.

I was to be moved from the Furthest Nursery to the attic, where, George said, I wouldn't be influenced. Frank smirked from the doorway of the nursery as I lugged an armful of frightened toys up the sinister stairway. Each stair groaned and sighed. I stopped halfway and looked down at George who stood on the landing frowning. I considered dropping a spinning top on to his head, and escaping, but his hair was hard and crinkly, like a helmet, and I didn't know then where I would run beyond the brick walls of the long garden, or the sweet shop on the corner, and there was always the matter of strangers and their penises to consider, so I trudged on.

The attic was so low and cramped that George had to bend double to enter it. It was a small intense room with leafy wallpaper and a sloping floor. The moment I walked into it I knew it was full of unresolved misery. In Jean's absence, Carmen the cleaner had tried to make it nice, with pictures on the walls of innocent animals and a jungle bedspread, but underneath it smelt mothy and festering. Carmen came in and opened the window, and an ivy tendril curled over the sill. I sat down on the bed, feeling ostracized. I could hear Frank and the toys shrieking and warring in the distant country of the Furthest Nursery.

I wondered what I was supposed to do in my attic?

I shut my eyes and wished for company.

There was suddenly a strong and unbearable smell, of spa water and flatulence. I heard scratching. A queen bee flew drunkenly into the room. Someone breathed in my ear. I tried to call out but my voice was a shrill cantata. I ran downstairs, past a radio playing hissing random music.

While Jean was in hospital George had taken over the domestic organization of the house. He was building a luxurious cake with sponge finger scaffolding, and cream filling. He stood in the dusky kitchen holding an egg whisk in his right hand, with a silk scarf tied around his head, whipping egg white into a stiff frenzy.

I tugged at his heavy trousers and he tutted as if I was a missing ingredient. 'What?' he said, wrinkling up his salty nose.

'Help!' I moaned.

'Do you want to do some cooking?' said George. He was like a man let loose in a ladies' underwear shop. I climbed onto a high stool, and played with a grey lump of pastry left over from a chicken pie. George was piping cream onto the roof of the cake. For a while I forgot all about upstairs. I could hear Carmen banging about, wildly polishing in spasms.

I made the pastry into the shape of a bird. Its wings slumped and it bent its head towards me. The cake was leaning over to one side. George patted it with a non-stick spatula and looked alarmed. My ears were getting hot. 'What's the matter?' he said.

'I don't like it in the attic,' I whimpered. He picked up a crystallized strawberry and gazed at it as if it was a nipple.

'Did you see a ghost?' he asked sadly.

The pastry bird tried to fly, then fell off the kitchen table.

I tried again. 'It smells!' I yelled, into the quietness.

'You'll get used to it,' crooned George. 'It's only a room.'

A cherry slid off the roof of the cake and a dollop of cream avalanched after it. George was getting irritated.

'I want to go back to the nursery!' I screeched. (I don't know why, but I did.)

'Don't be silly,' he jabbed, and Frank galloped in holding a plastic jet that he hurled maniacally into the air. It nosedived into the side of the gateau and George covered his eyes with a gesture of helplessness. Frank wrote something down on a piece of paper, then scooped up some stray cream that had landed on the floor and looked at it quizzically.

'It's the wrong consistency,' he announced. 'And I don't want her back. She gets on my nerves.'

'I know that,' snapped George, brandishing his spatula at me.

Suddenly Carmen stood squarely at the kitchen door, holding a mop and bucket as if they were a spear and shield. 'What's going on?' she said, as if she was in charge.

'I don't like my room,' I spluttered.

'Her cheeks look funny,' Carmen said solidly. 'She's got the mumps.'

George brightened and looked at me paternally. 'The mumps?' he repeated as if it was a new recipe for a cake. 'Poor buttons.'

I felt my cheeks. They were hard and full of unpronounceable words.

Frank whistled through his teeth.

I clambered down from the high stool. My legs were pastry. Carmen ushered me upstairs to the bathroom and wiped my face with a cool sponge. Then she pulled off my clothes and sprinkled talcum powder on my belly so that it looked like a doughnut. She led me back up the attic stairs. The smell had disappeared. I was too wobbly to protest. She tucked me up in bed and stroked my damp head.

'It's good to get the mumps,' she said approvingly.

Her hands were dry from Ajax and her bare leg had one virulent varicose vein running down it in a blue river.

'It's a nice room really,' she said, glancing around, picking a rose from her patterned overall and placing it in a vase that appeared by my bed.

For a moment it *was* a nice room. The presence of Carmen dissolved my fears, and I slipped down under the sheets into a dark peace. I fell asleep with Carmen sitting there, a wholesome weight on the edge of my bed, guarding me. Downstairs George had remade the cake into a splendid mountain and was letting Frank lick the contours of a large and sticky wooden spoon, while explaining the physics of cake decoration to him.

The Kingdom Of Leaves

Days later, I was swollen up into a delirious caricature of my former self. The mumps made me feel as if I was encased in a swarrn of hostile bees. I lay counting the stings. In front of me there was a blurred flurry of fat wings. I was tangled up in a weighty Victorian nightgown, that clung to my body whenever I tried to move. When a doctor came I asked him to take me away, but he just patted my heavy jowls with his dry hands, and told me that darkness was good for the mumps, and winked at Jean who had just returned from the hospital wrapped in mummy-like bandages, with a fierce and battered face. She stood bravely in a dress made of alabaster that smelt of sherry. The thermometer rattled on the roof of my mouth, and his stethoscope was unbearably cold and flat against my back. The air was yellow as old Lucozade, brewed in foggy factories in Watford.

After the doctor had gone Frank appeared, carrying an

oversize astronomical manual, and sent by Jean to catch the mumps. He stood there, breathing deeply, looking down at me scientifically.

I was so hot, it was as if I was strung up on the top branches of a leafless tree in the midday sun. My tongue didn't fit in my mouth. My heart was bubbling.

Frank shook his head like a doctor, then stood at the window, squinting up at the sky. He was studying the eclipse. In my Savannah dreams the eclipse was happening above my head. He opened the book and started to read in a ponderous, poetic tone. It sounded like another language.

I groaned.

'What do you want then?' he enquired politely.

I said, 'Rain.'

What sort of rain?'

I told him, croakily, that I wanted the heavy stormy type rain that bounced when it landed.

Frank sharpened a. pencil and coughed authoritatively.

'Imagine,' he lectured, 'that you are a citizen of the Kingdom of Leaves.'

I nodded. Frank was drawing on the wall. I was reptilian, and helpless.

He drew me a map of a country that was beset by continual monsoons. It was soothing. He recited geographical facts about the country, where, he said, the rain was so ever-present that people lived under huge elephantine leaves the size of houses, and were wet all the time, with their faces streaked with mud, and leeches sucking at their skins. No-one was ever ill in the Kingdom of Leaves, as diseases were washed away daily down a thick, torrential river named the Sump. The population had skin of flannel and could wring themselves out. Fishes lived on land and tigers swam. Frank drew across the ceiling with sweeps of his pencil, stopping to peer into my delirium and fan me with tales of squelching, of incessant watery tracks on which one could sail to market on a twig to buy wet meat to boil in pans over a spluttering blue flame.

I wet the bed. Warm urine soaked sensually through the hot sheets and weighted the mattress. My temperature flew to a place where birds flapped their wings like seals, and my limbs were masts with sails attached to them. Frank put his pencil down and sniffed.

'Smells weird in here. Like mouldy books,' he muttered, and left as quickly as a gust of wind.

I fell out of bed trying to follow him.

I think I must have fallen asleep, but when I opened my eyes I saw a figure standing motionless by the window. She wore a long grey cloud of a dress and her face was small and indistinct.

I wondered for a moment if I might be dead. She reached out to me, then disappeared. The leaves around the window shuddered and brushed against the window frame.

I was drifting away, down the Sump. Blue rain was falling onto my white cotton nightdress.

Later Frank told me I never stopped yelling. He said that Jean wore earplugs and played Elvis Presley records. I remember only that I lived in another place for a period of time, and that I was always wet.

Wooing

How I hated the lottery! Theobald and I discussed the changes in our workplace with scorn and fury. The archaeological institute was filled with whirring machines, and there was constant drilling in the once quiet wings. I saw a skip filled with birds heads on plinths. It was somehow pathetic. The Head Curator had appointed a consultant who wore iodine-coloured shirts and who kept asking us questions about our movements. I did my best to confuse him with archaeological jargon. He obviously knew nothing about the museum's collection. He didn't understand that anyone can push a button and watch a video and leave the place with a plastic pencil sharpener and a frog-shaped pencil case, and still be none the wiser about the cultural heritage of ancient civilizations. Also, although Theobald was my friend, he was a very weak person, and I knew he would probably swing to the new way of thinking. I was in a state of constant anxiety.

*   *   *

It was in this insecure state that I decided to start wooing Eva. Even if I was disappointed in love, I reasoned, it was better than never having loved at all. In wooing terms every detail was important; clothes, facial expressions, conversation, timing, superficial impressions. I did deep-breathing exercises and ran up and down the stairs. If I was going to practise the art of courtly love then I thought that I had better be fit.

The next morning I stopped at a flower stall, run by a woman with the face of a tiger and a fur shawl wrapped around her shoulders. I stood there for ages considering the symbolism of different flowers.

The tiger said 'Somebody sick?'

'No,' I answered, although I suppose I was sick in a manner of speaking. 'What do you want then?' she barked. 'Roses for love, lavender for remembrance, daffodils for cancer?'

'What about irises?' I asked.

'What?'

What do they mean?'

'Oooh, they're very stately.' Stately. Eva was stately. Her back was as straight as an iris. Her eyes were blue.

'I'll give you two bunches for three pounds,' she snapped, already wrapping the flowers in paper with the gentleness of a butcher.

I started moving off. The flower seller touched my sleeve.

'Be careful,' she said, and squeezed my arm.

'What of?' Did everyone know what I was thinking?

She didn't answer.

This was one of the things that frightened me about the Public. They could be over-perceptive.

At the institute the Head Curator was standing in the room

of Arctic mammals, waving his hands about. I tried to skirt past him but he lumbered towards me. We stood in the shadow of a polar bear.

'Flowers Gert?' he boomed.

'Irises,' I muttered, trying to edge away.

'We must talk,' he whispered. 'There's going to be changes.'

'Oh?' I sniffed.

'You see, stuffed rooms like these aren't relevant to today's youngsters.'

How I hated his vocabulary. I didn't like his trousers either. They were big and corduroy and too long. I held the irises in front of me like a shield, and peered through them at his pavement face with its slabby cheeks and small, gritty eyes.

'What are you proposing?' I asked, creeping sideways.

'Humour!' His bulging eyes sparkled. The polar bear sighed. There's nothing funny about taxidermy. Not many jokes about holes in ancient pots either.

'Theobald agrees.' Theobald would have agreed with a mass murderer. Perhaps he will form a flea circus, or dress his gnats in dancing shoes, I thought, ignoring the Head Curator as he elaborated on a number of humorous examples, based in similar buildings in Rome, Madrid and Toronto.

What are you doing today?' His nose brushed the petals.

'Sharks' teeth,' I muttered. I was investigating a shark's tooth necklace from an island where the inhabitants believed that they became fishes at night and ate each other.

'Perhaps you would like to come upstairs and give a talk, to a school party?'

This was one of the Head Curator's themes. For years he had wanted me to become a kind of Rolf Harris; to leave my quiet room and sit in a glass box with a magnifying glass and ramble on to any old toddler passing by about the nature of my work. I told him, over and over again, that I needed peace and privacy.

'You could bring an object like a shark's tooth necklace alive!'

The image was disconcerting.

'No,' I said, 'I don't do talks.'

'Gert.' He stopped smiling. 'Things are changing. We live in a modern world. Ask yourself some tough questions. Like, what is the point of what I do?'

It was a thickly buttered threat, but I couldn't be fagged to take it seriously. My desk was an oasis after this conversation. I put the irises in a temporary bucket and settled down with my cross references. Coffee break arrived after I had written an extremely inaccessible paragraph about the necklace with no juicy detail whatsoever.

As I walked towards the canteen my heart was being eaten by sharks. Eva was standing in a pool of domestic light pouring coffee into a teacup, looking calm and efficient. I leant over the counter with the irises. There was a deathly silence as the rest of the museum staff watched with amusement.

'These are for you,' I whispered.

Eva looked at the irises and then at me. Her face was pale. I noticed that she had perfectly formed, white, modern teeth.

'Is it a joke?' she asked.

'No,' I said.

'Why then?'

'I thought they would match your overall.' I half smiled, an expression I had rehearsed at home, in an attempt to look suave.

'I see.' She took the flowers furtively and pushed them somewhere under the counter.

'How do you want your coffee?' she asked politely.

The canteen started to gossip. Theobald was shaking his head wearily.

The first steps in wooing had begun. I shoved feelings of embarrassment and exposure into my sweaty pockets and sat down.

Theobald leant towards me. What's the matter with you?' he said.

'Nothing,' I answered defensively.

'It won't do you any good. The powers that be are watching us all the time.' Theobald glanced furtively around the canteen.

'It's not illegal to woo!' I snapped, sounding like an owl.

'At your age!' exclaimed Theobald. This depressed me. I was only thirty-five.

'And why irises for God's sake?'

'I just like them,' I said.

They symbolize death I think,' muttered Theobald cheerfully. 'You should have got roses. She probably thinks you're a nutter.'

Well, I'm not,' I retorted too quickly, as Theobald smirked.

George Goes To The Crocodiles

When I recovered from the mumps, some weeks later, I was too thin for my clothes, my skin was sallow and I had heavy rings under my eyes. The light outside the attic was so bright that I had to peep through my fingers. I staggered to the bathroom. The first thing I saw was a group of American tourists up a tree filming me as I got out of the bath.

As I shuffled downstairs I noticed that the house had been redecorated and that there was a new floral carpet on the mezzanine. I wondered how long I had been lying in the morguish attic. It could have been months.

The family was eating breakfast. They looked different.

Frank had a new pair of rectangular spectacles, which magnified his eyes into large unwieldy marbles. He was eating a piece of toast cut into identical geometrical shapes. Jean wore shiny lipstick and a cloudy frock of pink linen. She perched at one end of the table glancing at her watch, and George sat at the other, hooting. My place was on his left side, not far from his mouth.

'So you're up!' he bellowed into my ear.

Jean took a pill from a small brown bottle and slipped it under her tongue calmly. She was wearing a necklace that looked like a string of wasps. 'Guess what?' she said, turning her watery face to mine.

'What?' I asked.

'Today we're going to the station.'

'At ten fifty-two,' interjected Frank dimly.

'What for?'

'To see your father off on a train.'

'He's going away!' Frank chirped.

'For quite a long time!' George boomed, raising his eyebrows. 'But I'll come back,' he continued, buoyantly.

I chewed a strand of Shredded Wheat. They looked at me, waiting for the next question. 'Where?' I asked obediently.

'He's got a new job.' Jean sipped from her bony cup.

'Crocodiles,' said George.

'Handbags,' Frank expanded.

'He's going to help run the crocodile farm,' Jean explained. 'Uncle Willy's.' The crocodile farm was in West Africa. It had been left to my father after Uncle Willy was eaten by his pet crocodile. It supplied crocodile handbags to Paris, Rome, and London. It bought Jean whole salmons and lavish soaps. It had provided the cash with which to buy our huge and uncomfortable house, and also to send Frank, later, to a sadistic educational establishment.

However, this was the first time that I had been aware of the world of work. Of course, George must have worked before, but I had never noticed. We had always lived off the crocodiles. Perhaps I saw a briefcase once lying on the desk in his room. Sometimes the telephone rang officiously and he answered with a careful, well-behaved voice. I looked at him again, trying to imagine him in this new role.

'Administration,' barked George.

'Skinning?' muttered Jean uncertainly.

'Everything!' He puffed up his heavy shoulders.

I secretly wished he would stay at home and make cakes. I couldn't imagine him skinning a crocodile. And where did the crocodiles live? Was it secure? What if a baby one crept out through a hole in the wire and hid under George's bed until it had grown to ten foot? And crocodiles were obviously not dependable, thinking of Uncle Willy.

'How are you feeling anyway?' enquired Jean politely.

Some distant tears fizzed in the ends of my fingers. 'I don't know,' I mumbled, calculating how soon I could leave home.

'You'll feel better in a while,' said Jean with a faraway look in her eye.

We all went to the station. Jean drove the car in a careless, American way, with one elbow hanging out of the open window. At the station she got out of the car very slowly, as if she was practising something she had only just learnt. The station was very clean and there were notices everywhere telling us to be neat. Pink hydrangeas grew in wheelbarrows. George bumped his head on a hanging basket. We stood in a row on the narrow, rural station waiting for the fast London train. Jean linked arms with George, but he was anxious about his tickets and kept rummaging in his pockets, searching them out, so that her arm fell away from his. I pulled at his trousers and he looked down at me crossly.

'Take me. Please take me,' I said. George was puzzled. 'Where?' he said.

To Africa.'

'I'll send you a postcard.' He picked me up and for a moment I was close to his thundery sad eyes and his shaven chin.

'Why can't you work here?'

'The climate's no good for crocodiles. It needs to be moist and hot,' and he smiled a stupid mad grin as if he had made a joke.

'But what about me and Frank?'

'I'll bring you a present,' he muttered quickly, and then dropped me back onto the platform, as the train came in screaming with rage. So I ran about in decreasing circles, yelling. Frank timed everything with a stopwatch. George was so agitated that he forgot to say goodbye and at the last minute he hung out of the window and blew kisses at us. The only lips he could reach were Jean's, and I stared at them as they embraced. I had never seen them kiss like that before. On the lips.

As the train pulled away Jean took a small lace handkerchief from her handbag and wiped her lips, but the kiss hung there in the air for ages like smoke from a firework.

Trouble With The Rubbish

It was all hospitals where I lived. Ill health and bad blood. In the daytime the area was crowded with doctors and people in tears, and sometimes women in dressing gowns who were trying to escape from the gynaecological wards. There was a low drone in the air as if all the poorly people were breathing together in miserable breaths, like one great unwell beast. It smelt of cut flowers and force-grown fruit. I think it affected me, living where I did, among healing scabs or decaying bones. Dustbins were filled with computer printouts from heart monitors, and broken chunks of Armitage Shanks plumbing. There were rusty wheelchairs and bedside tables down the back lane waiting for the rag and bone men. I could feel the electric currents emanating from the psychiatric unit. It was an area with the ambience of a busy morgue.

*   *   *

On Friday morning I parted my reluctant curtains and looked across the yard to the back of a hospital building which was opposite my flat. I saw two sour-faced women wearing large yellow rubber gloves stepping out of the dark interior. They wore overalls the colour of bleach bottles, and their manner was underhand, even shifty.

They were carrying two black plastic rubbish bags which they placed discreetly with my rubbish. This was not where they were supposed to put their waste. Hospital rubbish generally went in yellow skips with the word DANGER painted in black on them. I knocked on the window but they slithered back into their own territory, leaving their suspicious garbage on my patch,

I was unsettled. I dressed quickly and ran downstairs. I felt vulnerable. I lived on my own. I had very little debris. What one decides to discard is a very personal matter. I purposefully crossed the back lane and knocked on the handleless door. I could smell contaminated blood. No-one appeared and I returned to check that the bags were still there. I went to the front of the building which was craggy brick with a pompous main door. I pushed myself dizzily through a revolving door. Ahead of me was a maze of carpeted corridors. I wandered along them nervously, calling into cubicles until eventually a sleepy caretaker in a brown sacking overall stepped out from behind a marble bust of Freud.

'It's all closed up until Monday,' he said.

'I thought this was a hospital. People get ill at the weekend you know,' I snapped.

'It's a wing,' he muttered defensively. 'What kind of wing?'

'Keep your hair on! It's the loony wing,' he said with a grin.

Well, I have a complaint to make.' I looked at him fiercely. He seemed to have artificial ears, and they weren't a pair either.

'You have to have an appointment,' he droned on.

'This isn't a medical matter,' I said. 'It's domestic.'

'Medical or domestic, it will have to wait.'

'It's the cleaning staff I'm after!'

'They've all gone home now.'

'Who are you then?'

'Harry.'

We paused then, looking at each other. I felt a need to introduce myself by name, but repressed it.

'I mean what's your job here?'

'I don't work here. I'm from the other building. I'm security.'

'What happens here?'

'Therapy... counselling... drugs... the lot.'

I felt a sense of hopelessness. 'I'll come back on Monday then.'

'Suit yourself.'

I left him standing in an amiable stupor, and went back to the rubbish.

What, I wondered, was in those bags? Then I looked down at myself and realized my nightdress was hanging out and over the back of my jeans.

Later, after a strange afternoon at work with a magnifying glass, and a couple of flutters with Eva when I asked for warm milk in my coffee and she said, 'How warm?' and I became weak with the possibilities that such a question offered, I went to buy a bottle of Bull's Blood from Jimmy's corner shop. When I got there Harry the guard was there talking to Jimmy who had the teeth of a rat and the prices of Harrods. Harry's strange ears were covered by a balaclava helmet that an aunt must have welded for him out of a sock. With lavish sweeps of his fingerless gloves Harry was telling

Jimmy of the area he guarded; from casualty to the dental block.

'Who is guarding it now?' I asked him casually, wondering if I should go and help myself to a large parcel of morphine.

'I am,' said Harry. 'I look after everything round here.'

Then he winked at me, and I winked back. Or I blinked because I have never been able to wink. It's not a skill you learnt in the south of England.

Letters From Africa

George wrote to me from Africa. 'Dear Gert, I hope you are well...' But I wasn't well. No-one heard me when I tried to speak to them. Everyone was involved in their own private problems. Frank was lost in space, or squatting in the centre of a train set, his young head revolving as the toy train chuntered around the track. Jean had pasted herself into the pages of *Vogue* magazine. Carmen only came one day a week, and then she was generally too occupied to notice me as I slunk around the alcoves. I got on everyone's nerves. My mouth opened and closed. I said the same things over and over again.

'Don't make me go upstairs.' The words seemed to disappear, whenever I said them. They were sucked back up into the vortex of the attic.

A postcard from Africa arrived. It was a picture of a laughing black man with glistening teeth, holding a dead crocodile on a hook. He stood in front of a group of obese, sunny women wearing dazzling gold head-dresses. They pointed at the crocodile and laughed, or maybe at the man who held the crocodile. It was hard to tell.

The postcard joined the line of identical blue letters that lined the mantelpiece. The stamps were hot and lurid. The paper smelt of curry. The letters were very short. They talked about wild animals and intimate ailments. Sometimes photographs arrived, showing George on wide white verandas wearing a heavy straw hat. The black people always seemed to be holding trays and smiling as if their lives depended on it. George was taller than anyone else, and sometimes the top of his head was omitted from the picture, so that only his long nose and difficult mouth could be seen.

Jean had taken off her pink dress and put on a pair of slacks. She was growing a new layer of flesh that was pink and soft. Sometimes she let me watch *The Man from UNCLE*. Every night when she tried to send me to bed I sat on the hard attic stairs and wailed. It was like howling at the moon. Jean was following the Spock method. I heard her talking on the telephone to Mabel.

'Gert's driving me crazy,' she moaned. 'She's so nervy. She says she wants to move back in with Frank, but he's too sensitive. She drives him up the wall.'

Then she paused, listening to Mabel's frenzied chatter and eventually said, 'Oh Mabel! Would you?'

The next day Mabel turned up with her thin mouth and childless hips. She took her shoes off and opened a bottle of sweet Martini. Jean cuddled up to her and giggled. Suddenly the house was full of handbags and perfumed scarves. The two women wouldn't stop guffawing. They talked about the men at the typing pool where they used to work, and every time they said a man's name they snorted, as if the man was stuck up their noses and they had to blow him out.

When I walked into the room they blinked blearily and said, 'Cheer up Gert!' and I scowled at them, my eyes glued to Jean, waiting for her attention. She wiped my nose with a sweep of her silk handkerchief and told me to go and get the biscuit tin. I walked out of the room backwards and banged my head. When I returned they were standing in front of the mirror with their bras pulled up comparing nipples. Mabel's nipples were huge brown upturned saucers. Jean's were flat and reluctant. They were both saying, 'Wish I had yours.'

When they saw me they sniggered and hooked their bras back on penitently. A lipstick rolled across the floor. The television, which had been switched on ever since Mabel arrived, burst into raucous studio laughter. The two women were a fence that I couldn't climb over, so I went to Jean's bedroom and sat in the cupboard, letting the silky tongues of dresses fall on my face and holding the red shoes in my hands, making them dance with each other.

Mabel stayed for weeks. She treated us like dogs, that needed food and exercise, or squinted at us as if we were flowers that were difficult to grow in this climate. Perhaps she thought we weren't worth the pruning, the cutting and the watering. Sometimes, in the afternoons, we left Jean sleeping with the drowsy radio, and went for unrelenting walks that seemed to be all uphill. Mabel wore impractical shoes that twisted in the grass, and stockings that snagged on the thistles. If we lagged behind she whistled for us. Sometimes we stopped and she dispensed white bread sandwiches wrapped in greaseproof paper, and we wagged our tails. I couldn't stop thinking about her nipples, even when she was wearing a raincoat.

In the evening the two women laughed so loudly that the china dinner sets rattled in the cupboards. Mabel was unmooring Jean. She was quite oblivious to the fact that she was a mother.

Frank looked at the two women as if they were shooting stars.

Sometimes Jean stopped laughing and her eyes rested on Frank as if she had just found a shell on a beach.

She looked at me as if I was a letter she had forgotten to post.

Other Communications

Frank and I once experimented with telepathic messages sent from one room to another. We were both shocked to discover it worked We were simultaneously mentally naked, and confused. Which thoughts belonged to which twin? Were my desires for girls in gymslips in fact the lecherous adolescent fantasies of my twin brother? For some years we became silent and mentally blank, but gradually, out of devilment at first, I began to call him on our exclusive telephone.

'How's things, Frank?' I could hear sheets shift. I must have woken him up.

'Where are you?' His voice was deep, hoarse and shaky.

'I'm finding myself.'

'Why?'

I picture Eva.

'I see,' said the voice gloomily. 'So you haven't changed.'

'This is different.' There was a long silence, I could hear Frank stretching his arms and yawning. 'How are things?'

'Stony, slow. Very quiet until now.'

'You never call me.'

'I'm not supposed to speak to anyone.'

'Not even me?'

'Not even you, Gert. Look, I'm kind of busy right now. I'll get in touch later.'

'Oh yeah, sure.' Frank had never even sent me a Christmas card.

Then he drew a curtain across the conversation. Sometimes I tried to imagine what it would be like if Frank was living with me. I pictured him sitting at my kitchen table with his hands cupped over his ears, or the two of us cooking a meal together, arguing over the meaning of words like 'curdle' and 'finely chop'. He was so bloody obsessive. To be honest I don't know where I would put him if I had him. He was like an animal which was nearly extinct, with all its natural habitat gone.

Five Shillings

Soon there were so many letters from Africa that they kept falling off the mantelpiece. I worried about George, picturing him wading through swamps where crocodiles writhed treacherously in green mud.

And each night, when I went to bed, up the winding stairs to the ominous attic, I wondered if the strange figure I had seen would come back. I placed my blonde doll at the foot of my bed. I left all the lights on.

Sometimes I thought I smelt something, or heard skirts rustling by my head. When this happened I would scuttle downstairs to the Furthest Nursery and try to slide into Frank's bed without being seen or heard. I was like a stealthy reptile, nosing and twisting under the covers. Frank would wake up and push me out onto the floor, so that I often slept on the hard linoleum.

I heard Jean talking about me again to Mabel. She said she found me quite impossible. Mabel said I needed a good slap. Every night I wet myself.

Before Mabel returned home she pulled me into a thorny corner of the garden. I shied away from her, expecting the slap, but instead she gave me five shillings and told me to try harder. She hugged me and told me to smile. I forced the corners of my mouth upwards, and she squeezed my cheek as if to test the ripeness of a melon, and fastened the top buttons of her coat.

'You tell Mabel next time you have a problem,' she said. 'Don't take it out on Jean.' She tied a tight knot in her headscarf. 'She's more delicate than you think,' she said.

I nodded uncertainly, knowing that Frank would embezzle my five shillings for his telescope fund, and that I would end up giving it to him anyway.

The Farmer Wants A Wife

Frank and I were to be sent to nursery school.

Downstairs Jean was ironing two blue sailors outfits; a dress for me and shorts for Frank. The dress had small puff sleeves with virulent elastic, and was very long and unmanageable to wear. The shorts were more basic, although Frank complained that the sailor's tie was throttling him.

Jean drove us to the hall, which was surrounded by conspiring yew trees. She parked in the middle of the street and left the car door wide open. That's what she was like. She never locked anything, and never kept to the rules.

I was beginning to panic. I suddenly felt that I might as well be a suitcase being abandoned at left luggage.

Jean pushed us both in front of her and we found ourselves in a hall full of creaking toys and wide-eyed children. I turned around to cling to Jean's skirt, but, following the Spock method, she had nipped off, leaving us to fend for ourselves.

The boys were generally square and chubby, although later I noticed some thin stringy ones lurking behind radiators and under window-sills. Most of them pelted around the room in imaginary Rovers, bumping into the girls, who were frothy, with rubbery mouths and shining hair haloed with velvet hair bands. They leant over large pieces of sugar paper holding unwieldy crayons.

Frank started counting maniacally. I told him to stop, but he wouldn't. He was holding a bullet of plasticine in his hand as if it was a weapon that he might use. I ran to a vacant metal horse and started to rock to and fro in a disturbed manner.

A ferocious-looking woman with dog teeth blew a whistle, and everything stopped.

The woman told us that her name was Miss Lute, and that we must all sit in a circle. When all our legs were in identical positions Miss Lute told us that it was NEWS TIME.

A boy with shocking blond hair and a red neck stuck his hand up immediately.

'Yes, Terence,' said Miss Lute politely. 'What is your news?'

'My grandpa was sick down the stairs,' Terence shouted, then curled up into a snigger.

'Did he go to hospital?' asked Miss Lute.

'No, he died.' Terence burst into tears. We all made odd shapes with our lower lips.

'Oh dear,' said Miss Lute sweetly. 'Never mind Terence. Let's ask one of the new children for their news. Lucy?'

We've got a new baby. It's yellow, and I sat on it,' chirped Lucy.

'That's nice. Has anyone got any unusual news. Any surprises?'

'There's something nasty in my room!' I blurted. All the other children stared at me sullenly.

'I'm sorry. Say that again Gert.'

'There's something in my room. It smells.'

'You smell,' mumbled a sour-faced girl in a knitted frock.

'Please, please, can I go home?' I looked at them all desperately.

'But Gert, you're having a lovely time,' said Miss Lute. 'Do you need the toilet Gert?' Miss Lute was saying.

A dark arc of liquid slowly spread over the floor around me. I looked bravely at my captor. 'I want my mother,' I said. 'I'm wet.'

It didn't work.

For the rest of the morning I was ostracized. Miss Lute forced me to wear a pair of nylon slacks and an unravelling sweater she found in a cupboard. She made a big thing about it. Everyone smirked. Frank was mortified.

I sat in humiliation by the fuzzy felt. Frank, still counting, drew a picture of an abattoir, upsetting some of the other children. Miss Lute told him to play with the bricks, but he scared her by looking up at her with a face disguised as a barbed wire fence. He had reached two thousand and eighty-three when Miss Lute rang a heavy brass bell, and we were instructed to eat rusks, which tasted of recently ironed tablecloths. We were told to chew them thoroughly. Then we had weak juice, that must have been drugged, because afterwards we all lay down on straw mats and fell asleep, while Miss Lute sang 'The Farmer Wants a Wife' in a low monotone.

I heard Frank whispering a violent fairy story to a boy who believed he was a train. The boy interrupted Frank to let off steam. Miss Lute stopped her song and bravely slapped Frank with a heavy wad of silence, although of course that made no difference to him.

Then she growled, WE ALL PAT THE DOG.

After that we lined up to go to the toilet. I was last and the toilet seat was hot from other children's bottoms and the toilet paper had run out.

Then Miss Lute opened the door, ushering in the parents as if they were bad children that had been shut outside. She beamed uniformly at each of us as we passed.

Jean was outside, banging over her car door reading a magazine. She looked like a film star.

I looked back at Miss Lute from the back seat of the car, catching her expression just before the door closed. Her face was suddenly hanging down in morose folds, gone from round to oblong. And I realized, in the way that I was often to know, by some childish intuition that I have now completely lost, that she wanted a farmer, a child and a dog all for herself.

Reprieve

But after my first day at nursery school I was suddenly granted unexpected parole from the attic. This was because unprecedented winds had dislodged slates on the roof and subsequently workmen were brought in to fix the damp. Happily, they discovered dry rot, which everyone assumed was the cause of the smell, and the work went on for some weeks. I was briefly allowed to sleep with Jean, back in the inner sanctum of her white cotton bedroom, with jars of yogurty creams and watercolours of churches. I noticed how she muttered in her sleep and how her feet danced to some silent music. She would say things like, 'The ropes, I can't hold on!' or 'There's nothing to eat, we'll have to kill it'. She slept with a hairnet over her straw blond hair. Sometimes she smiled at me when she woke up. Great yellow smiles with butter spread all over them.

The workmen got more and more disenchanted. Some

days they didn't turn up. I heard the foreman discussing the atmosphere; he said it was putrid and that one of the younger men kept hearing scratchy noises. The others called the man a nancy and made fun of him.

The house was full of dust and untidy planks. This forced us out, usually to parks, but sometimes on more ambitious outings.

We decided to go on an outing to the zoo. When we arrived there was a humid rainstorm and soon we were all soaking wet. We each held a small, sodden paper bag full of peanuts. The spiky railings of the zoo were painted green, and as we walked through the entrance multicoloured birds beseeched us from high wrought-iron cages. The air smelt of hamsters. We seemed to be the only people there. Jean walked ahead swinging a white leather shoulder bag. Frank was looking through a pair of plastic binoculars. I sat down to get a bit of gravel out of my plimsoll. The earth trembled with the plod of elephants' feet.

We followed the signs that said REPTILES, and found ourselves in a dry and airless room filled with glass boxes. The snakes were cramped and lethargic. Not one could stretch out to its full length. I found myself immersed in a fat python that wound itself around an insubstantial twig. The snake breathed in and out. Its eyes were long and reproachful. I whispered its name, which was painted in gold letters above its box. *Lenny*. When I managed to turn away there was no sign of Jean and Frank. I began to run through the dark chambers. Lizards with leathery collars shrugged as I ran past. A chameleon changed colour. A boiled mamba moved in a sudden crack across its glass box. I bumped into a thin woman carrying a baby. She snapped at me with her fingers and the baby silently opened its gummy mouth. I ran on, through an archaic and tricky turnstile and found myself standing by a fetid toilet with a shabby door. I wandered inside, warily. A woman with skin like crackling was applying powder to her cheeks. She barked at me and I ran out again, panicking.

Thanks to Miss Lute's efforts, I managed to read a sign that said SEE THE MONKEYS and I followed it, running through a maze of mean cages containing mammoth shining beetles and tortoises with mould on their shells. I tripped over and my peanuts spilt all over the ground. Some sparrows soared down from a tree and began to gobble them up. Then I saw Jean, miles away, running in circles. She was the other side of several large fences. I shouted out to her, but I couldn't hear anything and she couldn't hear me. It was unbearable.

Then I did something that the zoo keeper later said was impossible, which proves how much I wanted my mother in those days. I scrambled over a difficult eight-foot fence, scraping my knee on some barbed wire, and vaulted over a moat that was littered with coke cans and crisp packets. I was suddenly in an oasis of tropical trees with a quiet pond in the centre. Jean had disappeared, but Frank was standing on the other side of the moat staring at me through his binoculars. He was trying to say something, waving his arms in delirious semaphore. I started to walk towards him. A crowd of Cornflake-packet people with sloping shoulders were gathering next to the fence. They were holding hands. I could hear Jean calling my name. Her voice was broken, as if I was truly lost. Frank was motioning me to sit down. Feeling puzzled, I planted myself under a shrub and waited.

Then I saw the crocodile.

It lay a few yards from me with a terrifying stillness. How ridiculous, I thought. What a coincidence. Then I thought irrationally, maybe it's George, dressed up.

It opened one eye.

Jean was there now. She stretched out her gloved hand, through the mesh of wire. All the attention was on me. I gloried in it for some seconds, and then the crowd gasped, as the crocodile opened its mouth and yawned.

Jean moaned softly, and I had the feeling that only I could hear it.

I wondered which part of me it would eat first.

Perhaps my hands, so I would never be able to carry a handbag.

A small monkey-faced man was creeping towards me holding a hoop and a fresh, bloody bone. He beckoned to me. The crocodile opened its other eye.

It scuttled a couple of inches. Everyone stifled a scream.

Jean fainted.

The man ran to the side of the cage and unlocked a door.

The crocodile charged. I ran.

The crowd hung onto the sides of the cage.

I felt its reptilian breath on me as the cage door closed behind me.

Jean had gone blue, and was slumped on a bench rolling her eyes. Frank poked me in the ribs. Some small boys wept because they were not allowed to have a go in the crocodile's cage. The crocodile was happily splintering the large bone into bite-sized pieces, as if it was a child's leg.

I was taken by the man with a hoop to see the zoo keeper, who had cagey eyes and boxy teeth, in a pillbox office. He shouted at me for half an hour, and I am sure that if he could have done, he would have whipped me. Jean revitalized herself and threatened to sue him. She was on my side.

On the bus home Frank treated me with a new respect. He

even let me try on his spectacles, which shrunk Jean's face down to the size of a pixie's, with a large pale nose. It occurred to me that I would have repeated the whole episode if asked. I imagined that I was coated with crocodiles' breath, like a sugared almond.

Jean said she would never go near a zoo again, and that she planned to complain to the highest authorities.

I saw the King of the Jungle bending his head wisely towards her, and the Queen of England nodding her vague and jewel laden brow.

It's a rather happy memory. That's why I'm telling you it. Part of the dry-rot time when I slept in the white peace of Jean's bed.

The Second Letter

Dear Gert,

Did you get my last letter? I have been very depressed. The room I live in is damp, and without Cameron it's really quite unbearable. I know you never liked Cameron, but if you had known him better I'm sure you would have got used to him. We were very happy. I am supposed to leave soon, but the landlord says I can stay a bit longer, until I find another place. He is a horrible man with one of those army faces. He wears a combat jacket. I know we haven't seen each other since you left, but you are my only daughter. I'm an old woman now, Gert. I've got so much I want to talk to you about. We should never have left things for so long.

I look forward to hearing from you soon. Perhaps you have been away.

From your mother

A Conspiracy Of Idleness

This inner narrative was wrecking my present. I felt as if I was watching myself disintegrate and flake away, like the dead irises I saw in the bins at the back of the canteen.

I couldn't concentrate on my work. I was supposed to be looking at ways to introduce primitive voodoo objects to the under-fives. I told the Head Curator that I must think about it carefully, hoping to deflect him. I was under a lot of stress, I told him; family problems. I tore up Jean's letter and flushed it down the toilet, although scraps of words, like 'daughter', kept floating back to the surface.

My inappropriate obsession for Eva had made me nostalgic and uncommunicative. At the institute bad behaviour was treated with benevolence. I never realized this was possible before. They were being horribly kind to me. However, this was obviously sincere. There was, for example, the matter of redundancies which put everyone into a semi-coma. The stuffed condor in the foyer hung its beak with doom, and several labels had dropped off the artefacts in the Egyptian section. Theobald complained of nightmares concerning birds' nests, and only Eva was consistent with her Nescafé and kettles.

Before then I had never really lied on purpose, at least not as an adult, but now I saw the infinite possibilities of pretence. My excuses grew like malignant tumours. Some days I phoned in with a voice that I didn't recognize myself. It cracked mirrors. Carol in the office developed a soothing tone and always agreed with me that it would be wise to 'take things easy'.

I discovered a conspiracy of idleness involving others who had practised the art all their working lives. I would drift to the toilet and mess around with the hand dryer. I examined my underarms in the mirror. Upstairs there was a mummified princess. She was the colour of what remains after weeks at the bottom of dirty coffee cups. She stooped with an awful anorexic hunch. Her womb had been removed, leaving a torn envelope of parchment skin. She was entombed behind glass in an endless room at the back of the museum. I wanted to ask the curator if I could take her out and clean her up a bit. I had an urge to cover her up.

Each day I met porters and delivery boys, cleaners and caretakers, schoolchildren playing truant, even a lady mayoress, all dawdling and dallying, eager to discuss the colour of the sky, bus routes, or the price of shoes. Like smokers, we supported each other in a mutual mission. One day I met one of the museum cleaners by a fish tank. She was talking to a piranha who listened carefully. I asked her if she knew where I could buy cheap bananas, and she told me the history of every kind of fruit you can buy on a market stall. Then she sighed and said, 'Better get back to work,' but didn't.

Instead she warmed her bottom on the radiator and complained about the mess that the public made. She said that once some workmen had come to do refurbishments, bringing dust sheets, and how the museum was closed for a week and it was lovely because there was no mess, thanks to the sheets. We both agreed that our lives would be so much easier if we too were covered in sheets. We wouldn't even need to wash. We arranged to meet again by the eel tank so she could show me her photographs of tulips in flower, although of course she never came. The idle never stick to their arrangements.

I didn't read the e-mails that appeared on the screen in front of me describing urgent meetings, wage cuts and developments. I would wander home after tea break and buy wine that tasted of ammonia, and lie on my bed smoking rolled cigarettes. I wrote letters to Eva which I made into kites and threw across the room, and I rewrote my messy life in chronological sequences, then scrumpled it up, so that my flat became a fire hazard.

Learning To Dance

You see, I really wanted to make Jean happy. It was my life's work, and the main reason why I said I wanted to learn to dance. Not for myself, but for her with her weak ankles (my responsibility) and dreams of be-bop and jive. I said I wanted to be a dancer when I grew up, and that really made her perk up. I was worried about her. She sat around a lot. She drank a lot of gin. She didn't have many friends.

The second reason I wanted to dance was to spite Frank, who had large feet and thin arms and no sense of timing. This, I thought, was one way of demoting him from his smug position as most favoured twin, and at first it seemed that my plan was actually going to work.

When I told her about wanting to dance Jean went straight out and bought me pink satin ballet shoes, a leotard and a stiff tutu. She touched these things as if they were precious. As soon as we got home she made me put them on and point my toes, then she clapped with a kind of disappointed pleasure, flexing her own delicate feet with empathy as I skipped around the room.

I was to pas-de-bas with a dozen small girls in front of an ageing woman called Miss Palms in a heavyweight tweed suit, who was lame in one leg and who tapped time with a thorny stick.

I had become a dour-looking child. I had a heavy fringe and protruding eyes. My jowls were heavy, and I had developed a sophisticated sneer. I used it lavishly in those first sessions at the dancing school. The piano player's fingers creaked and we hardly ever saw her face; only her hunched brown cardigan. The room was wooden, like a ship, and once in it we were trapped and couldn't escape. I danced with a girl who had no fingers. Her hand kept slipping out of my grasp. We were told to be trees, or animals, but I felt more like a bird trapped in a closed room. Sometimes I ran blindly into the walls and saw stars. After a few weeks I was experiencing my usual bouts of contempt and disappointment.

I knew this got on Jean's nerves. She wanted me to be wholehearted. She wanted me to enjoy the things she'd laboured for; social ease, accomplishment, sharp toes. Throughout each lesson Jean sat gazing crazily at my legs, nodding encouragement, biting her increasingly shredded lip.

(What was the matter with her? Did she miss George? Did she have regrets? Why didn't she do something with her life?)

One day Miss Palms lost her temper with the piano player because she wouldn't play the polka fast enough. She grabbed her by the back of her neck, and threatened her with her stick. We stood and sniggered, as if it was a joke. The piano player was not amused, and slammed her fists down on the black keys, making an ugly jarring chord. There was a pause that was the colour of thunder. Then Miss Palms growled, 'You're being a naughty girl, Jemima,' and we all stopped giggling and froze into the shapes of gravestones.

What were the mothers doing? They have disintegrated in the picture; women with no opinions. Perhaps they were laughing? None of us was. Our childish sense of survival forbade it. Maybe they were scared too?

Miss Palms dragged Jemima from her stool by her ear and displayed her limp and cardiganned shape to the class, Jemima was pleading with her.

'Don't Florence, please!'

She shook her as if she was a mongrel, and her spectacles fell off and lay on the floor like broken bones. Miss Palms stared at them and then at us, then blinked. We all waited.

When she finally dropped her, with a look of utter disgust, Jemima sagged down to the size of a child. Miss Palms sent her sidling back to the piano, her figure turned from brown to pale grey. She played then, as if her life depended upon it, slamming her poor old fingers down on the keys. The polka was transformed into a discordant, modern jangle. We danced as if we were possessed; stamping the splintering floorboards beneath our feet.

Miss Palms wanted everything to belong to her. I only wanted Jean and the balmy scent of her bed at night. The shape of her blond head asleep on the white pillow. I was dancing my heart out just to stay there.

After the violent incident at the dancing class I always associated the polka with fear and suppressed violence, even though, as time went on, I realized that things were not quite as they seemed.

I even began to understand the nature of dancing.

One day, Jean and I were halfway down the lane when Jean realized that I had left a ballet shoe behind and made me run back to collect it.

The room smelt of coffee and cigarettes. I peeped around the door. Miss Palms and Jemima were dancing a waltz, and the piano was closed. Jemima had taken her cardigan off, and was wearing a short sleeved flowery blouse with a lace collar. The only sound was their feet and the drip of taps from the toilet. They both had their eyes shut tight. Two cigarettes lay closely in an ashtray, with entwining threads of blue smoke ringing up to the ceiling.

I stood there, entranced. Jemima opened one eye and her expression told me to leave before I was seen. I ran out of the building, somehow exhilarated and relieved.

I did learn to dance. I have certificates to prove it. But the thing I learnt from Miss Palms was far more mysterious. It was as if I had seen something I wanted, but it was so far away that I couldn't quite make it out.

We were coming up to the exams, and Miss Palms was teaching us the cha-cha-cha, as well as encouraging competence in free expression. Free expression, like all dancing, was not what I thought it was. We were told to maintain a certain attitude or Miss Palms' thick stick would make marks in the parquet floor and thud out a reproval. We weren't allowed to flap our arms, but had to move them as if they were underwater.

The mothers sat nervously at the back of the hall while we enacted this complex ritual, comparing our skills. Jean often looked disappointed.

When it was time for the cha-cha-cha exam we waited in a queue outside the door, while the hall shook with raunchy music and small girls' feet. I was last, and I saw Miss Palms yawning as I walked through the door. A tall woman in a pink acrylic suit smiled at me. She was the examiner. I was meant to dance with her. I could hardly reach her waist. I was supposed to curtsey but when the music started I dropped dramatically to my knees in a gesture of grand adoration. The woman in pink giggled. We had to start the whole thing again.

Dancing with the lady in pink was oddly pleasurable. My head sank into the pillow of her belly which gurgled with giggling, and she tasted of freshly sprung corsets. She was being the man, and all I had to do was follow. It occurred to me that all I ever wanted was this kind of leadership and my feet fell in with hers mesmerically. I didn't want the dance to stop, but it did, with a resounding cha-cha-cha and I was sent away, leaving the women to confer on the subject of my swivels and turns.

Later I got a certificate with a seal on the top. I had passed with honours. I stuck it to a wall in the attic, but it soon dropped down onto the floor and became mildewy.

When my feet got too large for my ballet shoes I stopped dancing, although I still have dreams about free expression, in which I become a belly dancer with the pink lady and our inner thighs begin to sweat as we roll our bellies to the flutes of snake charmers.

Harry

I went to the corner shop to buy cigarettes. I was off work again. Harry was everywhere, lurking in the canopies of car parks, looking up at empty conker trees. He circled the dental hospital with its green windows and cabinets full of molars. He poked in the skips with his mottled nose. At night he guarded the back lanes and incinerators. He ambled to Jimmy's shop and I heard him making lewd remarks about young nurses; filling the long uneventful nights. I never went back on Monday, like Harry told me to. I watched for the women, ready to pounce, to catch them red-handed.

I spoke to Harry as I passed him in the back lane. His head must have been on the boil all the time, because the balaclava was so thick. No wonder he thought of sex in his woolly world. He stopped me and beckoned conspiratorially. I ambled up to him, curious. He pointed at the tarmac, and we both examined the remains of a stolen car; a small pile of blue, shattered glass, an emergency breakdown card, a keyring with a blurred photograph of a child encased in plastic, and the tracks of tyres swerving on full throttle. There was a moment's silence; a homage to the excitement of the thieves and the euphoria of hitting the coast road at ninety miles an hour.

Harry said, 'Happened ten minutes ago. Brand new Nissan.'

I liked Harry. I found this surprising, as he was a man with no morals. He seemed lonely as an isolated virus. When he slept, back on a green settee in Westerhope, he said he dreamt of his ancestors who were Roman soldiers guarding the wall in a dreary line, their thighs freezing under their tunics. It was in his blood to guard places and things, he told me. His father had been in charge of the city's car parks. His grandfather had carried Victorian explorers' handbags while they swayed into the desert on camels.

Provoked by this intimacy I started to explain our first meeting, and my concerns over garbage that was not mine. About the glum women who never spoke, who came from nowhere. I even told him about the lottery grant, and the Head Curator, and the Egyptian mummy who nobody cared about. As I gabbled on a sea wind gathered and blew us closer together. I could see the tyre marks on Harry's cheeks and his pink eyes peeping.

'What do you think is in those rubbish bags?' he asked mysteriously, as if he already knew the answer.

Bad experiences. What else could come from a state psychiatric unit but terror and misery... mothers' grimaces, fathers' infidelities, a nightmare concerning a Persian carpet and a smothered kitten, a Catholic childhood, or raw silence?

'I don't know. I don't like to think about it,' I said eventually.

'You should be careful rats don't gnaw the corners,' he murmured. 'There's plenty of rats here. They play together at night. I see them larking about. Whatever is in the bags could leak out. Maybe it already has. You could catch it.'

'Why don't you speak to them?'

'Rats don't speak.'

'Not the rats, the cleaners.'

'Them too. They won't even give me a cup of coffee.'

Harry lit up a Silk Cut; pulling his balaclava down and exposing a frail moustache.

'I don't go in there unless I have to,' he whispered. 'There was a man went in, looking for a dentist. Got the wrong place. I knew him personally. He had an abscess in his molar and he was howling with the pain. It took him hours to get out, because they got out the forms, and no-one knew what he was talking about so they mistook him for a loony. He nearly ended up in Ward One Hundred.' Harry paused for effect. 'But he kept opening his mouth and showing them his teeth and in the end they let him go and he ran out and found his car had been stolen. It was a Nissan, like this one.' Harry shook his head, relishing the moment, exhaling smoke like a car exhaust.

Then he whispered in my ear, 'That's what they're like in there. Unsympathetic.'

He turned and whistled, as if he had a dog.

Walking through the smells of amalgam and surgical spirit, skirting the black bags that slumped on the streets and listening fearfully for rats' teeth, I went home, worried.

Frank

'Are you there Frank? I can hear your tin cup scraping across your stubble. Frank?'

'Gert, why don't you calm down?'

'What do you think about Frank?'

'Shades of light. Breath.'

'Do you think about the old house?'

'No.'

'Why not?'

'Because it's incidental. Unimportant.'

'How are things?'

'Same.'

'Does anyone converse?'

'Of course not.'

'What's the point of it then?'

'There is no point.'

'Do you ever miss George?'

'No.'

'Me?'

'No.'

'I got a letter from Jean.'

'So?'

'What shall I do?'

'Whatever you want.'

'You're no help are you?'

'You could write back.'

'But I can't.'

'Why not?'

'I don't know. I can't face it.'

'Don't then.'

'You are no help at all.'

'Look, will you stop disturbing me. I'll have to start the whole ritual again now.'

'What ritual?'

'Everything. Washing. Meditating. You know.'

Eva And The Cream Bun

I had noticed Eva was sighing a lot. Her straight back had a subtle sag and her coffee was slightly less hot.

Then I saw her standing at the flower stall. She was wearing a tailored jacket that flared at the waist and a cobalt blue scarf that spread over her shoulders in a wave. She was buying some irises. I had meant to glide past her without being seen, but I sailed too close and she looked up and waved.

I stopped and said, 'Eva?'

I was filled with guilt then, because I looked her straight in the face and knew I had somehow deceived her. I had thought about her so much I no longer knew her.

'These are for my bloody mother. It's her birthday,' she said.

'Ah.'

'She's seventy-six.'

'Your mother!' I echoed.

'That's her name. Iris,' said Eva.

Then she looked at a man's watch on her perfect wrist and up at me.

'Do you fancy a coffee?' she said.

I was very hot. The back of my neck was vibrating like a cat on heat. I remembered a café near by with small tables and bone china cups. I mumbled, 'Yes,' and dumbly walked beside Eva who began to chatter. After that it was easy because all I had to do was nod while Eva talked. We ordered a pot of tea for two and two portions of gluey cake. Eva played with the cream that lay in a glut over hers and then pushed it over to me. She was preoccupied, upset, and enigmatic. It was like winning a date with a famous person. Maybe she thought I was boring.

'You're from the south aren't you?'

'Um.'

'Well that doesn't matter to me. I don't mean to be rude, but people round here are like that... about southerners... I never thought of you as a southerner. I've watched you at the museum. You look foreign. Did you know that?'

'Ah.' Was that a compliment, or was she merely referring to my Germanic ankles?

'Did you think I was crazy, when you saw me dancing?'

'No, not at all. I thought I was seeing things.'

'I was practising, that's all. For a competition.'

I raised my eyebrows.

'Amateur ballroom,' said Eva brightly.

There was a creamy pause, then she said, 'Thank you for the flowers. No-one's given me any flowers for years.'

'Don't mention it.'

'It wasn't some gimmick, was it? The Head Curator didn't tell

79

you to buy them did he?'

'No!' I exclaimed.

'It's just, well, he's got some weird ideas hasn't he?'

I nodded, and told her about the voodoo objects. Eva shook her head in disbelief. Then she wiped her mouth with a napkin and leant towards me.

'I've never been anywhere. Other countries came to me. On boats. I'm right near the quay... in that big block of flats with the clock that you can see from the other side of the river. My daddy was a watchman, and my mam made pies. Fish pies. Do you like fish? You should come up to ours and have some fish pie.'

'I'd love to.'

'Except she's a bit of a handful.' Eva pointed at her head. 'Barmy.' Then, 'Why did you give me the flowers?' she asked suddenly.

'Why not!' I shrugged.

Eva frowned. She was trying to work me out, looking at me the way I once looked at an undated artifact.

'Chrysanthemums are my favourite. Irises symbolize death. Chrysanths are all about life and change and that kind of stuff. I don't like irises.'

'So why are you giving irises to your mother?'

'They're her favourite flower, that's why.'

We paused. Eva looked embarrassed. 'Do you get out much? I go out with Gwenny, my friend.'

'Your friend? With ginger hair?'

'How do you know that?'

'I saw you meeting her.'

Watching me were you?'

I shook my head, unnerved. 'No, I was just on my way home,'

Eva grinned suddenly, sitting back in her chair.

'We go to the clubs... Fat Betty, the Continental... and get pissed, you know. I hope you don't mind me talking like this.' She waited for a reaction but I was muted by a large walnut.

'The truth is I'm putting off going home. She won't go out, so that means we both stay in... and I'm in charge of the birthday celebrations. I made a cake last night. It's nice. It's a fruit cake. But all she's got is the telly. I shouldn't be going on like this. When she walks she says it's like walking on knives. Like the little mermaid. Walking on knives! It's Gert isn't it? Not Miss Hardcastle. Can I call you Gert? It's a nice name. The truth is, about the flowers, that I wish she was dead. She was a bloody awful mother and now I'm stuck with her.'

I took a large gulp of tea, and opened my mouth to speak, but the tea had gone down the wrong way and was driving a ravine somewhere up the back of my nasal passages. I started to splutter. Tea seemed to be dripping out of my ears. Eva stood up and landed on my side of the table. She bent over me. Her lips were near my ear. Her hand was flat on the centre of my back. She tilted me forward and I started to breathe. A steady river of tea dripped from my nose and ran in a brown thread over the tablecloth. I could smell pastry and security on Eva's scarf.

'It's all right, Gert,' she said. 'Breathe slowly. It's only a hiccup.'

Dusty Springfield

For a brief period in this chronology I became a girl in a sticky-out dress with an indulgent mother. The cha-cha-cha certificate had helped. I was making an effort. Jean wanted to school me in all the arts that she had neglected. I was a debutante before I reached the age of six.

The piano was a gift from George. It came in an African envelope in the form of a sales receipt. He had bought me a baby grand with a velvet stool. It was delivered the next day by tone-deaf men with stumpy legs. I made Jean check inside it for crocodiles, which she related to Mabel on the phone with much giggling.

And then she telephoned Mrs Hesp.

Mrs Hesp had blue fingers, the colour of varicose. She was my piano teacher. She put the metronome on the piano and set it off like a brisk disapproving tongue. We were stuck in the scale of C. Her house was a hole with a piano in it. I was at the bottom trying to play 'The Cuckoo', my fingers clumping over the wide white notes.

These are the words I learnt from Mrs Hesp; manuscript, cleft, lento, bars, flats, sharps - the hard words of musical agony.

At home I was playing a different scale altogether. Jean played music hall songs in wild scattering chords. She got lost in the tunes, fumbling and tripping, lolloping from chorus to verse. After she left the room the piano would hum with nostalgia. Then Frank would start, crashing his spidery hands on to the aching keys, playing Schoenberg, and disjointed modern jazz, fighting with the keys, bruising them and making them defiant.

It was my piano after all, not theirs. When the room was empty I would creep in, in my Shetland jersey and forget-me-not skirt. I would play stories. I played the story of the brave girl who destroyed a city, starting with the tinkling of paraffin flames, or the love story of the brave girl who leapt an impossible chasm to reach her sweetheart. I played until the room was full of me. Someone would always come in (was it Carmen, or Jean?) and tell me to shut up, and by then it was usually night although the curtains weren't drawn, but I had spun myself so high and taut that I couldn't come down. I was mute with music. They would slam the piano lid down on my fingers to stop me.

That was why I got sent to the piano hole to see Mrs Hesp and to play 'The Cuckoo' in the scale of C. It was an exercise in repression.

I had reached school age. Try and imagine the sum of my parts, with my cha-cha-cha diploma, and my unsettling relationship with Jean who had weak ankles. My father was lost to crocodiles. We used his letters to light fires, as the paper was very dry and inflammable.

The school had wire all round it. It was high up, above the town. Through a six-foot fence I could see a row of terraced houses with meek curtains and polished letter boxes. I whispered to passing strangers on the way to the shops to get me out. I tried to pass messages to them written on scraps of toilet paper, but they didn't turn their heads.

I wore a hat in the shape of a door wedge with thin elastic under my chin. Frank had a flat cap. Our clothes were weighty with name tapes. We stood in the playground trying to be invisible, drinking from dwarfed bottles of creamy milk with straws. Our ties were strangling us, but if you took your tie off then Mr Whitebait, the headmaster, led you to his parlour with the picture of Winston Churchill above the mantelpiece and attacked the palms of your hands with a baton. I couldn't believe that he dared do this to Frank. Frank was Einstein. After the beating Frank's face turned so white that it glowed at night.

The school was very expensive. They knew nothing. The nature teacher was drunk and couldn't say the word primrose. 'Primrose,' I said to myself, and wished for oblivion.

I was so well behaved that adults loathed me. I was good in an artificial way. I crossed my arms as if I had a rifle stuck in the base of my spine. I listened so hard the words became foreign. I did my homework twice. That is why Mr Whitebait made a scapegoat of me. I had a victim mentality. I liked to suffer and I selflessly believed it took the spotlight off Frank.

The other children were strangely vacuous, with uniforms that looked as if they were cut out of a catalogue. They had straight hair and teeth and carbolic cheeks. At playtime they ran in circles as if powered by an invisible motor. They were the progeny of policemen and traffic wardens, reared under the auspices of the Church of England. They had mothers shaped like caravans.

At first, when Mr Whitebait made me chew the chalk I thought he was joking. He was talking about a pop group called the Monkees. He said, 'Who listens to the Monkees?' and I stretched my arm high up in the air, because although I didn't listen to the Monkees I thought it was a yes question.

'I expect you watch "Ready Steady Go"?' he went on, pleasantly.

All the little policemen looked at me.

'Yes. Yes. Yes.' I spluttered.

'And who is your favourite singer Gert?'

'Dusty.'

'I beg your pardon?'

'Dusty Springfield.'

Frank shook his head.

Mr Whitebait turned his smile upside down and took a stick of chalk out of his pocket.

'Chew on that Gert,' he snarled. 'And consider the eleven plus.'

It tasted sweet, like candy dust. I swallowed most of it. The class roared with laughter. I laughed too. I swallowed it. Dusty Springfield.

When Winston Churchill died his big blubbery face was in all the newspapers. Mr Whitebait told us to cut him out and stick him on our bedroom walls. I cut him out twice and for days he stared down at me in duplicate as if I was Hitler. I asked Jean to take him down, because I didn't dare. She scrumpled him up callously and said, 'That's enough of you and your sleep walking!'

I asked her what she meant

'You,' she said. 'You've been walking up and down the stairs at night waking up poor Frank. Don't you remember? I got up and took you back to bed and you said you were looking for a book, but it was nonsense.'

'What did I say?'

'I said, "What book?" and you said, "The Complete Works of Dusty Springfield."'

Around this time Frank wrote to Jean to ask if he could see a psychiatrist. He was sitting in the top branches of a beech tree at the end of the garden, waiting for a reply.

But she just ironed handkerchiefs and changed the furniture around.

The Third Letter

Gert,

Why haven't you written? Are you still angry with me? I know we didn't always get on, but you were such an imaginative and difficult child. I was very young. Surely after all this time you want to see me at least. I'm not a monster. I'm nearly sixty. I've got palpitations. Let's forget the past and start again.

Perhaps you can't forgive me for not getting in touch sooner. After you left home I was not myself. I fell in love with Cameron. Surely you must know how that feels? I forgot everything. I wanted to put it all behind me. I had to get out of the house.

I shan't bore you with sordid details, but put it this way, I am in a desperate situation. The landlord says I can do cleaning work for him, temporarily, but I can hardly bear even the smell of the streets around here. It stinks of trains and chips. I never noticed when Cameron was alive.

Perhaps you're not a letter writer? I'm sorry I'm not on the phone. Please write soon.

Jean

Christmas

What should I give Eva for Christmas? An ornament? A book? A pot of honey? Or shall I buy her a card, and if so, what shall I write inside it, and what should the card signify? Should it be flowery, serious, light-hearted, large, small or abstract? What do you give a love object?

What do you give someone you don't really know?

I was sitting on an underground train, concentrating on this question. It was snowing and the passengers waiting on the platforms were solid and furry. The carriage was crammed with pensioners, defensively clutching concessionary passes, with mighty felt hats pinned to their heads and overlarge gloves. When they moved there was a sound of crackling polythene. They looked at the snow with disgust, and stamped their feet on the floor to shake the flakes off. Christmas approached like a tunnel.

What should I give her? When I got off the train I was no clearer, and it was only when I began a tedious walk through a shopping mall that I decided to buy us both a holiday.

George Comes Home

Dear George,

   I have reached a decision. You should see the way that Gert bites her nails and mutters to herself. Frank is also going through a difficult time. He will only look at me through a telescope. You see, George, when we married I wanted a proper home, but what have I got? Children who never smile with psychiatric disorders and a sofa I can never sit on.

   It can't go on. You must come home.

When George came back the house was neurotic and tidy.

   When he stepped off the train we didn't recognize him. He was red and scaly from the neck up, and his hair had grown thick and ragged. When he saw us he sighed before waving.

   At home he dispensed strange ornaments; skeletal wooden

horses, wiry African heads, bead pictures, necklaces and bright blankets. He gave me a stick with a long mane of hair stuck to it that I swished about, catching the back of Frank's knees. I asked him about the crocodiles, but his own face had closed down, as if all his wires had been snipped. I wondered if his brain had boiled in the hot sun. I was unsure if the man sitting at the end of the table was really my father. Jean served up boiled beetroot and roast beef and he looked at his plate as if it was an impossible problem.

And Jean acted happy and lit a candle in the centre of the table which reflected in the pupils of her eyes, like love.

The Lost Au Pair

Next thing I knew we were on holiday. It was supposed to be Jean and George's second honeymoon. We were staying in a pink cottage by the sea. Botanical plants grew on ledges in the cliffs above us. The sea was so blue it looked artificial. It was in a seaside resort with shells encrusted in the walls. A spindly pier stretched out into an impenetrable mist. There was a book shop that sold postcards of women with vast fleshy bottoms, and encyclopedias, shackles and sailors' hats, and sweets shaped like pastel-coloured pebbles. Boats jiggled together and sung in the evenings. A toy train chugged along the promenade driven by a man with no legs in a kiss-me-quick hat. Sometimes a cannon went off and it felt like our insides had sunk to the bottom of the sea.

Everywhere was steep. The waves crashed against the harbour wall and curled over themselves. Frank said there was too much noise. He was trying to write a novel. I looked over his shoulder and saw that his writing had almost disappeared. It was just spiders' footprints now. When he wasn't writing he played silent music on a bent piano in the front room. The sofa was high backed and deep and I sat there watching him. He hunched over the keys, concentrating, and from behind he looked as if he was sobbing.

I followed him everywhere. I couldn't help it. I wanted to talk to him about Jean and George. Frank knew something I didn't. He said I smelt revolting, but I still hung about waiting. Frank had changed a lot. He was trying to be like other boys, but he wasn't. He had bruises behind his eyes. George treated him like a girl. He called me Gertie and taught me nautical terms. He was quite different since he'd been away. He tried to introduce himself to us every day, but we turned up our noses and wouldn't give him even a courtesy nod. The salt blew the crocodile scales off his brow. We looked up at him humourlessly and longingly. He was the one who tried to keep the conversation going over cottage pie. Jean just looked into saucepans and listened to angry music on the radio; her face as doom laden as a black sail. Something was up.

When everyone was asleep I pulled on my shabby holiday clothes and walked out of the cottage. I went to the shingle beach and shouted. The waves egged me on. I could hear Frank dreaming; of places he had never been; of planets and universes. Then I saw a lonely woman on the two-bit jetty that lunged halfway into the harbour. She was crying and staggering like a sailor whose boat had steamed away without her. I called to her, but she didn't turn round, so I couldn't see her face, and I didn't think I wanted to see it, because I wouldn't know what to say. Whoever it was, they were dangerous, so I made myself forget what I saw, and the smell of the sea that particular night. Babies' tears, that's what it smelt like.

Then a Swedish au pair girl turned up with a white leather suitcase and dark glasses and we all stared at her as she sat in the front room of the dank cottage, wondering why she was there. She didn't match the furniture. George treated her like something he'd just pulled out of a bran tub. He said that now Jean could rest, as she'd been having trouble with her nerves, but as soon as Oona arrived Jean became twitchy and restless.

One day we were all on the beach, in the steep seaside place; George with his porous nose, Jean, Frank and me. Next to our huddled group two small boys with thin arms and sharp wet legs were digging sand as if they were possessed.

I was wearing a puckered bathing costume with a limp pink bow. Oona lay some distance from us; in the pose of a foreign postcard, wearing a white bikini that fitted her like a seal skin. George was reading an almanac and fingering a corned beef sandwich. He was stuck in a deck-chair. He wouldn't take off his shoes. He said he must go somewhere soon. Jean had nested beyond a breakwater. She was reading the obituaries in *The Times*, and her hair was contained in a daunting black scarf, which made her a landmark, even though she tried to be unnoticeable. She scowled at the boys ferreting in the sand, throwing up grainy storms with tin spades. The sand was black and their puny limbs were smudged with it. Jean ordered them off and fingered a Dunhill cigarette in the bottom of her beach bag. It was common to smoke outside. Frank was constructing an oil rig from lollipop sticks. You would only know he was part of our family by the way he pretended not to know us.

Oona knew how to sunbathe. It was in her genes. She lay on a lilo behind a frontier of suntan lotions and had a gadget, a pulpy plastic envelope, that rested heavily over her eyes. We wanted the lilo. It belonged to us, and Oona had plumped herself on it. Jean glanced at her with contempt. Oona, who George had got from an agency, didn't even know how to clean a lavatory. She was already homesick, and only pretended to love children in letters. I ambled about, looking at Oona, looking at Jean. I sidled up to Frank, who turned his acned back to me. I sloped back to Oona and tapped her firm, greasy thigh. She took off her eye cover and scowled. I attempted to explain the word SWIMMING to her, using arm movements. I pointed at the lilo and then to the bow on my chest. Oona shook her head. Jean was asleep now, and the death columns were blowing in wheels along the beach.

I started all over again with Oona, who wiped her arms with white cream, then got up when I was in mid-stroke, picked up the lilo and catwalked down to the calmish sea. She launched herself into the shallows and floated face up with her arms drooping languidly over the sides.

It was all very quiet. George's deck-chair was empty, and a seagull carried the remains of his corned beef sandwich high up in the sky. Jean was in the fathoms of slumber. I buried my leg in the sand, until it felt numb and dislocated from the rest of my body. I imagined that I was a one-legged person and waited for a kind passer-by to feel sorry on my behalf. Hours passed.

Then someone saw an orange cruise liner sliding along the top edge of the sea; like a ship in a novelty pen. The group of children all stopped digging, and got up to shout and wave, as if we were shipwrecked, desperate to be heard. I wrenched my dead limb from its cold grave and limped hopefully down to the sea. Soon there was an almighty wash and vast booming waves were crashing along the shoreline. We applauded, as if it was a passing parade, and ran about in the froth. Then, gradually, the wash slipped back to nothing. That's when Frank piped up, 'Where is Oona?'

We craned our necks and fanned our eyes.

Frank shrugged and picked up a pebble in the shape of a heart. I tugged at Jean's black headscarf and she slapped my hand viciously and woke up.

'Where's our lilo?!' I screamed piercingly.

One side of Jean's face was red and creased from where it had pressed against the breakwater. She was so angry that she pulled her cigarette out of the bag and lit it, trembling still from a nightmare about a stain on a Jaeger jacket.

'What?' she snarled. She did look common.

'Oona's floated off on our lilo,' Frank and I bleated in squeaking unison.

'For God's sake!'

The tide had seeped away by now. The family was a long way from anything. From the promenade we were a little clump of people alone in a daunting expanse.

Jean stood up and shrieked. Even the youths in the penny arcade heard her and the seaside town turned its head. She ran, still shrieking, towards the pier. Frank tried to roll himself into an invisible ball as she passed. The small boys cried and hunched their shoulders. I ran through the dipping rock pools calling, 'Ooonaaa, Oooonaaa!'

I sounded like a sea-bird. I was nearly hoarse.

'Ooooooonaaaaaa!'

On the quayside there was a dull bang and a flare whooshed above us. We cheered. A posse of men in yellow plastic anoraks galloped out of nowhere, crushing Frank's oil rig with big leathery Wellington boots. They carried an inflatable lifeboat, and disappeared into the sea after Oona.

George came back. His breath smelt fruity and he had mislaid his almanac. He squinted at the horizon and coughed. Jean put on his large flecked sweater and walked up and down like a hungry wolf. She told George to take us home, but he shook his big head. When Jean was like this it was better to do nothing.

When the men returned, some hours later, and the sun had quite gone, and the sea purred, and the family was a line of cold people wrapped in wet towels who waited, they brought back the deflated lilo. One of the men held it up, as if it was a skin.

'He's got the lilo!' chirped one of the boys helpfully.

Jean whispered the Lord's Prayer, and sent George tiptoeing off to the police station.

At the cottage we ate fish fingers.

I asked Jean, as she scoured the frying pan, 'Where is Sweden?'

'Look in the atlas,' she snapped and blew her nose on a dishcloth.

I went upstairs to the cabinet where the encyclopedias were kept. Oona's bedroom door was open; it smelt of wet bathing costumes in there, but I didn't go in.

I looked at the green map of Sweden; its head hung over the Baltic Sea. Like Oona, it was just a shape.

Frank was mending the lilo with a bicycle repair kit.

The next day Jean wrote a letter to Sweden. Her face was a church. George took us to a tearoom where there were cakes as big as bricks. We each drank a milkshake with a long straw and looked up mournfully at the waitress. It was meant to be a treat.

But for a long time I kept finding bits of Oona; her mascara, her raincoat, her Lypsyl.

Frank Disagrees

'Gert. Stop it.'

'Stop what?'

'Getting things out of proportion.'

'Do you mean Oona?'

'She was homesick. She didn't stay very long.'

'Are you saying that she never drowned?'

'Of course she didn't. She lost our lilo, that's all. Forgot about it and it drifted out to sea. You always make tragedies out of things.'

'So what happened to her?'

'She packed her bags after about a week and went home. Jean didn't like her.'

'And George did?'

'Yes.'

'Are you sure?'

'I'm sure. I can't bear it, the way you get everything wrong. I think you should write to Jean after all. She is your mother.'

'Yours too.'

'But I've got nothing. You've got a job and everything. Don't you want to make friends with her?'

'I just can't.'

'You have still got a job haven't you?'

'Yes. Go back to your breathing Frank.'

'I am, don't worry. One more thing. Stop remembering me as a kind of dysfunctional egg head.'

'You were.'

'I was just a little boy Gert, just like you were a little girl.'

And a door slammed somewhere in space, forcing me back into the unpleasant reality of the day ahead.

Learning To Communicate

That morning the Head Curator made us all have a meeting. We sat around the long wooden table in the Victorian conference room and Eva brought in coffee on a tray. Everyone gazed expectantly at the Head Curator who was looking at his hands on the flat table. I noticed how hairy his fingers were. They were almost apelike. He told us that he had been on a course to learn how to communicate properly with others. Then he asked us all to hold hands. I was sitting with Theobald on one side and Marcus the botanist on the other. Neither of them had hands that I would normally consider holding. Tentatively, I asked 'Why?', and the Head Curator frowned at me as if I had burped or farted.

After we had held hands, he ordered us to turn to the person on our left and tell them our worries.

'How long have you got?' I smirked, turning to Marcus who had gone a deep shade of red.

'I'm worried I might lose my job,' whispered Marcus. 'I've got five children.'

'Yes,' I murmured, sympathetically.

'What about you?' he asked.

'I'm worried about everything,' I told him, feeling tearful.

'Five minutes is up,' boomed the Head Curator. 'How does everyone feel?'

'Great!' announced Theobald, who had just confessed his worries about his knees to Carol from the office. She in turn had unloaded her anger about dog mess in the area where she lived.

'So, on with the business!' announced the Head Curator. 'Redundancies!'

At this point I drifted off, too aware of Marcus's repressed sobbing to engage in the discussion. I suddenly remembered another incident, and another museum.

History Lessons

I was on a school trip, walking down a steep hill with all the other children, in a line, on our way to look at Mr Whitebait's version of history. It was autumn again, and the trees were heavy with bulging conkers that we were not allowed to collect. They hung above our heads in inviting prickly balls. We were supposed to walk in a military fashion, with our chins abnormally high, and our feet stamping the slimy leaves on the pavement. The nature teacher clung to the rear of this parade, staggering slightly, and Mr Whitebait led us, chanting war songs and slashing the path with his ferocious cane.

We walked along by the river which was overflowing, and stared at the angry swans down by the sluice. I stopped suddenly to point at a magical trout that was perfectly still in the rushing water, causing a pile-up and a boy called Roger to fall over and hurt his knee. The fish darted away. I stared at where it had been dumbly, ignoring Roger's roars of pain as he picked the grit out of his skinny knee. The nature teacher slurred 'Oh, Gert!' and comforted little Roger who had blood on his sock. I apologized several times, and a flock of swans glided up and listened to me, cynically. Then Mr Whitebait, who was miles ahead, roared at us, and we had to hobble on.

I began to worry about the insides of the sandwiches that Jean had packed that morning. She tended to hurl expensive ingredients in between stale bread, with slices of hard butter. I didn't want anyone else to see how inept my mother was at the basic domestic task of lunch-making.

We traipsed over a narrow bridge made of twigs, through a geriatric gateway between two flint walls, and past the lily pond where I had met the stranger. The goldfish goggled at us. The water lilies trembled.

'This,' announced Mr Whitebait, 'is the site of the Battle of the Mercenaries.'

We wrote this down on small notepads. I wished someone had told me earlier. I looked down into the water and saw that the gloomy bed was indeed matted with soldiers' hair.

Then we were walking down my street, and to my embarrassment ordered to stop in a line to look at my house, while Mr Whitebait and the nature teacher pointed to the plaque above the front door. I kept silent, hoping that Mr Whitebait wouldn't embarrass me, but of course he did. Frank and I had to stand and answer questions. Luckily none was asked. The windows were reassuringly blank and uninformative. Then Mr Whitebait blew a whistle and the front door opened, and Jean and George were standing there, waving. Jean was wearing a lace apron, and had flour on her chin. George had his arm loosely around her shoulders, and he was laughing. Perhaps he had oiled his hair, because it lay on his head with the shine of a patent shoe.

They performed for a few minutes, and then, as if by clockwork, retreated again to the innards of the house. A church bell began to ring. Frank smirked at me conspiratorially, and I raised my little fist in a victorious gesture. Things were going rather well.

Then Frank reverted to his anonymous identity, walking in the shadow of Mr Whitebait's hideous hat.

No-one else but me saw a thin hand waving from the tiny attic window, or heard a tubercular cough, or noticed a small swarm of hungry bees hovering above the chimneys on the house.

We marched on towards the museum, which was a ponderous building with closed eyes and a dark mouth. Mr Manners, the curator, was there to meet us, dressed in military regalia with a monocle pressed into his eye socket. He put his hand on our heads as we passed through the dark orifice, as if he was feeling the quality of our skulls.

Inside we were instructed to take out our notepads. The first room was a round foyer with colourful, imperial maps in gilt frames hanging on oak-panelled walls.

An ancient and speckled receptionist laboriously handed us each a ticket, which I instantly began to eat.

We were divided into groups. I was with Melanie and Andrew, who held hands and had black, ironed hair. They looked at the ground, as if history was all beneath their feet. I put my own hands in my pockets. We were sent down a corridor lined with bulky bronze heads. Each one was a famous person, but they all appeared remarkably similar, as if they were cast in bronze against their wishes. We were not supposed to talk.

Andrew and Melanie hung slowly behind me, and before

long I was yet again on my own. I slipped through a door into a cavernous municipal room that was full of stuffed birds, and loitered under an albatross, wondering what to do next.

I wrote, 'Albatross, wing span fifteen foot', in neat writing under 'Battle of the Mercenaries'.

I ignored the wide eyes of a frozen barn owl, and tiptoed past an animated woodpecker, nailed heartlessly to the branch of a tree, its beak pounding the bark. A button said PUSH ME and I did. At once the air was loud with hammering and squawking, and several large birds flapped their wings. I escaped from the room, sure that I could hear breaking glass as a vulture threw itself against the confines of its exhibition case.

I lurched headlong into Mr Manners, who had changed into a janitor, and was wearing a brown overall over his uniform, sweeping a corner of the room. It was very quiet. My whole school had disappeared into the recesses of the museum.

Mr Manners said, 'Are you interested in history?'

His white hair needed oiling, his teeth were rusty, and his nails were too long. The skin around his left eye was dented.

'Perhaps,' I said, holding my notepad as if it was a hand grenade.

'Come with me,' he rasped, and walked to a door with a notice saying EMPLOYEES ONLY. I hesitated, thinking of Mr Whitebait's cane and the button that said PUSH ME.

'It's all right,' said Mr Manners.

It seemed to me that Mr Manners belonged in a glass case himself, but still I followed him. It was like walking into a cave. We were in a room that was flanked with pipes and lockers. In the centre of it was a desk that was covered with coins and bones, and asthma inhalers.

Mr Manners removed his brown coat, and put the broom in a cupboard.

'Sit down,' he ordered. I clambered onto an uncomfortable swivelling chair.

Mr Manners pulled open a large flat drawer, divided into hundreds of compartments. Each was labelled, and contained a relic – a gnarled root, a butterfly wing, something wet and red, dried leaves, gold dust, bright beads, silver threads. I gasped hungrily and leant towards it. It was a playground of substances. I longed to tell Frank, who could have photographed it with his camera eyes and described the drawer again and again.

'This is my collection,' murmured Mr Manners. 'This is my work.'

I nodded.

He gathered some blue dust in his fingers and sprinkled it onto a metal plate. He struck a match, and suddenly the room was filled with cracking golden triangles, exploding into the air with flamboyant pops.

I yelped with excitement. When the last pop had fizzled away, I felt as if the backs of my eyes were scorched with the memory of them.

'Would you like to choose something?' he spread his hairy hands out generously. His knuckles were white conkers and his fingers were long and crooked. 'Anything you like.'

A glass bead glittered from one of the compartments.

'That.' I pointed to it, and it glowed even brighter.

'You shall have it,' whispered Mr Manners, scooping it out of its cavern. 'It has some qualities. Early Egyptian. Don't swallow it, will you?' I held the bead in my palm. It changed colour, turning a deep azure blue. I put it into my pocket. Then Mr Manners clasped his big hands around mine and smiled.

'I'd better go,' I squeaked.

'Not yet,' he grunted. Then he was rubbing the ball of our hands against his trousers, and there was something stiff under there; a piece of wood or a bone. His face was red and drops of sweat were gathering in the bags under his eyes and in the pores of his nose. I was perplexed. He let go of my hands and started to scrabble with the buttons of his trousers, reaching in and waggling the thing wildly. I just sat there, redundant, watching on until he stopped and sighed to himself, closing his eyes and hastily zipping up his fly. He seemed to suddenly realize I was there.

'Sorry about that,' he apologized. 'No harm meant.'

I nodded, confused.

Would you mind letting me have some of your hair?'

Mr Manners quickly flashed a fine pair of scissors around my head, snipped off a lock of my dark, childish hair, and placed it in the empty compartment where the bead once was. I noticed there were several similar locks of hair kept in the great drawer.

I shivered. It was as if a beetle was walking over my scalp.

Mr Manners laughed conspiratorially.

'Can I go now?' I asked politely.

'Carry on!' he boomed, closing the drawer with an abrupt movement. I slid from my chair and ran out of the room.

I was suddenly surrounded by Rogers, Melanies and Andrews, and Mr Whitebait was telling us the contents of the Roman arsenal in alphabetical order. I fingered the bead in my gabardine pocket.

Afterwards we ate our sandwiches on a grassy hillock, above a mass burial ground of plague victims.

I was curious to know the contents of the others' Tupperware boxes, but happy enough with Jean's efforts, which were pleasantly ordinary. A wedge of ham, a melted chocolate finger, a sliver of cucumber and a robust tomato.

After lunch we ran about, and I threw the bead at Roger, who said I had nearly blinded him and cried all the way home.

I wonder if all Head Curators are wankers?

Harry

'I'll tell you something', said Harry, as we queued up patiently in Jimmy's corner shop, 'that you may not realize.'

I waited. Harry had dramatic timing and didn't like to be interrupted.

'I have personal links with someone you know.'

I felt my usual sense of dread.

'Someone dead,' he went on.

'I see.'

'Aren't you going to guess?'

'No.'

'You see them every day.'

What was he talking about? I had enough to deal with without listening to the deluded ramblings of a hospital caretaker.

'Very dead.'

'How long?' As we were stuck in the queue there was no

option but to participate in Harry's game.

'Thousands of years.'

'Well?'

'Female. A princess.'

'The mummy at the museum?'

'That's right. My grandfather was one of the people who helped to ransack the tomb. He always felt very guilty about it afterwards. Said it was like walking into a woman's bedroom with a torch, getting mud on the carpet.'

'You're joking!'

'I thought you'd be interested. Personal links,' he mused proudly, buying twenty Silk Cut and four bars of Galaxy.

'How nice,' I said politely.

Swimming

You see, all my life I lived with danger. Danger emerged in the most innocent of pastimes. It's amazing that I am still alive to tell you all this.

At some point during this period I went swimming. On the way to the baths a rag and bone man passed in a horse-drawn cart. He looked out of place in a traffic jam of buses, as if he had just ridden out of sequence, from another time altogether. I thought about him as I entered the municipal baths, wondering if people saw me like that, as a person who doesn't match their surroundings, an antique surrounded by modernity.

The swimming baths were very old, and smelt of feet. Getting undressed was cold and difficult. I couldn't unlock the lockers and when I took my trousers off, they fell into a puddle of dirty water. When I emerged in my black regulation swimming costume the cobalt pool was completely empty apart from one old woman with an artificial leg that she had abandoned at the side of the pool. She surged up and down the blue water with enthusiasm, while I delicately lowered myself into the shallow end and splashed about feebly.

I started swimming laps in awkward high-school breast stroke, with my head held up and out of the water. I passed the old lady. She was wearing a pink bathing hat and had no teeth. We saluted, then swam on.

I swam twenty lengths then staggered out of the heavy water, exhausted. As I was about to leave a flock of goose-pimpled schoolgirls flew into the baths and hurled themselves suicidally into the water. Their screeching laughter made me feel old. One child was left behind on the pool's edge. She was about eight with terrified eyes and unstylish hair.

'Get on with it Hermione!' yelled a teacher with a thyroid neck.

The child shook her head. The other girls jeered and splashed her.

'What on earth is the matter now?' sighed the teacher, as if Hermione was always behaving this way.

The child pointed at the water with wide fearful eyes.

Then the teacher blew her whistle, so loudly that it made waves in the water.

To our horror, we all suddenly noticed that the old lady was no longer swimming, but floating, face down below the surface. The girls all quietened into a still, cold ripple, and the teacher leapt into the water fully clothed, along with an army of attendants who had all been skiving around the coffee machine, instead of doing their jobs.

The old lady was lying on a towel now, surrounded by young,

muscly men in shorts. They were giving her the kiss of life. I shuddered; what a bizarre awakening. Then her toe twitched and her fingers uncurled and we were suddenly aware that for a moment we had all stopped breathing, and swallowed great gasps of air.

She sat up grinning, holding tightly onto the hand of an attendant who looked like Hercules.

'She always does this,' he said to no-one in particular. 'Every Saturday. It's a syndrome.'

'OK everyone, to the side!' yelled the soaking teacher, oblivious to Hermione who slunk into the pool, still pale. She could have thanked her. Hermione should have got a medal I thought. I smiled at her as she shivered in the pool. There's another one, I thought, who'll end up working in a quiet place, trying to be invisible. Afraid of everything.

Other Rivers

By the time I was eight years old, Hermione's age, I had already been haunted, nearly eaten by a crocodile, maimed my mother, murdered an au pair girl, and all the other things that you already know. No wonder I was a nervous type. You might think that was quite enough for one childhood, but there is more calamity to endure, and I don't see why I should let you off the hook.

In the time when Jean and George were pretending to be in love I decided to have swimming lessons, which was a skill that Frank flatly refused to learn. I spent Saturdays immersed in water, and my skin was covered with scales. I went to Mr Valentine's River Club. It was in a fenced-in part of the river, enclosed by trees, so that when I was there it seemed like a separate country. It had damp pastel bathing huts, and a diving board soggy with wet coconut matting. Mr Valentine was a dappled trout, who was once a champion swimmer, but who lost his little finger in a bar brawl, which affected his strokes. He kept the finger in a pickling jar in his office, and showed it to us mournfully. It looked like a prawn. This experience made him dry-skinned and melancholic, and when he was not teaching swimming he drank gin flavoured with Angostura bitters, and slumped in a deck-chair under a shadowy straw hat by the side of the pool.

At first I thought Mr Valentine must live in a bathing hut, as he never changed his clothes, and he never went home. At eight o'clock he blew his whistle and ushered the last breathless child out of the wooden door.

Once Jean forgot to collect me, and I peeked through a dry crack in the fence to see him dive gracefully into the empty meridian water, and disappear into the murky depths, leaving only stray bubbles rippling on the surface. I believed, then, that he lived on the river bed. His hair was mossy and green, like the slime that grew on the surface of the diving board. His skin was covered in splashes of a muddy colour. Mr Valentine was amphibian.

By day the pool was filled with shivering eight and nine-year-old boys whose parents wanted a quiet Saturday. Every week they would line up at the side of the pool with hunched shoulders and white fingers waiting for instructions. Although we had never heard Mr Valentine shout, we all obeyed him as if he might one day explode and drown us all.

He had a long pole with a harness attached to the end, and dragged me up and down the pool. Through him I learnt the crawl and the butterfly, breast stroke and back stroke.

One day he said that I didn't need the harness and told me to dive into the cold eely water and swim.

'Trust me,' said Mr Valentine, waggling his stump of a finger.

I jumped in.

I cascaded down into the deep unknown territory of the pool; down to the muddy bed with its river worms and sharp stones. I re-emerged like a jumping fish. I found that I could move through the water by merely flapping the ends of my toes and the tips of my fingers.

After that I soused myself in the river. I was not afraid of it. It ran through my bed at night, and all my dreams were underwater. I knew its character; its fast places, and its slow pools.

Suddenly the River Club was confining and cramped. I swam a length in a couple of seconds. Mr Valentine watched me as I flashed around the pool like a large goldfish in a small bowl.

One day he said casually, as I stood dripping, watching a large girl lolloping about in the shallow end, 'You need a bigger sea,' and I knew that he was right.

So instead of paying to swim in Mr Valentine's guarded waters, I found other places where the river deepened and whirled. When Jean left me at the River Club on Saturday mornings I waved goodbye, then switched from human to fish, sneaking away to the wide waters beyond the swimming pool. She had no idea what dangers I explored. I swam through underground pipes. I jumped off wooden bridges. I curled up under waterfalls.

I would return to the River Club at the end of the day, to be collected by Jean, scratched and clammy, webbed and silent. My hair was so wet it didn't dry until Monday, and I left mud and water everywhere I went. Jean thought it was nice that I had a hobby, although she wrinkled up her nose when I walked into a room.

I never liked swans; the slit of their eyes, the dirty down of their wings, the crack of their beaks or the snake of their necks.

The town was filled with them. They gathered at every sluice.

Swans were the self-appointed guards of the river. They supervised the river banks like secret police.

Although I didn't realize it, they had been watching me for a long time, waiting for their moment.

One day I was swimming in a broad quiet place in the river. The banks were high with buttercups. The air scraped with crickets.

I imagined that I was swimming the Channel. I swam slowly, conserving my energy. I sank into the silky green water. I turned over on my back and blew softly at the clouds. I was invisible, a trout that was so still it couldn't be seen. I didn't notice the nasty throng of swans that gossiped together by the bank, hissing quietly to each other, treading the calm water, thinking they would teach me a lesson.

The first thing I felt was the ugly scrape of a swan's leg. They surrounded me. I didn't move at first. I heard their harsh hearts beating under the soft feathers. I prayed to the Queen, gliding through her palace, while soldiers marched below her window.

That's when they attacked. I couldn't see anything, just wings, and waves of swans, pythons of swans, awakened lions of swans, pecking at me. I struggled in the water, turned and dived beneath them. Friendlier ducks were screaming and calling the police. I thought of the headline in the local newspaper 'Swansong for Gertrude Hardcastle!' One swan twisted me into a knot, the other spread its enormous wings and lunged at my throat. I writhed in the dangerous water. I grasped some reeds and started pulling myself up the muddy bank. The swans were cackling. They struck at my blue ankles; they wanted to kill me.

Then Frank was there, holding a long branch. He was

insulting the swans in a language I had never heard. He slapped one about the face with his bare hand. He dragged me out of the river. We ran, Frank cursing the swans. I was covered with blood and marks like snake bites.

When we got home I said to Frank, 'How did you know where to find me?' and he looked sideways and confided, 'You know I can hear what you're thinking. I always know where you are.'

Jean and George were unaware of this incident. They were meeting a princess at a civic dinner. Jean was wearing an eggshell hat and George was drunk and talking much too loud. Much too loud. The princess noticed him and shuddered, then fanned her elderly royal face with a fan made of white swan's feathers.

A Letter From Mabel

Dear Gert,

Your mother Jean has recently been in touch with me about her circumstances, which sound absolutely dire. I would like to take her in myself, but I am at present the lady captain of the golf club here in Woking, and I have a very busy schedule. I don't feel I am in a position to really support your mother, and frankly I don't think it's my responsibility.

I would imagine you would want to welcome her with open arms. Think of all she has done for you! You were a very difficult child. You were always making up awful stories, and disrupting dinner parties. It was obviously attention seeking. Several times I suggested to Jean that she sent you away to some kind of boarding school, but she never did. You hardly ever smiled, and were consistently ungrateful even though you never wanted for anything and were born with a silver spoon in your mouth. Why have you not been in touch with her? Do you understand how desperate she is? We all say and do things we don't mean at different points in our lives, and it's important to learn to forgive. Don't you think she's been through enough?

I shan't say anything about this letter to her. I just hope you pay some attention to it, and do something.

Yours sincerely
Mabel

The Dunkirk Spirit

Christmas came and went with a flurry of municipal bells, and neon reindeer leaping across the high street. As usual I spent the festive season entirely alone, despite another pleading Christmas card from Jean, depicting the Virgin Mary hanging onto Jesus surrounded by vindictive cherubim. I was still trying to pluck up the courage to invite Eva to come away with me. Instead we exchanged cards in the toilets. I chose an image of two angels kissing, and she gave me a snowy landscape with glittering stars. I welcomed the advent of the cabin-fever months. January was as cold and dark as Siberia, and the institute felt huge, damp and empty, with threatening winds rattling every window. All the staff felt under siege, and appeared each morning in armoured rainwear.

After the meeting when the Head Curator warned us that our livelihoods were on the line the Dunkirk spirit infected the staff at the institute, and this was particularly advantageous in the development of my friendship with Eva. Since the choking incident in the café we had engaged in several long conversations, but now everyone's emotions were raw, and it was confiding time.

We talked together earnestly in the toilets at the museum. I savoured every detail I learnt about her life. She was born within yards of the scaly quay with its shining wet cobbles and stench of sack and lobster. She grew up in a gingham dress and sand shoes, catching crabs and shutting the door when the storms came. She never lost sight of the sea. The queen (I believe it was the same princess who held the swan's feather fan) came in a pompous hat to launch the giant ships that dwarfed the terraced houses, and cruised away, splattered with champagne, to Japan or America. Some weeks the quayside would be filled with Russians, or Italians, or men with beards of froth from Norway. They came and went with the tide. Eva told me her skin was good because of her diet of fish oil and seaweed. She danced too, in a dress embossed with a thousand sequins, and her partner was called Adrian and they were like brother and sister. Her room was full of prizes, she told me, silver trophies and gold medallions. Her mother was waiting for her father to come in from work with his lamp, although he was squashed fifteen years ago between two tugs pulling in different directions. Eva cared for her mother; washing her bent back and wiping her old nose. She was an only daughter. If she didn't work, Eva confessed, she would go out of her mind. There were times when she watched television programmes about euthanasia. She wanted a life, she said, beyond foxtrots, tangos and bedpans. She wanted to know what made other human beings tick.

She had a lad but she didn't love him. When they kissed her

mind wandered and she never let him stray inside her buttons. She wanted a lad who could conduct a conversation. I told her that I'd never met a man who could hold my attention, and she nodded and looked into my eyes until my ears popped.

The toilet was the colour of fly paper, and it got very cosy in there after the hand dryer had been on for an hour. The Head Curator informed us that the whole building would soon be utterly reorganized, from the toilet to the roof, and that we would be joining the new breed of museum which was accessible and immediate with hands-on displays and quizzes. He believed we were hopelessly antiquated, and stared at my hands as if they had no potential. This policy would have implications for Theobald and his gnats, for me and my vessels, and Eva and her Nescafé. The Head Curator asked me to consider the Egyptian section and have a brainstorm with him the following week. He felt the mummy was under used, and I told Eva how I kept going to commune with her leathery, melancholic face, and how much I feared for her future. Eva knew what I meant. Not only was she beautiful, she was also understanding.

Becoming A Horse

A horse was stronger than a swan. When I was eight I became a horse, which was better than being a boy or a girl. I was a palomino with a swishing tail. I galloped to breakfast. I snorted and neighed. At school, alone, I cantered the perimeters of the playground. I ate grass. I stayed as long as I could in the garden, pawing the rose bushes with my hooves, jumping the garden furniture. I shied away when Jean came to catch me and galloped up and down the garden path until she lassoed me with her apron strings and led me to the horseless attic where I had to become a girl until dawn.

Being a horse was very demanding. I needed a lot of exercise. I had a grooming kit with which I brushed myself down at night.

I was very happy. Horse hide protected me from Mr Whitebait, from strangers, and from other children, and even, I thought, from ghosts.

But one night, when the moon was full, I woke up and felt an overwhelming presence in the attic. The room seemed to be full of rustling, and faint whispers. I began to sweat, and fumbled feverishly for the light switch. Then something cold touched my face and I reared up in bed, as a clammy hand caught me by the mane and jumped on my back. It felt like a great wad of poetry, squeezing me until I could hardly breathe.

I crashed down the dangerous stairs, with the thing clinging onto my neck. I writhed and rolled on the landing carpet, but it hung on sniggering. I screamed and bolted further down into the labyrinth of the house and quill spurs cut into my sides. I charged outside, and careered up and down the street, which was empty of tourists, and murky as cobwebs.

The lights were going on in the house. George was looming up at the window, pointing down at me as I neighed to him desperately.

They followed me down into the street, Jean and George, wet from sleep and angry from their own bad dreams. They grabbed me by the shoulders and shook me.

'She's sleepwalking. It's Dusty Springfield all over again!' Jean wailed.

I slumped down onto the hard pavement. The weight flew from my back leaving a trail of ink in a stain over my father's face, which he wiped away as if it had never been there.

He picked me up. I pleaded with him.

'Don't leave me!'

Jean had gone to read Doctor Spock by candlelight.

George carried me back upstairs. I could feel his heart beating through his nylon pyjamas. He was embarrassed. He tried to leave me at the door of the attic.

I twisted away from him and scuttled downstairs. He thundered after me. I sprinted down the long corridor to the Furthest Nursery. Frank was sitting up in bed, calmly awake. Frank claimed that he never slept.

George was calling down the corridor. His voice echoed. It sounded as if he was shouting from the bottom of a well.

I looked around desperately. More than anything I didn't want to return to the attic. My sides still remembered the clasp of ghostly knees.

Jean was striding up the stairs, pulling on a pair of plastic gloves. She was chanting my misdemeanours in a rosary.

Frank opened his mouth. 'Here!' he commanded.

'Where?' I bleated.

Frank pointed with his finger.

With one last yell I leapt into the air.

I jumped into Frank, and he swallowed me, just as my father's hand reached for my neck. For a while I was sliding through darkness, and then I was suddenly in a neat, dustless room. A sign on the wall said PLEASE DO NOT DISTURB.

Some mathematical magazines lay on a hexagonal table. The walls were embossed with pale algebraic symbols. There was a distant sound of typewriters.

I sat on a square chair and swung my legs. It was a little boring. There were no pictures, and although there was one door, as if leading to a doctor's surgery, I was unwilling to barge through it.

I chewed my sleeves. I bit my fingernails.

In the pockets of my pyjamas I found a blunt pencil. I nibbled its dry wood. Then I had an idea. I licked the lead, and wrote upon the bland wall GERT WAS HERE!

Next to the words I drew a horse and a fish.

When I had finished I looked proudly at my contribution to the white walls.

The room began to shake.

Then the door opened and I saw a flight of steps leading up.

The vibrating reached earthquake proportions. I ran up the stairs. My legs had lengthened and I was able to sprint five steps at a time. Behind me there was a sound like an almighty roaring wave. I turned around, terrified. White horses with watery manes were galloping behind me.

I reached a plateau. I was on the diving board at Mr Valentine's River Club. I curved into a perfect arc, and dived.

I landed in a pool of vomit. My parents gazed down at me, horrified. Frank looked over me, his eyes bulging, his mouth open.

My pyjamas were completely wet.

No-one spoke. Jean took Frank and I to the bathroom and washed us in tepid water while she wrung out our night clothes. She rubbed us angrily with a gritty towel until our skins burnt, then fed us both pink medicine from a bottle at the top of the cupboard. Frank moaned that his stomach ached. Then Frank and I were tucked firmly into our parents' bed. The light was left on. We curled happily into the oversize pillows. I don't know where Jean and George slept. Maybe they sat up all night because in the morning the house was full of bottles and ashtrays and George had a red mark on one side of his face.

I woke up human. All my horse sense had gone.

Frank said something was gnawing at his insides, and later he blamed me for his dodgy digestion, but I never got the chance to go back and rub out my name, so I suppose it's still there, disturbing Frank's white interior.

Shopping With Eva

One day in the toilet Eva asked me if I would like to go into the town with her.

'What for?' I asked, dumbly.

'To shop, of course,' she said.

So the next day, which was a Saturday, we met under the statue of a naked golden lady with upturned breasts who balanced above a clock. Eva had a hungry look about her. She grabbed my shoulder and pushed me into a huge department store; the kind of place that I would normally avoid. She started to dart around, while I watched, listlessly fingering the odd brassiere strap. Normally I would spend a minimum amount of time in such shops. I bought all my meals from Marks 8c Spencer, which I was afraid was giving my skin a kind of cling-film texture. I bought my clothes from Burton; men's shirts and square jackets, and hard, cardboard jeans. I never bought anything in a sale.

Make-up departments in stores made me feel like a man in drag.

Eva seemed to know everything about shopping. She kept on quoting makes and brands that I had never heard of. She was only interested in bargains. Her hands filched their way into the back of the store where unspeakable scoops went unnoticed.

'Come on Gert!' she rallied, while I held the carrier bags uncertainly. I suppose for her it must have been like shopping with a disinterested boyfriend. I think that I was beginning to get on her nerves, so I tried to be enthusiastic.

She bought Italian shoes for a pound, silk flowers at five pence each, smoked salmon for fifty pence. If I attempted to converse she didn't answer. She had a glazed, mesmerized expression. In fact, one might have thought, looking at her sad figurehead eyes, and serious expression, that she was depressed, or certainly eccentric. In each new shop she stopped for a moment, feeling the atmosphere, fingers twitching, waiting for inspiration. When she did move, she was fast, like a hunting dog at the neck of a fox. Lambswool sweaters for five pounds, Brazilian fruit squeezers for nineteen ninety-nine (apparently that was very cheap).

Assistants were afraid of her. I noticed them moving closer together when she walked through the automatic doors. Sometimes they pressed secret bells under the counter. Plainclothes detectives drifted around her helplessly. She was an outlaw, a highway woman of the High Street. Oil of Ulay, slightly damaged packaging, one pound. Ten yards of crushed velvet, eight pounds.

'What's it all for?' I enquired dimly, craving her attention. We were sitting at a bus stop, surrounded by bags.

'I sell it,' she said glumly. 'Do you think I live on my wages? I do the job because I like to get out of the house.'

She licked her lips. A bus appeared and we both got on. It was filled with strappy girls in blue shirts carrying school books. We sat upstairs in the front seats. Eva grinned. She was beginning to relax.

'I have two talents,' she boasted loudly. 'Shopping and dancing. Otherwise I'm just like anyone else.'

The rest of the people on the bus all stared at her. She was alarmingly beautiful, in a bright red coat with a rabbit fur collar. Her hair was so shiny it looked wet.

'You're amazing,' I mumbled sycophantically. An old lady sitting behind us in a fishnet scarf nodded in agreement.

'Yes,' said the old woman. 'She would look lovely in fresh snow.'

We both gazed at Eva lovingly.

'Stop it,' she shouted suddenly. 'Stop looking at me!'

The lady blushed and pulled out a trembling shopping list.

'I never bought any rouge!' she moaned.

'Rouge?' Eva asked, looking apologetic. 'You want to buy that in the shopping mall under the Swallow Hotel. It's very dark, like going into a cave. There's a chemist there.'

'I know it,' whispered the lady, bent towards Eva. It was as if they were dealing in heroin.

'Go in quietly,' muttered Eva, 'and go to the very back of the shop. There's a basket there filled with old lipsticks. Nothing special.'

'Yes.'

'Put your hand deep into the basket,' I saw an image of her reaching for fish in cold water, 'and you'll feel some little round tubs. Bourgeois. Fifty pence. Best rouge on the market.'

'Thank you.' The old lady winked gratefully. Eva clicked her heels together.

'Isn't this your stop Gert?'

I left her then.

I didn't know what she made of me. What talents did I have? Why did she make me feel simultaneously weak and powerful? Why did I love her?

Doctor Diamond And The Gullible Heart

After the night of the horse Jean took me to the doctor. I expected to be seen again by the dry, rummy doctor who I saw when I had the mumps, but he turned out to have died. We sat together in the waiting room for hours while a toddler in a blazing jacket whirled around the small space, knocking old ladies off their chairs and hurling broken toys at innocent people's legs. His mother was reading an article in *Woman* about child murderers.

I wondered why Jean never noticed my physical injuries? The swans' bites for instance? Was she afraid that it was she who had inflicted them on me? Increasingly, my image of her got more and more hazy. She seemed to float above the ground. She was not dissimilar in her presence to the intangible shadow that inhabited the attic, although she was a lot better looking. Why didn't anyone take any interest? What were they up to?

'Gertrude Hardcastle!' a nurse yelled into the waiting room, making everyone jump. Jean yanked me to my feet. She had an angry expression.

The stony nurse led us down some back stairs to another room, that had a torn scrap of paper with the words *Doctor Diamond* written in felt tip on it pinned to the door.

Jean tripped and cursed, and then marched in with a hostile lurch.

Doctor Diamond's surgery was obviously temporary but not unpleasant. I observed her mantelpiece with mute interest. It was covered with rosettes. A drying rose stood in a thin vase on her desk. A beam of sunlight crossed the room.

Jean snorted and sat down. Why was she so annoyed?

Doctor Diamond must have been about the same age as my mother. She reminded me of someone from the television, with a suntanned neck, and a mane of black hair. She had a gold ring on her middle finger that Jean eyed with suspicion.

Jean growled, 'This child won't sleep. She's feral in her habits. She hallucinates. I feel as if I'm going mad!' and blew her nose.

Doctor Diamond laughed inappropriately, and asked me to strip off to my vest and to lie on a hard high bed so she could investigate my physical body.

Her brown hands smelt of saddle soap.

Jean stared, watching her with trapped-bird eyes.

'Open your mouth wide,' instructed Doctor Diamond.

'There's nothing wrong with her mouth,' Jean muttered. 'It's her bloody brain that's round the twist.' Then, 'It's not my fault!'

That's why she was angry.

Doctor Diamond ignored Jean and sifted through my hair with a metal comb, then peeped into my ears with a fierce torch. She prodded the skin around my temples and tweaked at my eyelids. She ferreted around in the back of my throat, and banged my chest with a dull spoon. She told me to bend and stretch. She pulled my fingers and toes. She karate-chopped my knees and listened, with a melancholy expression, to my ribs.

Jean interrupted, 'Are you a student?'

'No,' she murmured. 'I'm just here for a week.'

'Typical,' grumbled Jean.

Doctor Diamond said to me, 'Do you like horses?'

'No,' I answered.

She clicked her tongue and shook her head. 'Fishing?' She searched about in a drawer and pulled out a bag of orange boiled sweets and offered me one.

I refused.

'Dancing then,' she enquired politely. I shrugged.

'I've tried everything,' said Jean crossly.

'Perhaps this is part of the problem,' Doctor Diamond suggested with a sweet bulging in her cheek.

She sauntered over to the window, thinking. Her teeth were milky white.

'You say she won't sleep?' she purred.

'That's right.'

I waggled my tongue.

'How long?' she asked, gliding back to her desk.

'A long time.' Jean blushed, squeezing the straps of her handbag.

Doctor Diamond looked slowly at Jean for the first time, taking in her thin body, and the dark shadows under her eyes, and wrote something on a piece of paper that she handed over.

'That's for you,' she said with a kind wink.

Jean was relieved. Perhaps she was addicted to tranquillizers?

'Is Gertrude eating?'

'Yes. She's eating.'

The doctor returned to her seat and drummed her fingers on a sheet of paper. I yawned. It felt as if we had been in there for hours.

'What about her father; I mean your marriage?' she asked Jean suddenly.

Jean smacked her pale lips together and coughed.

'What do you mean?'

'Any particular tensions?'

'No.'

There was another breathy pause.

'There's nothing the matter with her physically,' she announced breezily. 'Apart from a gullible heart.'

A gullible heart? I preserved the phrase and placed it up my sleeve, so that I could look at it later under a magnifying glass.

'Is that a defect?' snapped Jean, pacing up and down, looking like she might kick the furniture.

'Not really. I'm sending her to see a friend of mine,' she decided with a manly flick of her hair. 'She needs to talk to someone.'

She wrote another note.

'It really isn't my fault,' Jean protested with a ragged cry.

'I know,' sighed Doctor Diamond sadly. 'But she's just a child isn't she?'

Jean looked at me as if for the first time. What did she think I was? A dog?

'Gullible heart!' muttered Jean as she dragged me down the street. 'She must be a student. I've never seen her before.'

Some of Doctor Diamond had stuck to my skin, and I could still smell her on my hands. I thought the opposite. I thought

Doctor Diamond was on my side. And even though I was only eight I believed that she too had a gullible heart, and in this condition we were comrades.

Frank

'Gert, are you there?'

'Is that you Frank?'

'You were always getting into bed with me, do you remember?'

'Yes.'

'You were like an animal, snuffling and snorting and pulling the covers off.'

'It was the only safe place that's why.'

'Is that what you thought?'

'Yes, that's what I thought.'

'I miss you sometimes Gert. No-one ever gets into bed with me here.'

'Or me.'

'How did we ever get to be so alone?'

'That's what I keep thinking.'

'My stomach doesn't ache any more.'

'Oh, good.'

'Gert, you've got to stop blaming everyone.'

'I'm not. I'm just thinking things through.'

'But where are you going to end up?'

'Don't ask me. Look at you.'

'But I'm different. We were always different.'

'You mean you were cleverer.'

'No. I was weaker.'

'Are you telling me to pull myself together?'

But Frank didn't answer. He was always doing that. Walking off just as conversations got interesting. Disappearing.

Carmen Leaves

A few days after we went to see Doctor Diamond I was lying on the polished lawn looking up at a cloud in the shape of a train, that ran along rails made from the tracks of aeroplanes, carrying Japanese tourists home. Inside the house my parents were shouting. Carmen, our cleaning lady, had handed in her notice. Her overalls, that hung in the cloakroom, had disappeared. For days Jean had worn a tranquillized, overcast face, and roamed the house in a dreamy fret. George wouldn't stop laughing, and the more he laughed, the more the mercury in the barometer in the high parlour rose.

That day it was very, very hot.

'You!' Jean stood by the garden door, swaying, and blackbirds changed places in the trees.

'Why me?' bellowed George.

The clouds curled into shoals of slippery mackerel and swam

across the sky.

'It's your fault Gert's not normal. The doctor said so.'

'What am I supposed to have done for Christ's sake! Anyway Gert's fine!' George's voice drummed a steady beat. 'Gert needs knots.'

'What are you talking about?'

'She drifts about. She needs tying down.'

'What do you know about children?'

'I'm just saying.'

'She's disturbed!' There was a stormy pause. Then Jean yelled with the force of a hurricane, 'KNOTS!' and guffawed nastily.

The laugh stopped as abruptly as it had started. The mackerel were replaced by inky scribbles. It started to rain.

Jean herself was drizzling softly.

She breathed out loudly, 'And Carmen.'

'What about Carmen?'

A drop of salty rain fell onto my lips.

'You know what I mean.'

'I don't know anything. I thought she had bad legs.'

'Bad legs? Sure!'

The clouds turned into a great gaping mouth. The argument travelled up the stairs and re-emerged from another window.

'She might end up in a mental home!'

'There's nothing the matter with her.'

'How do you know? You don't know anything.'

There was a crash, followed by loud moans and sobs. A door slammed. George's footsteps mashed the pavement as he strode up the street.

Jean wailed, 'What will people think?'

The clouds reared up and became a psychiatrist. I closed my

eyes. I was suddenly terribly tired. I could hear Jean's feet on the grass. They sounded weary too.

'Gert?' she mumbled.

I didn't answer.

'Gert!' she barked.

I sat up. I was covered in wet grass cuttings.

'Carmen has gone,' she said.

'Why?' I asked nonchalantly.

'Because of her legs,' stated Jean grimly.

'Oh.' I lay down again.

'Gert,' Jean started again. 'Do you know how lucky you are?'

Her face was a brown paper bag. She was twisting her hands into parcel string. She wanted something from me but I wasn't sure what.

'Oh yes,' I said.

'Good,' said Jean and turned back to the house.

What I Thought

Carmen was cleaning the back parlour; a room with no windows, like a priest's hole. It smelt of mice and punishment. It was a room I never played in. She was on her knees, polishing the rough oak floorboards when she heard a noise behind her; a scuttling and a hoarse breath. She swung round, rag in hand and there was George. He was so tall that he filled the whole doorway, and the room was suddenly dark. He walked in and looked at her. He was green. He held out his hands. They were claws, and his mouth was full of teeth. His eyes were narrow slits. He got down on his knees. Then he bit Carmen's ankle, so that it bled. She fought him off with her fists and sat on him, but she knew that once he had got the taste of her blood on his lips he would try again. That's why Carmen left. That's what I thought anyway.

The Cotton Club

I made the mistake of asking Eva out without having any particular destination in mind, so she took control of our date like the captain of a ship. I was to sail into more foreign territories; in this case, a wine bar.

I was nervous and alarmed. I thought I was the lover and she was the loved, but I was beginning to feel courted myself. I spent hours getting ready and ironed my clothes twice. When I put them on I looked like a cutout, I inspected my shadowy face in the mirror. It was the face of a person who was unused to light. I had creases round my eyes. My hair was cut in a schoolgirl bob. My mouth still had difficulty smiling.

I was meeting Eva and her best friend Gwenny at the Cotton Club, a wine bar in a part of town where I would never normally dare to go. I couldn't refuse.

On the way there a labrador got on the train without an

owner. Everyone asked the dog what it was doing, but the dog didn't answer and was aloof. It got off three stops later. The train was misty with hairspray and men's aftershave. Everything shone apart from me. Young women glittered and boys had a patent sheen. I looked at my reflection in the train window, and saw how papery I was. I was used to being with Eva in the toilet, but I didn't know how I would feel in the Cotton Club, without a hand dryer to fiddle about with.

In fact, I had done so well with Eva that I was cracking under the pressure. Perhaps I was deluding myself, I thought. I had no idea how she saw me. And if she got to know me would she find me too intense? And of course she could be heterosexual through and through; revolted by any overture. But there was something about the manner in which she held her head that gave me hope. I was sure she wasn't a man's woman; she was too undiluted.

The first person I saw when I pushed my way through a crowd of naked arms was the bright woman whom I had seen meeting Eva outside the institute. She turned to me with a warm look of recognition.

'This is Gwenny,' said Eva. 'I told you about her.'

Gwenny had the flanks of a racehorse and a short sharp skirt. She fell over Eva like water splashing against a rock. She stamped on the ground with her fierce high shoes. She cooed.

'Oh Gert... so here you are!' and the words made me feel as if I might belong.

Eva gurgled with mirth and kept looking at me as if Gwenny was a wild child she couldn't control. They both had bare shoulders and red lips. I was out of place in a man's shirt, but for the time being that didn't seem to matter. When they spoke to me I laughed in response. If my attention strayed then Gwenny would nudge me and wink.

We were standing by the door of the Cotton Club, holding white wine and sodas. The place was a mass of moving bodies; arms above heads, carrying drinks; standing around the bar as if it was an auction, shouting and waving money at the slippery bar staff.

When Eva went to the bar I was left pressed up to Gwenny's tasselled top. She leant towards me and shouted.

'Eva talks about you all the time. She says the old institute wouldn't be the same without you.'

'Vice versa.'

'What?'

'I feel the same.'

'Say it a bit louder... the speaker is next to my ear!'

'She's wonderful!' I shouted as the record stopped. Gwenny's face broke into a grin, and if she had a tail she would have wagged it.

'Are you married?'

'No.'

'Going out with anyone?'

'No.'

'Are you not that type?'

Our eyes met. Gwenny tapped her nose. I wasn't sure of this territory. It might be safe, and on the other hand, it might not.

The Cotton Club was decorated with plastic ferns that swept across your face. There was a wet T-shirt competition going on behind a screen with images of the Deep South painted onto it. The staff wore raggy shorts and cut-off vests. We were jammed into a sweaty embrace with each other. I was very close to Eva and we were all drunk. Redundant miners' sons passed pints of lager above our heads. The whole room was moving with the beat of a familiar song.

Then two vested boys elbowed into our affectionate triangle and stuck their fat chins into my face. They had shaved jowls and wet necks and Eva and Gwenny insulted them gleefully. The boys asked the same question over and over again.

'Are you coming to Fat Betty's with us?'

Gwenny and Eva refused vehemently, and the words bounced back and forth, but even I could see it was a ritual of which I was not part.

Then one of the boys jerked his sharp thumb in my direction.

'Who's this, your brother?'

Eva and Gwenny howled with laughter, their arms around my shoulder. Eva screamed, 'That's Gert... she's a lass, you great idiot!' and the boy frowned at me strangely for a few seconds. He knew. He had smelt me out.

I told them that I had a headache. Eva and Gwenny walked me down the street to the train station; one on each arm. The lads followed, jeering and whistling. It was a Spanish dance around us, with stamping feet and arms in the air; a drama happened every yard. A girl wept on the cobbles; a half naked man cupped the blood running out of his nostrils and wiped it into the hair he had shampooed so carefully. A couple kissed as if they wanted to meld into one tongue, a group of five danced a jig, three men embraced as if they had just scored a goal, a huge woman in a long black dress berated a taxi driver with a twenty pound note. Eva and Gwenny implored me to stay, to come to Fat Betty's, but I was too scared by it all. I couldn't keep up.

After they'd gone, merging with the boys who waited with their tongues hanging out for me to disappear, I was at a loose end. I didn't want to go home where I would be faced with my own social failure. I walked away from the train station and out of the crowds to Paradise. As I walked into the small bar there was a concentrated hush. It was ladies' quiz night. From Sodom and Gomorrah to a girl guides' camp, I thought. I whispered my order to the barmaid who had a pencil in her hand and was trying to remember the names of the seven dwarfs. Irritated, she poured me a whisky, and informed me I'd missed the history section.

I sat down randomly, next to a lesbian dentist who was bent over her quiz form as if it was a mouth.

When the quiz ended the bar collectively stretched and cheered, and everyone ran to it. I was drunk; so drunk that I stayed very still and pretended I wasn't there.

Then Barbara, my ex-girlfriend, appeared, her light hair done up in the style of a light bulb, and in a leather jacket that was ripped around the collar.

'Gert, I'm back!' she bubbled. 'I thought I'd find you here,' she said, and tripped off to get more drinks. I was rather pleased to see Barbara. She looked blurred and French. She plonked herself down after kissing me three times and started to tell me about Marseille. She had met a crane driver there called Monique who spat and rode a motor bike. She showed me a photograph of her and Monique astride the bike. Barbara was smoking Gauloise which I thought was a bit of a cliche. I asked her if she was in love, and she leant over to my ear and whispered, 'Monique was very butch. She's got a beard and everything. I had to get away from her... you know,' and pulled up her sleeve to show me what looked like hard pebbles on the skin of her arms.

'Cigarette burns,' she sighed happily.

'Monique did that?' I was horrified.

'No, I did it. That's why I came back. Monique said I had to pull myself together. She doesn't like smoking.'

It was hard to follow Barbara's logic, so I just patted her hand.

'Poor Barbara!' I muttered, but she beamed back at me and went and got me another whisky.

I started to tell Barbara about the institute, and Eva, and the Head Curator but the words were falling out of the wrong side of my mouth. I think Barbara must have taken something because she laughed whenever I spoke. After I had fallen off my chair she said she'd get a taxi for us both and take me home. Then I was in the street with Barbara and vomiting onto a neat pile of blue broken glass which reminded me of something.

You should be careful rats don't gnaw the corners.

I swung on Barbara's lapels and snorted. I breathed all over her with my foul breath and told her she was my best and only friend.

Then I passed out.

*   *   *

I woke up in my own bed shouting for Barbara who appeared in a motherly fashion and said shush. She climbed into bed beside me holding a plastic bowl which she put helpfully under my chin.

I pushed the bowl away and Barbara told me to go to sleep, and I did, with my head under her arm, smelling her French perfume which reminded me of gutters.

Then I was dreaming rhat I was standing in the street with Jean. We were outside the Cotton Club, which was closed. It was just before dawn, and Jean stepped gingerly across the uneven cobbles, gathering her coat around her. It had a stain on it, the colour of blood. Starlings were yawning and shuffling on the ledges. The pavement was covered with the remains of the previous night; bits of clothing, uneaten chips, jewellery, broken bottles, coins and vomit.

We tiptoed along together. Then, gradually, I realized that we were not alone. People were appearing from back alleys and behind parked cars. They were a race I had never seen before, with the wrinkled features of pixies. They started to sift through the rubbish that lay around us, pocketing anything that shone, searching for lost earrings, watches and cufflinks.

Jean appeared bleak, as if this was a world she would rather not know about.

Then as the light broke there was a sound like a vast wave; a deafening roar of rushing water. From around the corner came a corporation cleaning machine, which gushed green slimy disinfectant, and then with whirring brushes, Brilloed the pavements clear of all that was left.

As it approached, this dragon, the scavengers retreated, arms full of their findings, mumbling, and rattling the coins in their pockets. Then, as the sun came up, the cleaning was done and the road was spotless.

Jean turned to me and said, 'Now do you see how lucky you are?'

I woke up on the floor, freezing cold, with the plastic bowl lying upside down beside me. Barbara had gone, leaving a torn piece of paper stuck to the toilet bowl, that I only saw when I vomited. It read, 'Au revoir, ma chérie.'

I supposed she must have gone back to Marseille. I actually wondered if she had been there at all, or if I had dreamt her up too, and written the note in my sleep.

First Attempts

Dear Jean,

    Thank you for your letters. I am sorry I haven't been in touch before but...

Dear Mum,

    How dare you write to me after all this time. I...

Dear Mother,

    I am not well. I had a dream about you...

I tore each sheet of paper into tiny squares and scattered them around me like snow. My flat was a mess.

Rosa Van Durk

Jean took me to see the shrink recommended by Doctor Diamond.

I was in an oyster shell of a room with an elderly bohemian. Her face was a long brown violin that examined me quizzically.

She handed me a pencil and a pad of paper and said, 'Draw.'

I looked dumbly at the pencil in my hand.

'What is it?' asked Rosa Van Durk.

'I can't draw.'

I put down the pencil and looked into her eyes that were as brown as field beans. Was this another gullible heart?

'There's a thing in my bedroom. It's been there since I was three,' I croaked. 'I'm not safe,' I said bravely. 'Things happen.'

Rosa Van Durk nodded and asked me to draw a picture of the thing that frightened me.

Hesitantly I attempted to create an image that was something like the figure I had seen and felt. When I had finished it was just a grey scribbled cloud.

'A poet died in your house?' asked Rosa with a sweep of her ebony hand.

I nodded, scared.

'Is it her?'

I blinked.

'Are there other things?'

I shrugged. There were things I couldn't put my finger on. Silences. Gaps in between words. Miseries that you couldn't name.

Rosa wrote something down in a small leather-bound notebook.

'When I was young,' she continued conversationally, 'I lived in Germany. Like most small children I was afraid of certain dark holes in the house. It was an old country place. I was especially afraid that monsters would come and take away my parents.'

She paused.

'And one day they did. I hid in a dark hole in the very intestine of the house. I heard them. So my fears were true.'

She spread her branchy arms out.

'We must assume then,' she went on, rather intellectually, 'that what you see and hear is real, not imaginary.'

I breathed out. Perhaps it was the first proper exhalation I had experienced for many years. I breathed in. My rib cage expanded. I unrolled my tongue. An iron rod that had been clamped to my spine was gently removed. My hair began to grow. My fingers rolled open. My eyes closed.

Rosa Van Durk removed her round glasses and rubbed them on her draylon trousers. She was wearing a complex pair of hoofy shoes.

'Yes. This is the way forward. We will remove it. This thing that lives in your room. We will put it to rest. Then it won't meddle with your happiness and safety any more.'

'Will everything be all right after that?' I asked.

'After we have removed it we will discuss any other problems.'

'How will you do it?' I asked curiously.

'Whatever it is, it's probably scared like you. It can't leave the house. We will entomb it, in another place. I have a place in my house where I keep children's bad spirits. I shall put it there, with the others,' Rosa Van Durk said slyly. 'And I shall keep the key.'

She ushered me out of the beaded room, with its lowered blinds and low shabby chairs. Jean was waiting in the hallway, reading Freud.

She jumped up and said, 'Excuse me asking, but is this on the National Health?'

'Of course,' answered Rosa, nonchalantly.

Then she led Jean into a curtained parlour and whispered into the bowels of her ear. Jean gradually nodded and shifted from foot to foot.

I was being an eight-year-old. I swung on the banister. I made faces at myself in the warty hallway mirror. My gullible heart had been given a tonic and my hair began to fall into place.

On the way home from Rosa's house, as Jean and I drove along the country lanes filled with wild roses and cow parsley, I started to sing. I sang, 'The farmer wants a wife!' and Jean joined in, and for a while we were unselfconsciously together, riding in the same direction.

Ward One Hundred

I was finding it hard to endure everyday life, and at the same time deal with the mysterious rubbish which continued to pile up at the end of my garden. I stood alone, staring at a black plastic bag with a sense of injustice and fury.

I marched towards the hospital and into its stuffy corridors. Harry was not about, but an elderly receptionist was combing her grey hair and listening to a Walkman. I shouted 'Excuse me!' as viciously as I could, and she slowly teased the headphones from the innards of her ears and looked at me plainly, as if I was just one of the regular shouting customers.

'Who keeps putting plastic bags in my garden?' I shouted, banging my fist down on the desk. 'It's not hygienic!'

'I know,' she soothed. 'I'll call main office,' and dialled mysteriously.

'I have a lady here', she whined, 'who is a little upset about her refuse.'

'Your refuse, not my refuse!'

'She's a little upset. Shall I send her up? Oh I see. Ward One Hundred. Yes.' She immaculately replaced the telephone. My head was full of wires.

'I'll take you up myself,' she offered courteously.

We walked along awkwardly together, her in front, tapilappying on tiptoes, and me stamping along behind her. Then Frank suddenly called, screaming into my telepathic signal box,

'Gert!'

'What?' I snapped out loud. The receptionist turned round and for a moment we faced one another in the narrow neck of walls.

'Sorry,' I mumbled.

'Gert!' screamed Frank. 'Don't go up there!'

'Where?'

'To where she's taking you.'

'We're just going to see someone from main office. It's just a stupid domestic thing Frank. Go back to sleep.'

'But you don't want to go there. I know about those places.'

'Well, what am I supposed to do then?'

'Please don't go Gert.'

'You mean that you're actually concerned about me?'

'Yes.'

'About time,' I sighed, touched.

I tapped the receptionist on the shoulder.

'Where are we going exactly?'

'To see someone important.' She showed me her watch. 'We'll have to hurry.'

'I'm afraid that I haven't got time for this right now,' I said, backing away. 'I'll come in another day.'

'If you're sure.' She stopped and smiled. 'It's up to you.'

'Yes, it's up to me.' I turned and ran, leaving her standing marooned in the jugular corridor. She put her Walkman back on and listened carefully.

'That's the spirit,' whispered Frank. 'Stay away.'

'OK,' I bleated, as I revolved through the great wooden doors, into the bright daylight.

The Exorcism

The day Rosa Van Durk came to the attic, with a black bag and a butterfly net, George was away counting crocodile skins in London.

Rosa wore a long matted green woollen coat, even though it was summer. She appeared in the hallway in the guise of a hedge.

She was in a very jolly mood, and peered into all the rooms with dancing feet and elaborate movements of her arms. She accepted a sherry from Jean who was dressed for the occasion in overalls.

Frank had taken up photography and was documenting the visit. He stood behind a tripod with a black hood over his head. I couldn't help thinking that he was seeking attention when it was really my day, not his, but Rosa completely ignored him, as if it was perfectly normal to be photographed while exorcising spirits.

Rosa ran her fingers along the mantelpieces and peered out of each window.

Then she announced 'I will go alone!' and strode up the stairs in the direction of the attic. I was quietly afraid. Rosa Van Durk was just an old lady. I thought of her bravely hiding in a dark hole. Yet my gullible heart was full of admiration for Rosa Van Durk. She told us to wait for her in the hall, and on no account to follow her. Frank took a loud photograph of her back as she climbed up the stairs.

Jean and I waited, listening. Jean was perplexed. Frank took another picture of me and Jean. I still have it. We both look guilty.

We heard loud thumps, and bangs and then Rosa's authoritarian voice barking a series of words that had a rhythm.

There was a demonic squawk, and a waft of yellow smoke drifted out from under the low wooden door.

Jean shook her blond head and started to run up the stairs, but I clung to her ankles. Upstairs Rosa was singing something that sounded like a hymn.

A river of ink was dripping down the attic steps. There was a terrible, nauseating stink of camphor.

Jean called out, 'Mrs Van Durk? Are you all right?' but there was no answer, just an unearthly clamour. It sounded as if the room was bursting with voices.

Suddenly the door opened and Rosa emerged in a stream of light. Her grey hair was flying in all directions, and all the buttons had dropped off her green coat. She was holding a shoe box. There was no sound at all now, only our breathing. Rosa walked past us, down the stairs, with the box held in her outstretched arms.

We followed her. I was very impressed.

Downstairs Rosa told me, 'It's in the box. I am going to take it home and put it in a safe with all the other children's nightmares. She won't bother you anymore Gert.'

Then she turned to Jean. 'You can use the room now.'

Jean was staring at Rosa as if she was demented.

'Have you fumigated it?' enquired Jean, as if Rosa Van Durk was from Rentokil.

'I have,' said Rosa, winking at me. 'It could do with a hoover.' Then she turned to Frank and said, 'No more pictures please.'

I blew a kiss at Rosa Van Durk as she stepped carefully out into the street. A row of tourists watched her tiptoe along the pavement, box in hand, as if she was carrying an unexploded bomb.

Jean turned to me, looking perplexed. 'Happy now Gert?'

'Yes!' I blurted, and then ran about feeling childish, jumping on the furniture, whining for extra pocket money. And then I threw my arms around her, and I cried, and when I lifted my head Frank was standing staring at us through the lens of his camera, but both his hands hung limply down by his sides as if he had lost the use of them, so that's the photograph I don't have.

Eva Takes Me Dancing

After the Cotton Club Eva treated me with even more affection, although I caught her shaking her head once when she looked at me, as if I was some kind of lost English eccentric. She often came to see me in my moist darkened basement, and once put her hand on my neck as I examined a potsherd, making me have near-death palpitations. Gwenny sent me a card. It was a picture of a woman astronaut grinning from the bubble of her space helmet. Gwenny had written, 'She reminds me of you. Let's go out again soon.' Her signature was flamboyant and curvaceous. I stuck it above my desk, and found it strangely comforting.

Then Eva invited me to come to the Jarrow Ballroom Dancing Championships. I nervously agreed. She said she would meet me there, and that I could watch her dancing with her partner Adrian.

The evening of the championships was so dark that even the

street lights seemed to have lost their beam. It was a night when the city felt soaked in silence as if it might never awaken. Perhaps it was to do with February, and poverty. Or a lost football match.

I put on a pink T-shirt in an effort to appear feminine, and painted my lips in matching cerise. I looked clownish and eager. I examined myself carefully in the mirror before I left the flat. My eyes were cloudy with unrequited love, and neediness was pinned to my front like a badge.

A taxi sounded its horn outside, and I slipped out into the dead night for my second rendezvous with the extraordinary Eva of Shields. I told myself that already my life was changing. My hibernation was nearly over. In the taxi it was warm and furry. The cab had fairy lights around the dashboard and a plastic sign saying HAPPY NEW YEAR, even though it was well into February. The driver was so fat that he spilt over his seat, and his bulging thigh touched mine across the handbrake.

'Going somewhere nice?' he drawled, not looking at me.

'Hope so,' I answered, noncommittally.

'Student are you?' Taxi drivers always say this.

'No, I'm a taxidermist.' The lie jumped out so easily that I hardly noticed it.

'Fancy that!' he chuckled. He smelt of a slow divorce, this driver, and I didn't like him.

'Where are you from?' he probed, his massive leg pressing down on the clutch.

'A place called the Kingdom of Leaves,' I said casually. 'You wouldn't know it.'

We pulled up outside a shabby cinema with dark blue paint flaking off the walls, and a silver sign saying DANCING, that flashed on and off in a pulse.

'You're pulling my leg,' he muttered nastily as I awkwardly overpaid him. Then, as I disentangled myself from the seat belt and searched for the door handle, he grabbed my arm.

'I wouldn't mind stuffing you!' he quipped.

'Get stuffed!' I yelled, unaware of the pun. I pulled myself from the car, and slammed the door in an attempt to fuse his fairy lights. He swerved off violently. I forgot to catch the car number plate. That's the kind of thing that happens when I wear pink. I don't know how other pinker women put up with it.

Shaken, I walked into the once grand foyer of the building. I could hear distant sounds of sequins brushing together, and feel the heat of shoes tapping on a parquet floor. Inside the old cinema was as glamorous as the Ritz, with a deep pile carpet and golden chandeliers. I walked into the ballroom grinning and was nearly swept away by a tide of glittering dresses and tight, unmasculine trousers whirling in fixed lines on the dance floor. I saw Eva wearing a dangerously pink creation that might have been made from tropical birds' feathers. I waved, but she was concentrating on her performance and didn't look up. I sat down on a velvet seat and ordered a glass of water, determined not to get drunk. I wanted to drown in this vision; Eva dancing.

I watched the foxtrot, the samba, modern and improvised, the waltz and the flamenco with total absorption. Gradually I noticed Adrian, fluttering like a small moth at Eva's side. He was neat and quick, but it was she that held the floor. She was the controller, the vial for the roll of music that unfolded beneath her feet.

By the time the judges had come to a decision, Eva had still not seen me. To my despair she didn't win and the golden cup went to a snake of a dancer with an oily smile.

When it was all over the house lights went on, and the dancers disappeared backstage. Then Eva stepped out from a side door, dressed in a dark grey suit, carrying a suitcase, and saw me. My cheeks burned like the soles of a dancer's feet. Adrian was standing next to her, a meek and obedient shadow. He whispered in her ear and she smiled and pointed at me.

They came over, and I said, 'That was fantastic!' and Adrian sneered.

'Did you think so?' said Eva. 'This is Adrian, my partner.'

He kissed me three times on both cheeks. Then Eva enveloped me in her grand arms and I squeaked out compliments, flattery and approval. She cooed, 'Thanks for coming', and I could hardly cope. Love was surely not supposed to follow such an even path. Adrian gazed on grumpily, like an unwilling bridesmaid. His body was the shape of a pipe cleaner.

'So how long have you been... dancing together?' I enquired, like an amateur journalist.

'I've known Eva since I was three. I know everything about her. Her feet are my feet,' boasted Adrian.

I was getting jealous.

'And his feet are mine.' Eva pinched Adrian's skinny chin.

'I'll teach you to dance, Gert, if you like,' Eva offered.

Perhaps. I didn't answer. I was a long way from my feet. There was no connection between them and my head or my hands.

'Are you angry that you didn't win?'

Adrian's eyes narrowed, and he scowled like a ferret at the champions who were laughing loudly across the bar. 'She looks like a bloodsucker in that dress,' he snapped. Adrian grimly lit a cigarette. He turned to Eva. 'You missed a beat on the third turn of the last dance,' he growled.

'Now, now!' Eva sipped a gin.

'You always do that.'

'Don't start.'

'I can't help it,' he sighed. 'I hate losing.'

'I thought you were best,' I mumbled childishly.

'Oh yes,' Eva winked at Adrian. 'Gert's a big fan aren't you?'

Adrian turned spitefully to Eva. 'And you were a bit slow on the tango,' he sniped.

My hackles rose.

'All right Adrian, we'll talk about it later.'

He got up then and kissed her on the top of her head.

'So long, sweetheart.'

He skipped off, nodding at me.

'Prat,' Eva muttered, then winked at me. I nearly got down on my knees then and proposed, but at that second the lights flashed on and off and we had to leave the building. Eva had a taxi waiting, but this time it was driven by a thin woman who bred dogs. She told us all about her latest litter and I couldn't get a word in edgeways. Instead I gazed at Eva's profile against the car window, and the way that the street lights flickered across her features, and felt the currents that ran through my own body, like music.

When Eva got out of the taxi she leant towards me, kissing my cheek. Her breath smelt of violets, and I felt a strand of her hair falling across my face.

'I've got to get away from here,' she said as she looked up towards the flats where she lived. 'I'm going to die here if I'm not careful.'

I didn't have time to offer her an escape route. She was walking away, turning to wave at me as I sat staring at her with the taxi driver who was still talking about how to toilet train dogs. I would

ask her tomorrow if she would come away with me. I knew she
would say yes.

Daily Petals

We passed the eleven-plus. The exam was held in a vast vacant swimming pool that smelt of verrucas. The exam paper was aquatic blue and the questions swam in front of my eyes in a shoal.

When Mr Whitebait told us the results we were all hot and dehydrated from hurdling around the school field. The ones that failed loitered at the back of the small crowd of panting eleven-year-olds, their tails between their legs. Their faces turned from policeman blue to secondary grey and even I, Gert, felt sorry for them and embarrassed. Mr Whitebait smiled at Frank and said he had written himself off the paper and into the universe. He patted my head and called us the bright twins. Frank beamed at him with undisguised hatred. Mr Whitebait had shrunk and his skin was papery and yellow. I had an image of scrumpling him up and burning him slowly, like Jean had with Winston Churchill.

That night George announced that Frank would be sent to an expensive school beyond the city walls. I would go to the grammar school for girls. Neither of us protested. Neither of us wanted to go to school.

Soon Frank disappeared. There was a photograph of him wearing a multi-folded gown, on the mantelpiece in George's parlour. He held a book in his hand that he pretended to read.

Before he went we sat in the Furthest Nursery listening to a reel-to-reel tape recorder. His face was longer now, and had no childish neatness left. A moustache shadowed his upper lip. It was rare to see his face full on. No-one knew how to talk to Frank. At meals he crouched with his fingers over his ears as if he was listening to the palms of his hands. Sometimes I felt as if Frank and I were drowning in watery silence, and I tried putting my hands to my ears to see if I could hear the same things that he did. I think I heard figures adding themselves together, and then splitting apart. We listened to Captain Beefhart. Frank made maps of his songs.

Frank was sent to a school where beating was on the syllabus. In 1900 there had been an orgy of flagellation in the great library. It was as if he was going to a castle with no drawbridge and a wide moat. Everyone had forgotten we were twins.

Although the school was in a nearby town, Frank would be a boarder and would sleep in a dormitory and have cold baths. He would not be allowed to take his gown off except to play rugby and to sleep. I was sure that Captain Beefhart would not agree with this type of education.

After Frank went I listened for him, in the hollows of my ears. I could hear a game of cricket from behind a high wall. I hoped Frank was running, and that he wouldn't get bowled out.

Now I was just a girl in a sea of hefty girls. I had an echoing stutter and my chin was oily. My hair had grown into a long matted plait which I sucked obsessively. I had a hard boater to place on my head, a purse belt that I tightened nervously all day, great calves that had grown while I was asleep, and a blazer with steel sleeves. The school had a wide green lawn in front of its classical doors, and a palatial exterior, but round the back it was all Portacabins and hardboard, chipped toilet seats and leaking pipes. There were thousands of girls. The sixth-formers were angels. They flew about in groups. We were mice, scurrying from prefabricated hut to cloakroom, dragging our elasticated shoe bags behind us, squeaking.

We coloured in a lot there. They were very keen on maps and shades of tundra. I gazed at the teachers' faces, trying to understand what it was they wanted to impart to us. Some of them had mountainous noses, or wore dresses like Ordnance Survey maps. I followed the creases. When they talked of matrices and algebraic symbols I imagined them as people. When they told us of kings and queens, I saw them as algebraic symbols and mountain ranges. My first report said I was vague and academically confused.

I turned to sport.

Miss Reedcake, our form mistress and the PE mistress, led expeditions to a flat green field where we jumped over hurdles with pony keenness. We threw ourselves over the insubstantial pole of the high jump, and lurched and plummeted the length of the sandy long jump. We relayed in red-faced teams, and ran as if chased by poison arrows. Our knickers and vests were stained with pubescent juices.

'Come on yellows, blues, greens and reds!' commanded Miss

Reedcake from a primary position under a twisted beech tree.

I was discovering competitiveness and enthusiasm. It gushed through my young limbs in mercurial waves. It could make me over-emotional. The other girls had more restraint.

Watching Francesca made me weak. Her legs and torso were hairy and unappealing when she stood still, but when she broke into a sprint she transformed into a female Apollo. Her chest pushed forward, and her chin flattened to meet the wind. On the grassy flat she soared ahead of the others. I screamed with delight, and Miss Reedcake slapped me and told me to contain myself. When I fainted as Francesca cut over the finishing line, she left me lying face down on the grass so that when I came round my features were imprinted with daisy petals.

One day I bounced homewards from school, my hair sticking to my boater, ignoring the jeers from the jaded secondary school bus that passed each day, and walked through the churchyard with high grass and stopped, as I often did, to sit on a gravestone and cool off.

At first I didn't notice the man only a few yards from me. He was mottled and camouflaged by a lichen T-shirt. He scribbled in a small black book. He had dirty hair and the face of a crow. His knee bones jutted out under his trousers and he smirked as if he knew something I didn't. He smoked a fat unwieldy cigarette.

'Who are you?' I asked as I edged off. Lily ponds.

'An artist.' His eyes were tie-dyed.

Mr Manners strolled past, wheezing heavily, carrying a spade and a length of rope.

The artist dropped his fag end into the Pilgrim's Well.

It's very hard to leave someone who stares. I ran off down the public footpath, but I was interested all the same.

A Weekend Break

'Eva, why don't we go away?'

We were standing with the Egyptian mummy eating a bag of boiled sweets. Eva had noble weepy eyes. The institute had become almost unbearable. Theobald had a mobile telephone that he held upside down. Eva had been summoned to the Head Curator's office. The door had been tightly closed for ages. When she emerged she told me that she was on a month's notice. Meanwhile I had been told to re-apply for my job.

The Head Curator stormed about with a metaphorical dustpan and brush. He had swept out several antique filing systems and cleaning staff in the last week, and had a team of New Age archaeological and graphics graduates that flocked behind him with pocket-sized computers. The public had disappeared altogether and the quiet halls were filled with the sound of hammers. Eva was to be replaced by a dinosaur-shaped coffee machine, that dispensed lime green milkshakes. The shop was being stocked with miniature sarcophagi that were also pencil sharpeners, made in China.

The mummy had a stoical expression. I came to tell her, fearfully, that she was to be hauled down from her serene corner and bunged in the foyer, where a waxwork of a surprised pyramid plunderer would bend over her poor corpse as if stumbling over it for the first time. I said to Theobald that the curse of the mummy might descend on us. He replied that it already had and mooched off to supervise his desecrated gnats.

'Where?' asked Eva tearfully.

'Anywhere. For a few days... a weekend. I'll pay. It will be my Christmas present to you. Please.' A double room overlooking a lake, or the sea. I will profess everything, I thought. We will drink champagne in the en-suite bathroom. We will plan our future.

'I'd have to ask Gwenny.'

'I meant just me and you.'

'Yes. I'd have to ask Gwenny if she'd look after mother.'

Then, 'I'll go with you Gert,' purred Eva, and the mummy winked at me lewdly. Then Eva hugged me. For a second I plunged my head into her neck and grasped her taut waist. She hung on so tight I was beetroot red by the time she untied her arms.

After work I met Eva in the travel agent's. We pored over holiday catalogues for hours in a sweet fantasy of bounty adverts and striped umbrellas, but in the end we settled for Scarborough, for a long weekend break in a small hotel called the Navigator's Compass that promised log fires and a choice of kippers at breakfast. It wasn't quite what I'd intended but it was a cheap offer, and I heard the rusty merry-go-rounds creaking, the seagulls serenading, the chips dripping and hoped we shared a mutual view of charm. I paid the deposit.

The next day I rashly bought a car. It was a low green colour with rusty wounds around its shanks. I bought it from a man in an alley who had an Alsatian in a wire cage mocking me throughout the whole cash transaction. I was in a kind of euphoric daze. I drove up and down the wide coast road that skirted the North Sea and where all I could see was road and sky. It was the road that connected Eva and I, like a thin grey thread of spittle from one mouth to another. It had four lanes and was famous for tearaways. There was a radio in my vehicle, which spluttered Radio One out in spasms. I found myself weeping over the more sentimental episodes of Our Tune. It was a truly optimistic time; that brief period of contentment before the Navigator's Compass, in top gear, driving into the sharp sunset.

The Fourth Letter

Dear Gert,

If you won't write to me, then could you send me some money?

I believe you have a good job. A few hundred pounds would be helpful.

Don't send cash, as the post often gets stolen. Send a cheque.

I am your mother.

Jean

The Ornamental Shrub

Sometimes I saw Rosa Van Durk, usually in the distance. She wobbled along on an inconceivable bicycle, sporting a Panama hat and singing German folk songs.

I noticed how children stopped to stare at her, some shrinking behind their mother's legs, others greeting her with shining eyes. The latter, I assumed, were her patients. To us she was a goddess.

One day I saw her fall from her chariot of a bicycle. I ran up to her offering my arm. She had cut her knee and blood stained her tasteless trousers. She laughed at herself and tottered back onto her iron-clad feet. This incident worried me. Rosa Van Durk was mortal, and the guardian of my nightmares.

Another morning I awoke from a dream in which I was wearing a white dress and dancing, but the dress and my skin were made of glass, and everyone pointed at my inner organs; my beating heart, my rubbery intestines, my pulsing liver. A violin player struck up a tune and played the highest note in the history of musical endeavour and the glass broke. I sat up clasping my stomach in terror. Looking down I saw a brown sticky stain on the bottom sheet. Although I had read about menstruation I assumed the blood would be bright red. I was worried that my insides were faulty, like the plumbing of our old house that choked and spluttered.

It was dawn. The house was filled with cold, blue light. I climbed out of bed and searched for Jean, finding her at the bottom of the garden, planting an ornamental shrub. She was wearing a pair of baggy trousers, which were smudged with earth.

'What do you think?' she said, standing back.

She wore rubber boots and gardening gloves, and her hair was tightly pinned down, as if it might rise up and rebel.

The shrub was velvet green with scarlet flowers.

'There's blood on my sheets,' I confessed mirthlessly.

'Oh.' Jean stared at me with interest.

I followed her into the house. She was like an actress who had forgotten her lines. She put some bread in the toaster, then scraped Marmite on the toast and ate it slowly. I hung around vacantly waiting for advice, blood dripping down my inner legs.

When her mouth was still full of breakfast she informed me, rather casually, that my insides were soft and organic, like the roots of shrubs.

I gazed at her, chewing. George appeared with a bloodless face. She winked at me as if we had a mutual secret.

Later she handed me a crumpled parcel full of large knickers made of hard material, and wads of white pads that looked like they were designed to bandage war wounds. The parcel looked old, as if it was something her mother had given her and that she had never used.

Then, when she was sure that no-one was listening, she told me, in a loud, frantic whisper, that I should not dance, or pay any attention to the earthy stirrings of my body, and shook a finger at me as if I had already been disobedient, and shuddered.

Bad News

By the time I was thirteen, thanks to Rosa Van Durk, I had experienced some non-calamitous years. Exactly what happened in that time I'm not sure. I ate ice creams. I went to the cinema. I slept. And I assembled an enormous jigsaw depicting an ocean liner in a vast sea with a grey cloudless sky.

One morning George was reading the daily newspaper. He smirked to himself. I was digging into a resistant grapefruit, praying that it might make me thinner. A butterfly caught in the room was flapping around George's head. Several flies were nosing their way into the marmalade.

It must have been summertime, although everywhere in our house was always dark.

George said 'Oh,' and stood up, stunning the butterfly, and hitting his head on a dangling lamp which swayed from side to side, casting a theatrical spotlight on the table. He held the paper at arms' length as if it was suddenly distasteful.

Jean swept in wearing a vehement pink blouse. She scowled at the breakfast things, and poured herself a pungent cup of coffee.

'What?' she growled, pecking at a square of Ryvita.

'Bad news,' said George, tossing the paper in her direction, so that it landed awkwardly in the butter. He rubbed his head. His fingers were twitching and he left: the room suddenly. I knew that soon he would be bent over an impossible knot.

Jean folded the paper into a neat square and read as if she was wearing spectacles.

'Oh,' she murmured.

'What?' I asked innocently, spearing a stringy bit of pith from my teeth.

'Nothing.' A curtain crossed Jean's face.

I had the sudden sensation of being lowered into icy water.

Jean rolled the newspaper into a tight bundle, and put it in her pocket, and ran out of the room, leaving her coffee steaming.

But I already knew what had happened. A chilly breeze was blowing into the house. The chimneys rattled.

I bolted out of the door and made for Rosa Van Durk's house.

As I pelted through the irregular streets I saw other children, wide-eyed and nervous, looking out from their bedroom windows.

I jumped on a green country bus that slurred through winding lanes in a drunken stupor. Rosa's house was at the top of a tidy village called Broom. The front lawns were primped and trimmed with nail scissors, the roses were starched, the honeysuckle was forced, against its will, to curl around old ladies' heads. As the bus cranked to a halt I noticed that all the nets were hooked up, in craggy fingers, and that the tidy pensioners appeared to have been dragged through hedges backwards. A grandmother in a pink jumpsuit was frozen in a flower bed denting a row of pansies with her Zimmer frame.

Rosa's house was always a target for complaints, with its unruly raspberry canes, its bohemian garden ornaments, and its Germanic curtains. Now the whole village gazed sorrowfully at it, and even the cats howled.

There was a police car, with flashing lights, parked badly outside Rosa's cottage. Several windows were broken, and the front door gaped open. Rosa's belongings were scattered all over the place. Books hung from the trees, thin letters on blue paper blew down the hill. Rosa's walking stick was lying in a patch of nettles. A broken teapot crunched under my feet.

'What happened?' I wailed, to no-one in particular. A heavy policeman stomped up to me and with difficulty bent down to peer into my pubescent face.

'Did you know the deceased?' he asked slowly.

I nodded my head.

'When did she die?' I whispered, not really wanting to know.

'Last night. She was burgled,' said the policeman. Then he added gently, 'She had a heart attack in hospital. Was she a relative?'

'No,' I mumbled. 'She was my friend.'

A group of children with old faces, had gathered behind us. A cluster of elderly women, with honest, parchment eyes wobbled up the street, and a young, go-ahead vicar skated to a halt on a racing bike. The air was moist with tears. The villagers were sorry that Rosa had gone, despite her untidy garden.

We all felt as if we were witnessing something terrible and sacrilegious. A murder in a cathedral. The burning of a temple.

After Rosa Van Durk's death I became sullen and unhappy. I hunched up in the corners of rooms. I stole money from Jean's purse. I drank her sherry. I smoked her Dunhills and refused to sleep, and even though I was ordered to bed some nights, I simply crept back down the stairs and curled up in the linen cupboard, or wrapped myself around the water heater, or even stole out to the cold shed. I carried garlic in my pocket. My eyes changed from brown to dirty yellow. Fear followed me around, and I was pale and exhausted. At school I failed everything. I was cruel to the weaker children. I tied them up and left them in holes. I stuck drawing pins into their young skin, I pulled out their hair. They cringed when I walked past them.

I waited for something to appear. Sometimes I shouted into the caverns of the attic, telling the spirit to come and get me, but it didn't come, although I sensed a shadow behind me in corridors, and once I think I saw a figure looking down at me from the attic window. One day I burnt the poet's entire collection of leather-bound works in a pyre in the garden, but still nothing appeared. The fire stank of burning skin, and the words wound into the sky in italic grey smoke. George shook me and Jean followed me from room to room, shouting. I enraged them even more by silence.

I wore unwashed clothes, the hems encrusted with mildew, and painted my dour face with sticky white foundation. I resembled a Halloween ghoul. I spat at churches. I scratched my name on gravestones.

Jean wished I had never been born, and browsed angrily through the prospectuses of disciplinarian boarding schools. I waited for calamity, sure that it would come down on my head at any moment.

The Navigator's Compass

The first thing I saw when we unlocked the door of our love nest was a bookcase and on it the complete leather-bound works of Harriet Smiles. I tried to hang my coat over the bookcase, so that the books were obscured, but it dropped to the floor. I considered throwing them out of the window, but decided that this might alarm Eva who was sitting peaceably on the bed admiring the decor.

Our bedroom was plum coloured and perched on the upper turret of the Navigator's Compass. Eva had a suitcase made of iron with enough clothes in it to sink the *Titanic*. I lay on the bed and tried to look voluptuous, while Eva unpacked her array of nightclothes, day wear and cosmetic oils, pastes and enigmatic ointments. I had already emptied a carrier bag containing only a T-shirt and a packet of aspirin.

The room was mostly bed, with a vast coverlet inlaid with

pictures of drifting ships. Downstairs the theme was 'treasure' and the bar was a pirate's cave. It was out of season and the place smelt of dredgers and oil rigs. Eva had already made friends with the hotel dog, who was aptly named Endeavour, and whose legs were too far apart so that he creaked when he walked. I ordered a bottle of rum and some cans of coke. It was four o'clock and the sky was dark and milky. Scarborough had a wide and curving promenade with elegant lamp posts. It rattled and shivered with cold pebbles thrown up from the beach. Eva, having put her spotless underwear neatly into the mahogany chest of drawers, slumped down beside me and held my sweaty hand in hers in a gesture that was overtly friendly and companionable.

I poured us both a Cuba Libre, and we chinked the glasses together and giggled, 'bottoms up'.

'I hope Mother is all right,' said Eva, looking dreamily out of the window as if the answer might arrive by pigeon post.

We lay there then, in the half light, listening to seagulls and faraway fruit machines. I was about to speak, to confess everything, to offer all, to make the speech that I had prepared for months. I turned to Eva, but she was fast asleep, her mouth slightly open, her face calm as the night desert. I relaxed again. The bed floated into a longer twilight. It was peaceful to be stretched out in an unknown place. I dreamt for a while, of albatrosses and whales, of flying carpets skimming over flaking museums.

I woke in the glow of a candle. Eva was opening a bottle of champagne. She turned to me with a glass and her teeth glittered as she yawned and smiled. I had forgotten the speech, although fragments of it returned to me as I tasted the dry, sweet liquid.

I opened my mouth, but as I did, I smelt ink. A camphor fog filled my head. I put the glass down and Eva said, 'What's the matter Gert?'

'Can you smell something?'

'No.'

There were too many shadows in the room, colliding with each other. The shape of a thin head glided along the wall.

'Can you see that?' I screeched.

'Calm down,' whispered Eva. 'What's up?'

'Nothing,' I paused. 'Eva!'

'What?'

A voice was whispering in my ear, a cold clammy voice that spoke urgently, but incomprehensibly.

Eva grabbed my shoulders and forced me to look into her eyes. I saw her then. Another woman's features crossed Eva's face like a cloud across the moon. They were my mother's.

I screamed, and jumped away. I started to run, out of the bedroom, down the stairs, waking other residents, setting off fire alarms, forcing the lazy Endeavour to behave like a savage guard dog.

Eva was yelling from the top of the stairs. I heard an elderly guest mutter, 'Fucking dykes!' as I tumbled into the hallway.

Then Eva was there again. She was giving me water. I spluttered, 'I'm a haunted lesbian!'

'What do you mean, haunted?' Eva snapped. Behind her a platoon of guests looked down on me, lying in my knickers and T-shirt in the foyer of the Navigator's Compass.

'For God's sake!' cried Eva.

'I'm not well,' I bleated, and the assembled guests shook their heads.

The proprietor stepped forward and asked Eva to put me to bed, and whether I needed a doctor. Eva dragged me back to the bedroom where she administered aspirin with the aplomb of a registered nurse. There was something final about the way that she tore the silver wrapper. She tucked me into bed, pinning me down with the covers as if I was a dangerous animal and pragmatically drank the last of the champagne without offering me any. I watched her, my eyes full of need.

She opened the window and sat there smoking a long cigarette, not looking at me.

'One thing I don't need Gert,' she announced finally, in the voice that she used to speak to evasive shop assistants, 'is another invalid. Do you understand?' Then she walked out, slamming the door. I don't know where she went, but she disappeared for hours. I cried all over the maritime bed cover.

The room was dark as rum when she finally reappeared. She climbed into bed wearing a pair of scarlet pyjamas, turning her broad back to me and sleeping.

'Sorry,' I whimpered, as dawn cracked over the window-sill.

I could hear her wincing when I said it.

Trouble With My Face

At the grammar school I was being slowly boiled in the afternoon sun, which glared at me through the sheet windows of our prefabricated classroom. We had been making papyrus with glue and paper scraps. I sat at the back. I had stopped asking questions. The paper became a wad of sticky pulp. All I could think about was Captain Beefhart and escape. As I mulched on with my failed papyrus I told the Captain about my ambitions. I wanted to develop a sneer. I wanted to be pale like the man in the graveyard; pale as the stars that Frank traced through his telescope. I wanted to be so bad that badness couldn't reach me. If you can't beat it, join it, I reasoned.

I bent my lips into leering contortions, unaware of a ghastly silence in the room. They were watching me with a great repressed inbreath of mirth. Miss Reedcake held her fountain pen between two index fingers and let the moment ride. My moment of realization came with a frozen expression of hate. For a moment I was stuck; nose scrumpled, teeth bared, eyes bulging.

'What are you thinking about Gert?'

'Don't know.'

'Are you ill?'

'My face itches, that's all.'

The frog girls were smirking. Francesca winked at me helpfully. Miss Reedcake lifted me from my seat with her neat eyes and sent me along the dead corridors to see Miss Oar, the headmistress with the mind of an anchor. I was bleeding again and my sanitary towel was as damp as my armpits. I waited outside her office, peering quickly down into my cavernous knickers and gassing myself with the scent of rotting brown animal.

The red traffic light outside her office flashed to green, and I entered her office with Captain Beefhart strapped to my shoulder like a parrot. He disintegrated when she looked up. Her face was a nasty spoon. She was the enemy.

'You again.' She untied her mouth and cracked her tongue.

'I haven't done anything.' Yet.

'Your parents must be very disappointed in you.'

At that moment Jean was ambling up an aisle in the new Sainsbury's, tipping ten packs of butter into the trolley and deciding to try an avocado pear. She was having a good day.

Miss Oar's mouth was opening and closing. She told me I came from a good family; that I must learn to iron my face each morning, that I continually distracted the other girls, and that if I didn't start concentrating I would have to have corrective treatment.

She picked up a paper knife and twisted it in the air.

From now on, she continued, her terrible perm flopping

over her waxy forehead, I would always have to sit at the front, whatever the occasion, so that my face could be continually monitored.

I shrugged. So what. And stared back at her, mesmerized by a hairy mole on her neck. She dismissed me with venom and I swaggered back to Miss Reedcake.

I was slouched and indifferent. The other girls avoided me anyway and wouldn't lend me rubbers. Miss Oar was part of my corruption. She made me feel that nothing mattered.

I dragged my feet as I walked home, stopping at a waste paper basket to tip out the contents of my satchel. I swore out loud. I loitered at the bus stop looking for cigarette ends. I undid the top button of my shirt so that my vest showed.

I craved vice.

I lingered in back lanes and unsafe routes, hovering in the graveyard with my skirt rolled over exposing my naked thighs. When the artist appeared he surveyed me with a ponderous sigh, and wrote something in his black notebook. I sat on a gravestone with him. He didn't speak but he stared in a cruel way and offered me a Number Six cigarette. I smoked it with the ease of a practised smoker.

'Who are you?' he grunted after the stubs had left two black eyes on an epitaph.

'Gert,' I answered truthfully. 'I'm interested in art.'

'Fuck that,' he catapulted. 'You'll get me arrested.'

Then he leant back and ran his hard eyes over me.

'Gert,' he murmured, as if it was an idea he had just had.

Sibling Rivalry

'Frank!'

'What?'

'Fuck you Frank!'

'What for? I thought we were getting on rather well.'

'You got the telescope, you got the gown, you got the private education. What did I get?'

'You envy me that? Whips and cold baths! You were all right.'

'That's not the point. What do I get now? Begging letters! You don't get them. I do.'

'There's nothing I can do about that.'

'That's what you always said. Poor, delicate Frank who can't handle emotion, or upheaval, and mad Gert who gets the lot!'

'Have you been drinking?'

'Some. They spent more money on you.'

'Money is unimportant.'

'Maybe to you it is. I may lose my job, then what do I do?'
We are all responsible for ourselves.'
'Frank.'
'What?'
'Sometimes I really hate you.'

The Art Of Disobedience

At fourteen I learnt the art of lurking. I had already given up sleep. At night I tiptoed down the attic stairs and the whole house trembled with my disobedience. I slid out of the front door and into the street. I went to the graveyard with its stone angels and pagan gargoyles and lay under a tree which was an umbrella with a canopy of lungs. I made up miserable songs which I sang in a low monotone. I was always looking for the artist. I drifted to the water meadow and walked through clumps of nettles until my ankles grew numb elephantine skins. I walked slowly, wrapped in a duffle coat, hoping that something would happen. I stretched out in fields of dark buttercups, staring heavenward at the Seven Sisters and the Plough and I considered my insignificance. When birds began to call and the milk train shunted from the station I dragged home; cold and disappointed.

At school I was too grey and tired to be rebellious. A girl

called Emily from the fifth form had been expelled for stealing a blue coat from Top Shop. Emily came from the lands beyond the station, with bric-a-brac shops and dogs with teeth. She was rny heroine after that, with her chewing gum and her slanting eyelashes. I liked to think that she was free to loiter all night and day. Miss Oar tried to convince us that she had disgraced the school. She was not even good enough for Woolworths, she said.

In the evenings I wired myself up to the reel-to-reel tape recorder and listened to Bob Dylan groaning and the Captain growling, *Gimme that heart boy.*

I sneered in time to the music. No-one ever came to the attic. It had changed colour. The inside of my head was purple.

Jean was often in her nightclothes. When I slouched past her bedroom door she would coo my name softly and I would have to go in. She would just lie there in a sea of tissue paper, very pale, but not ill, she said, just resting.

I wouldn't ask her any questions in case her voice became tremulous. George was away fixing up a crocodile handbag factory in Rotterdam. Jean had a large cat with a silver face that guarded her. If I went in the room it hissed. When she got up she might listen to quiet trumpet music and write long letters on thin paper at the window. Perhaps the tourists thought she was a literary person. Perhaps she was.

A Box Of Chocolates

Jean asked me sometimes why I perpetually frowned. I told her that I had grown that way, since there was so little light in my bedroom, but the truth was that I skilfully applied make-up to my face in an attempt to make myself look ironic.

I had even fooled my own mother.

One day I was walking home talking to the Captain backstage in America. Then I walked into a thin post and looked up guiltily. It was the artist. He was whistling. My heart was a Ginger Baker solo. He held out his long fingers and in the centre of his palm was a blue speck wrapped in Sellotape.

'Do you want some acid?' he drawled. We were standing in the High Street surrounded by Conservatives and men's outfitters. I swallowed the pill. If it had been arsenic I would have taken it. I peeled off the yellow tape and plopped it in my mouth. It was so small that it was tasteless. He snorted with laughter, as if it was a great joke. Then he walked away. I followed him. He wasn't walking straight. He tottered to the graveyard and through the dim doors of the church.

Inside it was subdued and murky, and heavy like the interior of a dense forest. A choir was rehearsing in the vestry. They kept starting and stopping. The artist clambered into a pew and gazed up at the stained-glass window. I perched beside him; my satchel knocking prayer books onto the stone floor. At first I felt nothing. I noticed Miss Lute carrying a bunch of dried honesty to the altar. She wore a paisley smocking dress. She waved at me and I sniggered and raised my hand into a semi-salute.

Suddenly there was carpet everywhere; up the walls and covering the artist's body. Even the stone was thick with Persian designs and the air was full and solid. My raised hand left a shape behind it. The gigantic pulpit was an eagle flapping its wings; a group of gargoyles clustered together, chatting with clay mouths. I pointed at them, snorting with laughter. When I laughed bubbles rose up from my nose and spun in spirals to the fluted ceiling, where rafters clapped, and hymns hung in large drops of rain. The artist took my hand. We floated down the aisle to the pretty altar where the embroidered cloth writhed and heaved. Miss Lute was on her knees arranging great palm trees. She looked up and exclaimed.

'My, my!'

I beamed at her and swam on, full of love for Miss Lute, whose toy face was polished and wholesome.

'My, my!'

We were in the cloister, where the famous dead lay. The low walkway was full of people, outlined with lead. We arrived at a plaque in memory of Harriet Smiles, and there she was. I wasn't at all surprised. In fact I was glad to see her, full on. She sat on a marble plinth waiting for me. She wasn't a very attractive person, with a small weak chin, and hair parted abruptly down the middle. Her face was rather sheepish. She held out her arm as if to shake hands, but I shook my head. Then she cursed, and pulled up her horrible black taffeta skirt and showed me her legs which were made of glass and filled with scraps of screwed-up paper.

'Gert,' she whispered. 'Please help me! I've got melancholy.'

'Fuck off,' I said, enjoying the cut of the word. 'I don't give a shit about you or your fucking boring poetry.' I ran away from her then. Did she understand bad language? The artist had sailed off using his long coat as a rudder. When I ran after him it was like flying through a jigsaw. I found him by the river completely naked. He was face down on a wooden bridge. I removed my shoes and socks and put them in the water like boats. They floated off in opposite directions. My toes were all alone then, and sad, so I started the long wade to retrieve them. The river was much deeper than I thought and the current was strong. I plunged about in clumsy strides. Everything took days. I got tangled up in the weedy hairs that entwined themselves round my legs. I was very wet. I was like a fisherwoman. I finally baited my shoes.

I followed a path that was encrusted with jewels and shouted to the immobile artist who was washing himself with blue light. He didn't answer. I heard voices calling my name, and decided, stupidly, to go home.

When I got to the front door, smeared with river mud and weed, there was a crowd of people in the hallway, standing over the telephone ambiguously. There was Miss Lute and a policeman with a helmet on, George, still in his overcoat with airline labels attached to the hem, holding the telephone receiver as if it was a new invention, and Jean who resembled an inmate from the Kingdom of Leaves. She was wetter than I was. Her tears had soaked the front of her nightdress and her complexion was wrung out. She was striding up and down, followed by her silver cat. I smiled broadly. Everyone looked up from their drama when I opened the door. There were still Persian carpets flying out of the corners of my vision. I was stiff and weary.

Jean swivelled and shrieked, then slapped me on the side of my ear. It was as if a huge explosion erupted in my brain. I sat down. Their faces loomed over me like puddings, then swerved away to a huddle in the corner of the room, leaving me staring at a dancing porcelain figure on the coffee table, who kicked her legs high in a flirtatious polka. The policeman was the first to speak.

'Do you realize that it's the middle of the night? Your mother was out of her mind with worry.'

I could have replied that I too had been out of my mind, but I was too busy trying to remove my shoes which stuck to my feet and dripped on the floor.

Jean wrenched herself from the stage and disappeared through the French windows to sob. George loped after her. I could hear them blaming each other among the shrubs.

I was superfluous, as if I had interrupted a melodrama in which I had no part. They were so involved in the tragedy of my disappearance that it took some minutes for them to adapt to my presence. Miss Lute packed her bags righteously; as she left she grabbed my hand and trilled 'I suppose you think you're clever?' I shook my head at her dimly. Her eyes were too big for her head. They sparkled with righteousness.

I was left alone with the policeman. He was too large for the room. His legs seemed unbendable. He leant down and peered into my pupils.

'Would you like some tea?' I asked politely.

'No, thank you. I think we had better have a little talk.'

'Fire away,' I said glumly.

'At what point did the man in question accost you?' he asked, pen poised.

'What man?' I answered dumbly.

'Miss Lute told us that you were in the church with a man.'

'That's right. I waved at her. She was arranging flowers.'

'Yes. Well?'

'He's just a friend. I've known him for ages.'

'What's his name?'

'I don't know. He's an artist.'

'But you say he's a friend, and you don't even know his name?'

'He's just someone who hangs about; that I meet sometimes.'

'You arranged to meet him?'

'No, I just bumped into him.'

'I see. Where have you been exactly?'

'For a walk.'

'And did this man make any, er, suggestions to you?'

'No. He hardly ever speaks.'

Jean was wailing; waking up the street with her bellows. The policeman wouldn't stop sticking his pocked nose uncomfortably close to my ear.

'Gert,' he lectured. 'Life is a box of chocolates. If you eat them all at once you will be sick.'

'I see.'

He kept his eyes fixed on me.

'It is illegal to have sexual intercourse at your age. Do you understand?'

The cast was back from the garden. They stood solemnly in a curtain call. George had gone red as a Dutch tulip.

'You'll sleep in the spare room from now on!' he roared.

Too late, I wanted to say. If only they had moved me there when I was six. My lower lip started to sag. I was suddenly sorry for myself.

'That's right,' muttered the policeman. 'Remember Gert. Chocolates.'

Their faces burned with a supernatural fervour. I shut my mouth and forced myself to look downwards, afraid that I might say something goading and start the whole dialogue off again. I drifted off to bed. The policeman talked to my parents for a long time. I could hear his heavy vowels booming like a double bass through the floorboards.

The next day the attic was defumigated of Captain Beefhart and the reel-to-reel tape recorder. Even the dolls' hospice was finally removed. Everything was put in boxes marked 'Gert's adolescence' in the shed. I would have to live in a pink room with twin beds and a glass-topped dressing table. When I was not at school I was to be tutored by an unemployed scholar called Mr Berry. Jean got hold of my arm and squeezed it.

'Are you sorry?' she said.

'Yes,' I answered deceitfully.

'What is the matter with you Gert?' she asked intellectually.

'Nothing,' I answered, thinking of Rosa Van Durk's sweet face. I wished painfully that she was still alive. Talking to Jean was like trying to converse with a weather vane. She swung in all directions according to the climate. And George was a steeple.

Cramming

Mr Berry brewed me a cup of camomile tea and stared at me bleakly. He unfastened his collar, which was crumpled, and focused his vague green eyes on my private education. We were in a room with nothing in it, apart from a picture called 'The Second Stage Of Cruelty' which depicted a man with a contorted mouth beating a dying horse, and a child being squashed by a wheel. Far away, at the back of the picture, was a body being tossed in the air by an angry bull. I looked into this picture, which hung sideways on the wall, for inspiration when Mr Berry asked me a question I couldn't answer. It rarely helped. We sat opposite one another at a skimpy table, piled high with books.

George paid him five pounds a week.

I went to see Mr Berry on Thursdays and Saturdays. The term used for this kind of tuition was 'cramming'.

Mr Berry seemed crammed himself, living in a rented two-up-two-down house sandwiched in between grander houses with lion door knockers. Mr Berry didn't even have a doorbell, and I had to knock on the low black door with my bare hands. He was writing a book about Paradise. He said that he had been writing it all his life. He drank his tea from a cup with no handle, poured from a tin teapot that looked as if it had been kicked. His hands around the cup were long and feverish, and his fingers constantly twitched.

He didn't look up. He examined a fat text book on the table before him while I had a lined pad before me. At first it was like playing chess, then as months passed, he relaxed, and sat back in his chair, and I began to learn.

I don't understand why it was that I so wanted to please Mr Berry. I strove to hear his quiet approving compliments. I shrunk my wide and flamboyant handwriting and tried to absorb any fragment of knowledge. His face was made of medieval stone, with grey stubble on his long chin. If he smiled it was as if dust fell from his face. He was the only Irish man I had ever met and his voice was a medley of low vowels. He was mysteriously nocturnal. Mr Berry was teaching me about opium. We studied Thomas De Quincey and his condition. I had a delightful sensation of being off the syllabus and following whatever flight of fancy Mr Berry deemed appropriate. I could imagine Mr Berry in an opium den; his pale pock-marked face looking quite attractive in clouds of Eastern smoke.

My education at Miss Oar's establishment was diminishing. It was like studying two different universes. I had developed a superiority which made me even more unpopular with the neat girls with pony tails. Yet, something in me demanded that I made a friend, and I loped about with an unnoticeable individual called

Eileen, who lent me ten pences for the hot chocolate dispenser and was from the North, which made her words heavy as clogs.

There was something different about Mr Berry, I told Eileen one lunch hour in the bracken beyond the sports hut. He had a lodger come from Dublin called Timothy who dressed in tank tops and rode a racing bike. Timothy had fair hair that was nearly long. Mr Berry looked at him with a big, dusky smile on his face as if he had just remembered something hilarious.

Eileen smirked and pulled up a handful of grass with her teeth.

'What are you doing Eileen?' I asked.

'Being a horse,' she snorted and jumped to her feet.

I was supposed to follow her in a gallop over the field, but I bridled and said, 'Eileen, aren't we too old for this sort of thing?' I didn't tell her I had already been a horse, and would never be one again.

She squatted down again, disappointed. Eileen wrote a diary and smelt of sour dough. She was dyslexic, but I comforted her by saying it was cookery that afternoon and you didn't need grammar to make a passable meringue. At the same time I was thinking that meringue was very flimsy stuff and could sink into a depression. We waited in gloomy apprehension until the bell rang, then scampered to the classroom singing, as if relieved to have ended our compulsory leisure.

Those days I was completely alienated from my own body. I looked down on it with disgust. Workmen and schoolboys leered at it. No bra would hold down my postcard tits. Mr Berry didn't seem to notice them. He annunciated poetry as if it was an enchantment. Poetry seemed to stop my buttons from bursting.

It was relief to be there in his tranquil burrow of a room.

Outside it I was confused by vice. I was always looking for its root, but only found the lost leaves from the previous season. My school reports were so short it was almost as if I was becoming invisible. Jean was summoned to see Miss Oar, who described me as rude and apathetic, with some facial difficulty. Jean bought me some Hide and Heal, and begged me to try harder.

'Gert,' she said, 'you need qualifications.'

'Why?' I asked, foolishly.

'Because without them you could end up—' and she paused, trying to summon the worst image she could.

'In Woolworths,' I mimicked smugly.

To me, Woolworths was a bright, homely store, with piles of broken biscuits and cheap perfumes. There were no ghosts in Woolworths, and the girls who worked there seemed glum but content.

'Lost,' whispered Jean, biting her lip. The house shook. Something laughed from an alcove. The bees clustered around the clematis window.

Mr Berry wasn't particularly interested in me, but then neither did he disapprove of me. He was genuinely pleased when I wrote an original sentence. His shoulders would spread out and he would straighten his back.

'Good,' he would drawl. 'I think you've got the hang of something there Gert!'

Sometimes I think he found me tiring and childish, and then he would yawn and curl over his books and his voice would get softer and softer. He marked my work illegibly with a blunt pencil.

One afternoon, with cups of black tea in our hands, I lingered a few minutes after the lesson. I was stuck for conversation, but Mr

Berry beckoned to me and we went through the messy hallway to a back kitchen, which was cluttered and dirty, with tacky plates with take-away curries smeared on them in unstacked piles by the sink.

'This is Milton,' said Mr Berry.

He pointed at a grey parrot in a high wired cage.

'Don't go close. He has a way of frightening strangers. Say hello.'

'Hello Milton,' I squeaked.

'Good morning to you,' scraped the parrot.

'What else does he say?' I enquired of Mr Berry.

'Anything he hears and remembers, don't you Milton?'

'Fuck,' screamed Milton. 'I fancy that.'

Eva's Confession

We woke in the fug of fried breakfast. No-one would speak to us in the dining room. We fixed our eyes on our plates streaked with fat and gristle, and Eva played with the salt and pepper set which was in the shape of a galleon.

Next to our table an elderly man sang while chewing a fried egg. I had an overwhelming sense of being marooned at sea. I couldn't think of anything to say.

Eventually Eva broke the silence. Well?'

I pushed a spoonful of porridge to the side of my bowl.

'What was the matter with you?' she asked. 'Did you see a ghost?'

Between sips of cheap coffee I told her then, about where I grew up, and the attic, and even Jean. It all sounded incredibly puerile, but I stammered on, until the dining room was quite empty and we were sitting in a sea of stained white tablecloths.

'Does this kind of thing happen often?' Eva asked crossly.

'No,' I said.

'I thought you were normal,' she said.

'I am. Really I am,' I protested unconvincingly.

'Why don't you write to your mother?'

'I can't.'

'It's your duty.'

'Yes. I know.'

'I mean, she gave birth to you didn't she?'

'Yes, she did.' I was shrinking in my seat.

'It's not very nice when someone looks at you and screams.'

'I'm sorry,' I whispered.

'Forget it,' said Eva, slamming the salt and pepper set down in the centre of the table.

'Eva,' I talked to her hands. 'I want to tell you something.'

She looked up, forcing me to look at her. Her wide eyes were only a few inches from my own. I leant into her as if falling into a wave.

'I told you I'm a lesbian.'

'I heard you last night. Anyway I'm not daft, Gert.' Eva was suddenly bored again.

'I've never been in love until...' I continued. It was like surfing.

'Love!' snorted Eva.

'You know how that feels?'

'Yes I do,' stated Eva, twiddling her earring. 'Can I talk to you? I know I can trust you. It's a secret.'

Something was not quite as it should be. The compass swung creakily in the wrong direction.

'I'm in love with Clive,' said Eva, '...and I don't know what to do about it.'

'Clive? Who's Clive?'

'You know, Clive, the Head Curator. We've been having an affair for months. Didn't you notice?'

A jukebox was playing in another room.

You are the sunshine of my life...

'It started when you gave me the irises. I thought they were from him.'

'I never realized.' My voice had grown solid and motherly. 'Is he married?'

'Yes. He's got two children.'

'And you love him? The Head Curator?'

'Clive,' said Eva. 'Yes, I do.'

Imagine his clumsy hand on her cheek. Her hand on the back of his after-shaved neck. Her undoing his awful trousers. Did they kiss in front of the Egyptian princess? Did they talk about me? Did Clive say 'Poor Gert,' and did Eva nod her head sympathetically. Did she say, 'She's quite nice really, when you get to know her'? Did she say 'I've said that I'll go away with her for the weekend. I'm dreading it a bit, but I've said that I'll go, so I'd better'? Did Clive promise to leave his wife? Had he seen Eva dance all alone in a room full of glass cases?

Do they swear undying love? Do they drive down country lanes in his velvety Rover and swivel across the gear stick towards each other? Does Gwenny know? Does her mother know? If he loves her, why is he letting her go? Perhaps he said, 'Eva, it's my job, we don't need a staff canteen, a drinks machine will do, and anyway, my love, it's better this way. Soon someone will find out at the institute.' And she might have said, 'But what about Gert?' and he would put his finger to his moustached lips and tell her not to worry her beautiful head about me, and for a moment she would push him away, and then she would fall, into his adulterous arms, and I would be brushed away.

God Comes To Stay

Jean was visited by God. He came to her once while she was washing up, out of a sinkful of scummy water. God said, shop around, and so she spent each Sunday visiting a different church, tasting the flavour of the holy water, feeling the sun's rays through stained-glass windows, running her hands along the pews, enjoying their smoothness.

God did not visit George; maybe because he never washed up. The house was littered with hardbacked bibles and spineless religious pamphlets. Jean had begun to entertain vicars and nuns, and to eat dry religious biscuits and drink weak tea, and look curiously at the sky. She learnt a collection of hymns with high, slippery treble parts. She sung them at night. It sounded like she was gargling.

The Church of England was not enough for her. She told us that the congregation only cared about roast beef and Yorkshire pudding. She believed they were more concerned about their hats than their prayers, and the local vicar had sinus problems.

Mother's prayers were long and fervent. I heard her incanting and pleading with angels in her bedroom. My name came up often. Meanwhile George stooped in the hallway and loitered behind curtains in the guise of a devil. He played blasphemous lewd music on a gramophone in his high parlour, and sported an evil aphrodisiac cravat around his neck, and rubbed exotic hedonist oils into his wiry black hair.

Jean painted her bedroom white and hung a crucifix above the bed. There was an invisible electric fence down the middle, guarded by Jesus's unhappy eyes, that prevented George from ever touching her sacred skin. He took to sleeping in the Furthest Nursery, surrounded by sorrowful Meccano cranes left behind by Frank.

God also suggested that Jean did less housework, and that she did more for the poor and needy. I often saw her rattling collection boxes in the High Street and smiling graciously at squalid sights.

She packed up a box of decadent underwear and gave it to Age Concern. I imagined elderly widows in her peachy bras.

Meanwhile the plates piled up and the floor was covered with crumbs, and God was our new lodger, and we were constantly told to consider him. 'Do not speak with your mouth full as God cannot hear you. Too much television offends him.'

One morning, at dawn, I was awoken suddenly by a swallow that flew through the open window and hovered momentarily above my head, before flying out again, with a shriek of despair.

When I described this event to Jean she smiled at me beatifically and informed me that I had seen the Holy Spirit. I pretended to nod wisely. There was no point arguing about it. I didn't tell her about the mess that landed on my pillow, smelling of worm and drain. Jean wanted everything to be white cotton and lilies.

These days Jean picked me up at the school gates. She wore dark glasses and parked some distance from the school. This was at my request. On these journeys I looked hopefully out of the window for some trace of the artist, but there was none. One day Eileen accompanied me to the car, and Jean smiled at her encouragingly.

'Who was that nice girl?' asked Jean.

'Eileen,' I answered gloomily.

'I wish you'd have more friends. God would like that,' twittered Jean, who had swung south, and was in a fine weather phase.

'Girls,' she continued, 'of your own age.'

I didn't answer. I was watching a group of sixth-formers passing around a cigarette furtively. They were changing into high-heeled shoes, stuffing their flat school brogues into plastic bags. One of them smeared purple lipstick across her lips.

'Men,' Jean was saying, 'have no scruples, Gert.'

'What do you do all day?' The question popped out of my mouth with no malice intended.

'What do you think? Good heavens! I try my best!' she protested pressing her foot down on the accelerator.

But she was a mystery; her scent, her days, her thoughts. I liked being alone with her at times like that, in a car, sat side by side. When Jean drove she looked as if she knew where she was going.

'Why don't you ask Eileen round?'

'I'm not sure that I like Eileen.'

'You have to get to know her better.'

'I don't get on with girls.'

'Of course you do. Who do you get on with?'

Captain Beefhart, Thomas De Quincey, Milton the parrot, an artist who never speaks, Rosa Van Durk, Mr Berry.

She ushered me into the house. I had been under house arrest since the night I disappeared. I couldn't even open my bedroom door without being observed. George informed me that he had alarmed the stairs, and that any movement at night would set off a cacophony of angry bells. Although the attic wasn't being used they wouldn't let me up there. It was full of George's weather charts, and the walls were still covered with Frank's leafy drawings of the Kingdom of Leaves.

I just wanted to lay my hands on some opium.

Jean's Last Letter

Dear Gert,

Here is a photograph of me and Cameron at Battersea funfair. I thought you might like to have it. I have given up expecting a letter from you. I have been seeing a doctor about my fits, but I don't suppose you want to know about that. Obviously you can't bring yourself to communicate with me.

I just want to say I forgive you.

From Jean

Eileen Visits And Frank Turns Orange

Frank had started coming home at weekends and announced that he needed space, and Jean said, 'Have the attic', even though she must have known in the back of her mind that nothing good would come of it. I sometimes wonder if many of our problems would have been solved by lopping off the top storey of the house. I got hold of Frank and attempted to warn him against spending too much time in the attic, but he just arched his eyebrows and announced that he had joined a sect, so nothing could ever harm him.

'What sect?' I probed, as he walked away tinkling a small bell.

Meanwhile, I had troubles of my own.

Eileen had come to stay the night. Her broad smiles filled the sticky air. She was going to sleep in my room, in the other twin bed. Jean was pleased. When Eileen met my mother she was rubbing a marble Virgin Mary with a duster. Eileen stood with her mouth open. Jean turned on her and became elegant. She lured her into the garden with a large golden teapot. I followed with ham sandwiches. I could already hear Jean interrogating Eileen about her Northern history. They ignored me as I set down the plate. Eileen's accent thickened as she described cotton mills and bobbins, and her flaxen family.

I abandoned them for a while, wandering neurotically up the spiral staircase to find Frank. He was transforming the attic into a temple, with a photograph of a grinning guru in a frame hanging above the fireplace. He seemed bemused. Everything else was Zen, apart from joss-stick holders and a neat altar made from a shoe box with an apple on it.

I wondered how the God downstairs felt about it.

Frank sat cross-legged on the rug humming. I sat down with him, but bis eyes were closed and he wouldn't open them. He was wearing a cotton nightshirt. His mouth was fixed in a permanent private smile.

'How long have you been like this?' I ventured, but he ignored me. I attempted to close my eyes but the humming reminded me of bees, or perhaps fog horns, and I started to think of Oona. I could still hear the distracting conversation in the garden too, and Eileen plodding through each mouthful.

'It's not safe in here Frank,' I said, prodding him with a joss-stick.

Frank gave me a cosmic sneer. I muttered a threat to the room.

Then I left Frank and tiptoed down the familiar creaks of the attic stairs. When I got back to the garden Eileen's face was swinging to and fro with laughter. I had really gone off Eileen. They were on about church now and I was spiritually out of my depth. The two of them glanced at me benevolently.

Later as Eileen and I lay side by side in the twin-bedded room, each reading paperback crime novels, we could hear the ripples of guru song reverberating through the old house.

Downstairs Jean played 'Abide With Me' on the piano, while in the distance 'Je t'Aime' slithered in between the floorboards.

'You're a very lucky person, Gert,' purred Eileen, before switching out the bedside lamp without asking.

I pretended to sleeptalk. I rambled on and on like an encyclopedia. I could hear Eileen rolling about in her fine cotton sheets. I wished they would strangle her.

The next day Eileen and Jean went to a spiritualist church, dressed in tartan skirts and white lace blouses, and Frank chanted his way through several complex ceremonies, and I drank a bottle of dry cider in the shed while George tied a dozen knots in his high parlour. Then we assembled for a vegetarian lunch of murdered nuts and damaged sprouts with a glutinous Japanese gravy. Eileen had made a pudding with a damask top out of bread ends. It tasted of the New Testament.

For the first time I premeditated a crime. When the last saucer had been washed and dried and the house was calm and businesslike I suggested a walk. Eileen fetched her parka and Jean departed to her linen counterpane, while George mooched through yachting magazines and women's underwear catalogues, and did not notice a missing length of white nylon yachting rope. Frank had disappeared into Nirvana.

Eileen and I walked down to the river, with its banks of watercress and vicious swans. I led her into the deep undergrowth of small streams, muddy paths and insubstantial planks. Eileen's trousers snagged on sharp thorns and her stout shoes were flecked with chalky clay. She said, 'Shall we turn back now Gert?'

And I answered, 'No, the main path is just around the corner,' feeling like Gretel's errant father.

Through a hole in the jungle around us I could see a cricket field and sitting cross-legged in the centre of it was the artist, with his idiosyncratic hairstyle and bony shoulders. He swigged from a bottle. It was time to get rid of Eileen,

'Let's play horses,' I suggested casually.

'All right,' agreed Eileen, 'I'll be the horse.'

'And I'm the cowboy.'

That's when I tied Eileen to a tree. She treated it like a joke and so did I. I wrapped my father's rope around her plump body while she squeaked and whooped.

'Whoah, Silver!' I exclaimed. I tied a thousand knots until the tree was a cotton reel and only her mousy head emerged. I despised her even more for being gullible and good tempered. When I was satisfied that she couldn't possibly escape, I walked off. By the time I reached the artist her cries were indistinguishable from those of the wild ducks that flew overhead.

I had learnt not to speak to the artist. I just sat down on the grass looking preoccupied. He reached over and pulled my hair playfully. I thought he was going to kiss me, but he growled instead and gazed beyond me to an approaching female figure who swept towards us in a pre-Raphaelite nightdress. It was a pale girl with long straight corny hair. Her whole body swayed. She was the painting. She was the one he was waiting for.

When their eyes met I was suddenly outcast. My body did not have her feminine qualities. I jumped up and said hotly, 'Goodbye.'

She looked at me for a second, then gave me an uncalled-for look of utter contempt.

The artist sniggered.

I ran off. I kept on running for ages. I pulled myself up a hill which was so steep that I had to grasp handfuls of sharp grass, that came away and crumbled in my hands. Once at the top I collapsed in the centre of a ring of trees and looked down on the churchy fastidious town with its rivers and bones, its walls and its moats.

I saw the map of my childhood. The southern sun beat down on me. I craved thunder, and danger.

That's when I decided to run away.

This was not my town, and these were not my people.

The Coast Road

Neither are these, I thought, looking at the landscape of high-rises and a field of black and white football players dancing around a green field.

I was driving along the slow lane of a dual carriageway; driving badly because all the time I was dealing with the medley of stories that came at me with more force than traffic signs or speed limits.

Last time I saw Eva was when I dropped her off after our disastrous weekend. For the second time I left her under the huge clock near her house. She kissed me lightly and walked slowly from the car. I sat there, watching her, like some kind of stalker. She suddenly stopped and turned back to look at me. Her face was quiet and solemn. Then she disappeared into a shadow, her shoes clipping on the grey tarmac. Two perfect tears ran down my cheeks. Every time I thought of that moment I started to cry.

Since then I had more or less stopped going to work altogether. Eva was leaving anyway, to take up a new career in double glazing. She phoned me up sometimes, and her voice was full of guilt. Her mother had tried to swim to Norway after we got back. They rescued her when she was shin deep. I tried to be sympathetic. She said her mother should go into a home, but when she went to see one she thought that the inmates looked like dried fish, and the place smelt of burning photograph albums. When I think about it, Eva spoke as if she came from another planet altogether. Because of her mother she had to miss two dancing championships, and Adrian was threatening to dance with the woman in a snakey dress.

Meanwhile, Clive the adulterer was lording it in his new kingdom. The Egyptian mummy had been moved and was frozen in terror in a coffin in the foyer. I saw a schoolchild throw his sweet wrapper into her sarcophagus. Theobald was completely brainwashed, and could only say words like network and download. He acted as if I might hit him every time I saw him. I was someone to be avoided. An object of antiquity. Perhaps they would put me in a skip, I thought. I knew my days in the basement were numbered. I had to be re-interviewed the following week. Clive had forced me to submit a curriculum vitae. He said it was a mere formality, but I knew he was lying. Even my own desk was unfamiliar.

So I drove my old knocker of a car, up and down the high straight coast road; a miserable joy rider.

I didn't notice the traffic jam ahead, or see a line of helpful traffic cops waving us to a standstill. I drove merrily onwards and into the back of a white Volvo. There was the most incredible racket; a crash of metal on metal that echoed and splintered like a thunderclap. My whole body was thrown forwards in a magnificent crunch. I briefly thought, as my radiator exploded into an atomic cloud, that maybe I would like to live. Then the door opened and I dropped out, onto the hard road surface, and somebody dragged me clear of the explosive body of my hysterical vehicle. I was laid on a grass verge. I was momentarily conscious as somebody fiddled with my eyelids and had a moment of clear vision. Leaning over me was Jean. Among the screech of sirens and running feet I managed to grab her arm.

'What are you doing here?' I spat.

'Saving your life,' she said, cupping my bloody head in her capable palm.

Her eyes were as fragmented as my windscreen. I started to giggle wildly. Somehow, out of the entire population of a region, I had managed to collide with my own mother. Blood was pouring out of my nose. Before I drifted off I had one more thought, like a drop of water.

Jean cared about me.

When I came round I was in the hospital. I had finally qualified to enter its architecturally grandiose walls. Perhaps I could send a message to the psychiatric unit about the rubbish?

More Trouble

Eileen was still tied to the tree.

I shimmied down the hill, thinking of escape. It was Sunday. The bells were clashing in an awful charivari of flat notes. The afternoon was now half evening and I had blanked out Eileen entirely. I was too absorbed in my own adolescent condition to have a conscience.

I was wearing a long black dress with beaded tassels. It covered my ample body like a tent. I strode purposefully down the centre of the path. The river had divided and flowed either side of me.

When I got to the street there was a noticeable whiff of Harvey's Bristol Cream in the air. A dog wearing a black and white jacket, like a dinner suit, barked at me from the house next door and a woman with an orange cocktail cigarette in her thin lips frowned from an upstairs window. I stuck my finger up at her. I felt that wherever I went I was watched and monitored.

It was only when I saw the glow from my father's parlour that I recalled knots, and then Eileen. A silhouetted group of people stood indignantly in the middle of the street. I could smell morality coming at me in blasts. When she saw me Jean grabbed me by the throat, her lipstick smudged and her teeth in an ungodly snarl. Behind her were two people who I assumed were Eileen's parents in chunky coats, and my friend the chocolate policeman. They had a conspiratorial air. 'Where is Eileen?' gnashed Jean, shaking me so hard that dust flew out of my clothes.

I had the sensation of being the possessor of such a secret that I counted to ten before I answered calmly, 'Isn't she back?'

Jean shook me and managed to kick me on the shin before the policeman stepped between us.

Then God whispered into Jean's ear and she smiled apologetically at Eileen's parents who were standing officiously under their hats, looking like standard lamps.

'Where's our Eileen?' grunted Eileen's father. I remembered that he was a butcher by trade, and began to feel worried.

'What have you done with her you bad lass!' cursed the mother.

I mumbled something about a game and they stared at me as if I was a dead turkey.

Then I led them on the arduous walk through bushes and brooks until we heard the stoical chants of a hymn. The group marched away from me in the direction of the holy tree where Eileen looked angelically at the sky. I hovered, knee deep in a marsh hearing their happy reunion and waiting for the policeman to undo my numerous knots.

'I prayed to God,' announced Eileen happily.

I knew she would. I was dragged back by Jean, who had given

up trying to forgive me, and clearly wanted to cast me out. She pushed me across the threshold with a curse. Eileen was coddled with toddy and cake, then carefully parcelled in a cashmere rug and sent home with her huffy parents.

No-one asked for an explanation, although the policeman threatened imprisonment, and I suppose there wasn't one. I was the Mary Bell of the town. If they had asked me why I had tied an innocent girl to a tree I would have answered that, in the greater scheme of things, being tied up for a few hours is relatively unimportant. In fact, going on Eileen's experience it was positively beneficial. Later in life Eileen was ordained, and became a famous church figure. I like to think that I was responsible for her spirit, nurtured in lonely hours under the stars. She never even got a cold.

That night Jean put on a fretful frock and roamed the house with the agitation of a hungry panther. George cowered downstairs in his parlour, whistling through his teeth.

Upstairs Frank was humming loudly, as if he might burst.

I shut down my face and read a dictionary.

'Is it me?' she shouted eventually, standing at the bottom of the stairs.

The house clenched its corridors.

'Well?' she bellowed.

She raged up and down the stairs. I heard a door closing. George had slipped away.

Jean towered over me like Moses. She put her pale face close to mine and whispered nastily, 'What then?'

The house shuddered.

Inappropriately, I remembered a visit to see my grandparents in a furtive suburb of London. There were unintelligent chickens in the garden. On the wall hung a picture of a Spanish lady in a twirling red dress. I thought it was delightful. My mother's face was hard as glass. Her parents were sitting under tartan rugs eating small sandwiches and drinking Horlicks. The house smelt of dentures.

Jean was staring at me as if I was a chicken in her parents' garden.

'I'm in the wrong place,' I blurted incoherently.

'What on earth do you mean, the wrong place?'

'I don't know who I am.'

'You're Gert, that's who you are.'

'I want to be somebody else. I don't like it here.'

'And I don't like you,' she screamed, and our eyes met.

I shrugged dolefully.

Jean's face disintegrated into a depression.

She left me, bewildered, and went to bed.

Visitors

Eva appeared beside my bed holding a bunch of pink roses. I was glad that I was lying down. She looked embarrassed and eager to please.

I opened my mouth to say hello, but nothing emerged. My voice was an engine with no spark. Eva noticed my confusion and laid her cool hand on my mouth.

'You might have internal injuries,' she muttered and sat down, holding her flowers tightly. 'I've started the double glazing job. I have to stand outside supermarkets and attack poor shoppers with my questionnaire. It's embarrassing.'

I nodded unsympathetically.

'I've brought you a card from Gwenny. Here.' She opened a blue envelope. Inside was a card with a black and white picture of Marlene Dietrich in a suit, winking. Get well soon was scrawled among kisses inside.

'Do you want me to phone anyone? In the family I mean?'

I shook my head vehemently.

'Sorry about Scarborough.'

I managed a sad smile.

'Perhaps we should go away again?'

I frowned. No more trips.

'Look, I'll come and see you tomorrow. Perhaps you'll have a voice then.'

She bent over me and kissed my cheek. I stiffened, and shrank back awkwardly.

'When you get out of here', she looked around and shivered, 'we're going to look after you.'

Who is we?

'I mean me and Clive,' she whispered as if she heard my thoughts. 'We're your friends.'

I shut my eyes. Eva was leaving. A nurse loomed on the other side of the bed and stuck a thermometer in my mouth. I was very hot and confused. I felt as if I was in the back of a great limousine with Eva and Clive sitting confidently in the front. They had clothes on and I was naked.

Leaving

The next day, after school, instead of meeting Jean, I slid off in the direction of the train station. I removed my grey school uniform in the Ladies' Powder Room, and stuffed it behind the pipes of a British Rail toilet and put on a maxi dress made from nylon cobwebs. I bought a platform ticket from a machine, and when the old London train came belching in I got on it and huddled in the luggage compartment. I pretended to be a suitcase lodged behind a brown parcel. After a while we sloped into a nondescript and deserted station and I jumped off. I flew past a cardboard ticket collector disguised as a crow. Outside in the street I walked until I found a sign pointing North. I knew that was the right direction. I was aware that my blood was not of Southern origin. Each step forward was larger than the last. I hitchhiked, imitating with my thumb a movement I had only seen on television. Cars full of open-mouthed babies and frowning grandmothers sailed past, staring with disapproval. In this green landscape I stood out like Stonehenge. Then a purple and green saloon car swerved to a stop in a layby. I could see it vibrating with wailing Pink Floyd before I opened the door. The driver was loose and lanky and reclining on a leopard skin seat.

'I'm going to Glasgow,' he drawled. He was wearing a ring with a skull on it.

'So am I,' I announced and leapt in beside him. He looked like Coleridge and that was good enough for me.

The car was soaked with Arabic oil and several times I got green and car sick. The driver, Robbie, wore dark glasses and watched me vomit on the hard shoulder of motorways, while ferocious trucks with a thousand lights ripped past. As we drove into the motorway night, under the arms of thin bridges, shadowed by dark hills I couldn't see, I entertained him with an uneven and random selection of lies which he accepted with casual nods of his skeletal head. I described my fictional friends in Glasgow. I even told him their names, their family histories, and their hobbies.

He was meeting a man called Welshy who owed him money. Up on those hard roads I was miles from my pink spare bedroom. Ahead of us was a necklace of light flung into the sky. I told him my name was Frankie. Short for Francesca, the runner.

We stopped at a motorway service station where it became apparent that I had no pockets, and no cash. Robbie bought me a cup of cloudy coffee and told me that he was training to be a social worker. When he got out of his car his legs didn't seem to fit the top half of his body. They were short and fat. On the next table a leathery rock 'n' roll band were gabbling moronically and lurching over a greasy dinner. They were so dirty that no-one would sit near them. Their conversation was a battle of curses, that seemed to make no sense at all. The manager, who had forty-watt eyes and was dressed in a Teflon suit, came and hovered over them shaking his long managerial finger. They sniggered like small boys, and squirted tomato ketchup on the table. A family of four in plastic raincoats, eating salad sandwiches, were shaking their heads.

One of the band picked up a chip and threw it at the family. The manager raised his hands and marched over to them. It looked as if there might be a fight. The waitresses lurked around the cash desk pouting and urging the manager on. The family hid behind a pepper pot.

I looked on with wide eyes, wondering if I could manage to leave Robbie and join them instead. They seemed to be well-marinaded in vice.

The biggest and dirtiest man, who was wrapped in leather bandages and who had a scar on his bulging forehead, lurched to his feet and leered at the manager who was a tiny man in comparison.

Then there was a clap of thunder and all the lights went out, and everyone groaned together. Robbie muttered, 'Come on, let's get outta here,' and I unwillingly followed him out to the car. As we left the building I could hear the waitresses giggling hysterically in the kitchen. Robbie turned off Pink Floyd and started listening to Radio Four.

On my journey north I learnt to roll cigarettes. At first they were loose and flaky, then tight and airless, and finally as we passed through the border from one country to another, they were perfect. I rolled hundreds of cigarettes for Robbie, who thanked me wearily.

I slept then, dreamlessly, curled on the back seat with Robbie's heavy sheepskin coat piled above me. I could hear the miles disappearing under the car.

When I woke up we were in Glasgow. Everything was square and high; men, buildings, lamp posts. I could see a black beery river and the city seemed to be cloaked in medieval smog through which I could hardly see anything. It was like being in a cave. Robbie stopped in front of a chip shop in an archway. Grease hung in stalactites from the ceiling. I was hungry. I looked at Robbie, who removed his dark glasses revealing naked, uncertain eyes. He handed me a Scottish pound note.

'This is where we part Frankie,' he said, sternly. I must have looked perplexed because he got out of the car and opened the passenger door, motioning me to step onto the flagstones. He grasped me by the shoulders and looked firmly into my eyes.

'Why don't you use the change to make a phone call?'

'OK. Thanks.'

'Scoot.' He turned and left me, jumping in the car and revving urgently and disappearing into a tangle of foggy streets with Macintosh names.

No-one had ever told me to scoot before. I murmured the word to myself as I stepped into the hollow cavern of the chip shop, where a woman in the shape of a blown up white paper bag was holding an unhappy fish by the fins.

There was a clock hanging precariously above the bubbling oil that showed the time to be midnight. I ordered the chips and my voice sounded like a ridiculous flute in an orchestra of double basses.

Back out in the street all I could hear was cursing. Garrulous words seemed to come from all directions. There were men everywhere. I stood by a bus stop and put comforting chips in my mouth. A car pulled up and a voice said, 'You don't know where you're going do you?'

'No,' I answered cheerfully, 'I'm an existentialist.'

'You're a wee idiot,' sighed Robbie, who was obviously not nearly as full of vice as I might have wished. In fact he had a fatherly, sensible side which emanated from him in clouds.

'I was brought up by Evangelists,' he confided when I got back in the car. 'I couldn't leave you in the middle of Glasgow.'

He drummed his fingers on the steering wheel as if he had the weight of Glasgow on his shoulders.

'Betty,' he announced decisively.

Betty

The woman before me was vast and wide. She had me sitting with a mug of weak hot chocolate in a room pillared with reams of paper. Robbie had deposited me at the Sanctuary for Alcoholic and Homeless Women.

Betty regarded me with unsentimental concern. She was here to help, she muttered. Around her waist was a belt from which dangled many keys; every five minutes the door opened and a fallen face peered around it apologetically to request one of these to 'get the milk' or 'open the laundry'. I sat there miserably. Yet again vice had evaded me. I was completely safe, protected and in the arms of mercy. Where were the opium dens of my fantasies, the brothels, the ravaged bohemians, the fearful underworld which exists in Gothic detective stories?

Betty asked me a question. Her thick arms folded over her enormous breasts. 'What age are you?'

'Eighteen,' I lied.

'Do your family know where you are?'

'They're dead,' I said plaintively.

'Your guardians then?'

I didn't answer.

'For Christ's sake lassie, will you look me in the eye. Every day I see girls like you; give me a phone number and let's get this straightened out. I want to go to bed!'

I gazed up at her. She was breathing heavily. She appeared cross and a little pink.

'I don't want to go home.'

'So where are you heading then?'

'Nowhere.'

'This house is filled with women who have nowhere to go. Any one of them would give her eye teeth to have a place. You're from the South? You've got a voice like Princess Anne. What happened? Was there trouble in your house?'

Everything in the room was overused. The telephone was smudged with fingerprints. The chairs had been sat on so much they sagged like old ladies. Betty was too direct. I was in the presence of an overweight angel. She didn't like me at all. I could sense that in her weariness. Everything was distorted.

I didn't want to be rescued by Betty.

'Can I stay the night?' I enquired politely.

'You'll have to sleep on the floor. The place is full to bursting.'

'I'll make a phone call in the morning.'

'That's the idea. Glasgow isn't the place for you.'

'Can I have a bath?'

'No,' she barked abruptly. 'I'll give you until the morning, and then I'll phone the police.'

She jangled her keys ferociously. From upstairs there was a loud burst of classical music. Betty raised her eyes to heaven.

'That will be Mari, I'll have to stop her.' She ran from the room, leaving me sitting in her claustrophobic office with the window open. I glanced outside. It was nearly dawn. There was a drop of about eight feet. I tucked my dirty dress into my school regulation knickers and climbed out, scraping my knees on the brick before dropping to the pavement. Outside it was murky as a coal mine. I started to run. It was glorious; running in a strange city, through streets with no cars, out of bounds, oarless, unattached, without morals, without advice, in a pair of grammar school gym shoes that were once bright white.

More Visitors

One night in the hospital I had an attack of breathlessness. I was listening to the sounds beyond the ward; the cool vaporous hush of the morgue, the tea urns bubbling in the canteen. My body had something the matter with it, but my brain was unusually clear. The hospital was similar to the institute. Around me patients were suspended in their dusty white beds in an exhibition of illness and malfunction. Nurses kept drawing the screens around my bed and investigating my orifices with sharp lights. I was a pothole.

I had several visitors, but the best one was Gwenny.

After Eva had gone Gwenny strutted in swinging a handbag with clips in the shape of parrots. Her earrings were bird cages. She was the least stressful of my visitors, bringing a Nintendo Game Boy and a bottle of Jameson's. I stared at the monotonous squares descending from nowhere and my pulse rate settled to a calm beat. I voicelessly watched Gwenny flirting with the nurses. They even gave her a cup of tea. She perched on the side of the bed and held my hand.

'Are you all right Gert?' she asked as if she meant it.

I shook my head, and we sat like that for ages, with her sipping tea and squeezing my fingers.

After a while she said, 'Bloody Eva. I blame her mother.'

I raised my eyebrows. 'She was a strapping woman,' said Gwenny. 'Beefy, like they get up there on the coast. She was one of the fastest fish gutters I ever saw.'

I looked at Gwenny. In the fierce neon of the hospital, I could see what a pirate she was. She glinted.

'She used to disappear every so often... for months at a time. No-one knew where she went. When she came back she would stink; even worse than the smell of rotting fish. Eva's got commitment problems.'

I nodded, dumbly, and had a swig of Jameson's. My head felt pleasantly furry.

'It will be all right,' she whispered, as she got up to leave, tucking the bottle of whiskey inside my pyjamas and folding me into the bedclothes.

'There are other fish to fry,' whispered Gwenny. I was so relaxed that I slept for hours.

When I opened my eyes Theobald and the Head Curator were gazing down at me, as if I had just been discovered. The Head Curator held a huge bunch of multi-coloured tulips, while Theobald clasped a brown crumpled paper bag of overripe plums.

Still unable to utter a syllable I lay beneath them while they conversed across the bed about the progress of the Mammal Room.

Then the Head Curator looked down at me sadly.

'I am very fond of you Gert. I want you to understand that. Very fond.'

'So am I,' squeaked Theobald, blushing.

'We want you to get better,' the Head Curator boomed, upsetting the iller residents who started to sniff.

'We miss you,' whittered Theobald.

Such are the palliatives served up to the unwell, cooked up in the corridors en route to bedsides. Off they marched, with a last managerial salute to the whole ward at the exit.

By now my bed was surrounded by flowers. My view of my fellow inmates was obscured by stems and petals. A face peeked through the foliage.

'I heard you were here off the nurses,' said a balaclava. Harry sat down furtively.

'I'm supposed to be guarding obstetrics,' he muttered.

I pointed helplessly at my mouth.

'They told me you'd lost the gift of the gab, so to speak.'

He leant towards me.

'The black bags are piling up, I'm afraid to say. I had a word with the Samaritans. They said you should complain in writing.'

I found I was able to raise one eyebrow and did it twice.

'That's the spirit!' Harry tittered.

Then he looked about, furtively.

'There's an awful lot of people stay in here for years. They get syndromes.'

I found his pessimism refreshing, even endearing.

'I expect you've got concussion; or shock. You're evidently not yourself. Oh well, I JUST POPPED IN...' Harry raised his voice, assuming I was deaf as well as dumb, or perhaps with the intention of impressing a passing matron. 'I'LL GO AND CHECK GERIATRICS!'

I raised my thumb in support.

'Oh, I brought you a book. I found it in a skip. It's about heaven and that.'

He pushed an earthy copy of *Paradise Lost* under the sheet, where it collided with the Jameson's, sending it shooting down my leg.

'KEEP YOUR PECKER UP!' he shouted, and disappeared.

I suddenly found myself thinking about Jean. Wishing she was there.

That's when I had this sensation of suffocating. I gasped and my face swelled up and thumped with pressure. Then I was underwater and crushed under massive waves. Bells started ringing and nurses scattered in birdy circles around the bed, pulling back the sheets to discover the whiskey, and scurrying off with it. A mask was pressed down over my nose and mouth and I stopped jerking about and began to swim. I was suddenly a great whale that could hold its breath for a hundred years. I descended down, fathoms deep, then; gracefully and fearlessly.

Henry And The Five-Pound Note

After a few days my grey dress was crusty with Glaswegian smog and torn at the hem. Glasgow was a large gentlemen's public convenience; tiled and stinking of urine and dog shit. I slept for two nights in the manky entrance of a subway. Already I had made the acquaintance of a dozen ghouls whose faces were camouflaged with exhaust fumes and river mud. Days were usefully spent looking for boxes and newspapers, and begging fifty pences off students who looked guilty.

We ambled down the precincts appearing bemused and deranged. Each time someone asked me my name I reinvented my identity – Dorothy, Emily, Jane, even Fred.

An old woman called Henry invited me for a cup of tea. She counted out the rough coins in halfpennies onto the formica counter. The proprietor considered refusing her custom, then relented, remembering Mother Theresa, perhaps, or Saint Francis and the lepers.

As we rattled to a table with our sweet china mugs she boomed loudly, 'You wouldn't be a virgin by any chance?'

'That's right,' I answered regretfully.

She sat me down and told me the facts of life.

I didn't really understand before, beyond the merest biological details. She was so graphic in her descriptions of bodily parts and their functions, from testicle to cervix, from masturbation to bestiality, from sodomy to blow jobs, that I retched into my mug.

'It's always best to be informed,' she told me dryly. 'You never know.'

'It's never happened to me. I've only ever seen two willies.' I wiped my mouth with a paper napkin. 'And that wasn't intentional.'

'It will,' she muttered grimly.

Henry was walking to Muck, where she thought she once had a mother, she said.

'Come too. I'll look after you!'

I peered into her eyes, which were oddly charming and extravagant, and accepted the offer. I agreed to meet her the next day in the same café.

'Where's your purse?' she asked.

I showed her that I was in fact without pockets.

She rooted about in her layers of clothing and produced a five-pound note.

'Buy some bottles of stout, for the journey, and a coat for yourself from the Sally Army,' she whispered maternally.

I nodded, tucking the note into my threadbare vest.

It was thundering outside. Henry reached over and looked into my palm.

'You've got a long way to go,' she announced finally. 'But you're trustworthy.'

I was touched by this compliment. No-one had ever trusted me before. I glowed with responsibility.

Although our discussion was at an end, neither of us had any particular appointment, so we relaxed in the steamy clutter of Mackie's Tea Rooms drinking from empty mugs for some hours. Henry showed me a black and white photograph in a silver frame of a sad girl sitting in a rowing boat.

'That's my daughter,' she told me.

The child was about eight. I examined the grainy picture and thought I could see Henry in the background, wearing a fisherman's smock and waving at the camera.

'Is this you?'

'Oh no,' she declared. 'Not me.'

The café owner threw us out at midnight and we parted politely under a curvaceous lamp post. I wandered towards my subway, thinking of Henry, and stepped on a boy with only one eye who was crouching in a puddle playing a guitar with no strings. He strummed it with his fingers and hummed. I sat down with him, and for a while we watched the feet of passers-by splashing past, afraid to look down at us in case we asked for our bus fare home. Then a policeman strolled up amiably and the boy grinned at him as if he knew him.

I expected to be invisible, but the man in blue stared at me and stopped smiling. Authoritatively he told me to stand, and then grabbed me with both hands as if he had caught a rare newt.

Gallantly he escorted me to the police station, which was granite and imposing. He squeezed my arm very tightly, steering me past a glass partition through which I could see Big Betty and

Robbie arguing over my juvenile face that looked up innocently from the pages of a national newspaper.

They saw me and tutted. I stuck my tongue out.

Unceremoniously I was deposited in a cell and informed that my father was flying to Glasgow in an aeroplane. I scratched GERT WAS HERE on the wall with a button, and hoped it would give the building a stomach ache. After some hours I was led into a brightly lit room and made to sit opposite a policewoman with a white collar and a defiant chin. She asked me patiently if I had experienced penetrative sex.

'Definitely not,' I said with conviction.

'You wouldn't know a lady called Henry would you?' I asked.

'Can you describe her? Did she corrupt you in any way?'

'Not at all.' I squinted, trying to see Henry's features, but ah' I could visualize was the blurred outline in the photograph.

'She gave me five pounds, that's all.'

'I wouldn't worry about that dearie,' grunted the policewoman, as she escorted me back to my cell.

But that's all I could think about. The dirty five-pound note that didn't belong to me.

Coming Home

George and I stepped off the night train. Our journey had been damp and silent, and I slept, or pretended to sleep, for the greater part of it. George read the same newspaper for six hours. He never asked me what I had been doing. I felt like a runaway animal. We walked down the hill from the station. He breathed heavily as if the air was difficult to catch. The town was full of bright windows and talkative televisions. I looked in at knick-knacks on mantelpieces, the dangerous swirling carpets of Southern sitting rooms.

I had a sudden memory of being three years old and holding his huge hand as if it was a raft. Now it might as well be a jellyfish. He was oddly reflective. He sailed ahead of me down the steep hill to our house, then stood outside, looking in. As I loped closer I could hear music. All the lights were on. The windows were open and the curtains were undrawn. We stood there listening to clinking and chattering. The silver cat peeped out at us and arched its back, hissing. When George opened the door, warm beery air flooded over us. The front room was full of candles. The table was heavy with large momentous cakes and the curling tongues of smoked salmon. Mabel staggered towards us with a sparkler in her hand, her eyes flashing with static.

'So you're back!' she squeaked.

Everyone looked at us then. The room was full of drunk women. They were clicking their fingers and licking their lips. It occurred to me suddenly that maybe they had eaten their husbands for first course, which was maybe why George was so apprehensive. They were dancing to raunchy hot chilli music. There were no handbags, only discarded shawls and lost shoes. I stared at them hungrily. George changed himself into a piece of rope and coiled up in a chair. The women sniggered.

Jean sashayed out from behind a cupboard door. God seemed to have gone on holiday. She had dyed her hair from grey blond to platinum and was wearing a glossy dress imprinted with trumpets, and a pair of sleek red shoes. I looked down at my feet which were like something from the ocean bed.

She eyed me with hostility. I stared back. My eyes felt like marbles in my skull. She rolled over to me and said, 'I'm having an old girls' reunion.'

'Where's God?' I asked nastily.

'Gone, gone, gone!' she chanted devilishly. 'Happy now?'

I tried to sneer, but ended up looking at the floor.

'These are my old friends.' She enveloped them with one sweep of her long pale arms.

'I think I'll have a bath,' I said casually.

'Go ahead!' Jean snapped, cynically. 'But you'll be paying

from now on!'

Someone turned the music up. They all started dancing. I staggered up the stairs feeling as if the whole of Glasgow was embedded in my head.

I could feel Jean, hot eyes in my back. This, I decided, was much worse than tears.

She never spoke to me after that. We moved in different spheres. George kept a file in his parlour titled GERT: DISAPPEARANCE, which contained newspaper cuttings, police statements and a cassette of Captain Beefhart's greatest hits.

It was the end of my formal education, as Miss Oar put her misshapen foot down and barred me from her gruelling establishment. I went back to Mr Berry, who calmly continued my tuition, as if nothing untoward had occurred.

And Jean pretended that she had no children and smoked at breakfast time and George began to talk to himself in public.

Escape

After a week in the ward I couldn't take it any more. The woman in the next bed wouldn't stop telling me about her ovarian problems, and eggs started to roll into my dreams at night like giant pods. The doctors were all junior and dropped their stethoscopes. They explained everything with naive smiles. Apparently, I was under observation, but no-one seemed to be looking, apart from Gwenny, who visited every day. I found her visits touching. I mean, she hardly knew me really. She would bring me an orange, or a kiwi fruit, and peel it carefully, then feed it to me very slowly. If I had been able to speak I would have asked her to get me out of there, but all I could do was smile gratefully and chew. After she had gone the air smelt of citrus and sparklers.

The nurses dressed me shabbily in darned paper nightdresses and occasionally asked me impossible questions about my medical history, which I answered with a nod or a shake of my head. They gazed down my throat with plumbing implements. They X-rayed my lungs, and twiddled with my larynx. They took my temperature and wrote coded messages on the file at the end of my bed. They turned off the lights at ten o'clock, leaving me rummaging about under pink blankets, wishing for pain killers and sleeping pills.

We were a ward of disturbed, faintly injured women. Opposite me lay a secretary who had gone blind for no apparent reason, and a teenager who had mysteriously turned a deep oyster yellow colour. On my right was the spinster with swelling eggs, cackling and complaining, and ringing the night bell so often that no-one heard it any more. Behind a pink curtain there was a bus conductress with a perpetual nose bleed. The nurses came out holding scarlet flannels.

At least I didn't ask for anything. Often the tea trolley wheeled past me as if I was invisible. The meals arrived on blue plastic plates with aluminium lids. Under the lids were indescribable meals, made from ingredients I had never seen before, piled indiscriminately on top of one another.

Frank whispered to me sometimes, but I didn't answer. I heard his soft feet on the cold stone, and his breath as he meditated cross-legged, silent and isolated. I wanted to speak to him, but I couldn't. I suppose it was always like that with Frank. My flowers had all wilted and all the visitors, apart from Gwenny, had dried up. It was like lying in a decaying greenhouse.

*   *   *

I waited until night fell and the matron was watching *Brookside*. The nurses flew about so fast they never noticed me anyway. I clambered down from the high iron bed, and put on the egg woman's slippers. Inside I was a grey mulch. My heart was beating in several different places.

I crept down the corridors in the guise of an escaping germ, aware that my nightgown was torn in several places, revealing glimpses of pubic hair and nipple.

I passed a group of Americans shouting at a doctor, who was red in the face with black sticky hair.

'Whadda ya mean, she got stuck?' yelled a woman with a chromium jaw. They were quite oblivious as I sidled past. A porter with a vast unmanageable hoover that pulled him wilfully along the perspiring linoleum floor didn't even look up. I wondered if I actually still existed until I was nodded at solemnly by a tiny Asian woman in a beaded sari gliding past me pushing a drip full of blue liquid. Her eyes were glittering and she was full of purpose.

Eventually I located a door, revolving all by itself. The reception desk was quite empty, and I scribbled a note on a scrap ripped from my paper hem. I propped it against an arrangement of dried flowers. It read GONE HOME. LOVE GERT HARDCASTLE. As I pushed out into the cold clean air I left the aromas of luncheon meat, tinned mandarin segments and margarine and smelt the incinerator instead. I decided I was quite content to remain mute. The journey home took five minutes. I had to break in having mislaid all the implements of daily life. As I climbed awkwardly with naked legs through the window I heard a yell. Across the road Harry was trying to communicate in semaphore.

'Do you want a leg up?' he mouthed.

I shook my head and clambered on. Harry shrugged and wandered off with his torch.

Once inside I put my clothes on and then got into bed, where

I sat propped on pillows drinking whiskey and wondering what would happen next.

George Builds A Boat

George was building a boat. No-one saw him making it, but each weekend he plodded off with cans of varnish and sandpaper and bags filled with shackles and pulleys. He came back smelling of burnt plastic, and gradually, over months, his back developed a curve from bending so long over his work, and his hair, instead of thinning with age, grew thick and tarry. The boat was blue, and he called it *Oona*, in memory of our lost au pair. It was meticulous and neat and had a little kitchen with a gas cooker and one tin cup, one plate, and one saucepan.

While George built his boat I sensibly taught myself the art of cake decoration. I was trying to impress Jean; to coax a word or a look from her stony face. My cakes were audacious and often multi-coloured. I made spongy structures, animals, buildings and abstract designs. I had a set of stainless steel kitchen utensils that George had given me for my birthday (I got nothing at all from Jean) which no-one else was allowed to touch. I notched and frilled, tweaked and fluted, glazed and crystallized. I was left quite alone.

Frank was now converted entirely to monkishness. He had shaved his head. I was used to this now and had learnt to bow slightly when he entered rooms. He lived in the attic all the time, and had stopped going to school in his gown. He was supposed to be going to university, but he was still too young. He had passed so many exams there were none left to take.

One day George invited us to witness the launching of *Oona*. It was the only occasion I can remember us all being together. We unwillingly tore ourselves from our introverted lives and made the journey to a jetty poking out precariously in a place called Orb. I went on the bus with Frank, who wore an orange robe. Jean drove separately in a car. She refused to even sit in the same room as me, let alone side by side in a vehicle.

The boat jutted out of a ramshackle shed. We lined up in a row watching George prepare for the birthing of his creation. I had made a cake in the shape of a wave, with a seagull flying above it made of marzipan, held in the air by a thin silver wire. Jean had brought a bottle of fizzy wine to break against *Oona*'s bottom. Frank hovered sadly, praying on the slipway, as if his hands had flown down from his ears. His robe clashed with the shingle. George was boyish in a wet towelling shirt and sailcloth trousers held up with string. He was a one-man band. Jean tried to smother her irritation as a rising gale blew her poncho tassels across her face.

Eventually the little boat creaked slowly down the planks and plummeted into the tarry water. We cheered, and I cut the cake; handing George a slice from the jetty as he fussed with the tiller. Jean took a photograph, but George was not looking at the camera. His eyes were set on the horizon. He was so tall that when the boom swung it nearly knocked him over.

Jean announced, too early, 'I'm going home,' and Frank and I shuffled after her.

George said he would tidy up and join us later. He hadn't eaten his cake and neither had Frank. He was planning a maiden voyage. We all looked forward to it. He made us feel guilty.

Finding My Voice

The next day Gwenny turned up at my flat, having gone to the hospital only to find a girl with an inflamed ear in my bed. The matron had told her that I was digging my own grave. She was carrying a bunch of energetic chrysanthemums.

I was very frail. In fact I could hardly stand. I opened the door fearfully. I had just opened a brown envelope and found out that the car I had crashed into on the coast road was a blue Reliant Robin, owned by an elderly woman who had just had her hips replaced. I was to be charged with reckless driving. I was losing my grasp on reality. Maybe Gwenny wasn't there at all.

Gwenny looked at me as if I was a small child. I pulled her into my flat. She said, 'You should be in hospital, you daft idiot,' and laughed.

Not being able to speak, I just shrugged. All the curtains were closed. We stood in the dirty kitchen like two shadows meeting in the twilight.

'You gave me a shock, when you weren't there,' said Gwenny.

She started moving around, picking up scraps of paper, and putting the kettle on. Almost to herself she muttered, 'I thought you'd died!'

I shook my head feebly.

'Why don't you get into bed?' she said kindly. Obediently I wandered into my grey, untidy bedroom. I could hear Gwenny singing downstairs.

Then she was creeping up the stairs. I pretended to be asleep. I could feel the intensity of her gaze as she looked down at me.

'Gert?' Gwenny touched my hand.

'Would you like a biscuit?'

I kept my eyes closed, refusing to acknowledge her. She sat there patiently, holding a plate of custard creams. I opened my eyes. It dawned on me then, as I looked up at Gwenny. Gwenny was beautiful. I saw her completely in focus, just for a few seconds. I saw into her thoughts. I smelt her childhood. I wanted her more than I had ever wanted anyone.

I grabbed her hand as if it was a life belt. My voice suddenly boomed out of my throat at top volume, gurgling up from the soles of my feet in great gushing words.

'I don't like custard creams!'

'What do you like?'

'Figgy rolls. Caramel shortcake. Club biscuits...' I pulled her towards me, reciting a litany of biscuits, forgetting Eva, forgetting everything but the taste of crumbs on Gwenny's tongue.

Closer

'Gert?'

'Frank, is that you? You sound louder than usual.'

'That's because I'm thinking about you a lot.'

'Me?'

'I'm worried about you. You've been weird. You might have died.'

'Oh, thanks.'

'And I was thinking about all that time when Jean didn't speak.'

'I didn't think you noticed.'

'Before I was ill. When the house was mapped out so that no-one ever met on the stairs.'

'Perhaps we were all ill.'

'And you just cooked food and carried on, and you didn't have anyone to talk to.'

'I had Mr Berry.'

'But no-one really close. It was awful. It was like ice.'

'What's brought this on Frank?'

'I just thought you might have died and I could have done something.'

'But I'm not dead.'

'No. OK.'

'Don't give up Gert. Please.'

My First Date

I was sixteen years old. My existence was entirely solitary. My mother hadn't spoken to me for over three years, my twin brother was too monkish to speak to ordinary mortals, and my father spent all his time bobbing about in *Oona*. If it wasn't for Mr Berry I think I might have killed myself, but I feared that if I did I would live in the limbo of the house along with Harriet who was, I believed, enjoying the general misery, so I continued with my education.

To my own amazement I got myself a job. I saw it advertised in a magazine. Cook wanted. Cooking made me feel useful. I loved to watch cakes rising in ovens with glass windows. The job was part time, and the restaurant was the Cowboy Saloon on the edge of a bypass, a few fields away from the small town where I lived.

The building was in the style of a cowboy's head, with a huge orange plastic hat for a roof. I was ordered to cook within full view of the customers in an imitation water hole. I sweated into the steaks while famished people drummed their fingers on their napkin rings. The orders lined up in hundreds on the counter, and plates were constantly returning with half-eaten shanks of meat on them, and complaints of 'too rare' or 'overdone'. The waitresses, dressed as Calamity Jane, despised me. They compared me to the day cook who was a man with a Clint Eastwood nose, and who cooked faster than I could read. Each night I cooked several cows. I heard their relatives mooing across the fields as I walked home.

At home I practised cooking for George, who chomped his way through sides of beef without making any comment. I made him Duchess Potatoes, Salmon in Aspic, Quails' Eggs in Lavender Sauce, Candied Lambs' Hearts and Anchovy Surprise. I watched him eating, and waited for a response, but he had no sense of taste. At one of these meals, he informed me in a low voice that the crocodiles were no longer paying. People didn't want crocodile handbags any more. His company, he confided, had unravelled and fallen into the hands of cheap alligator skin salesmen. I served him up a bowl of damsons and he gobbled them up two at a time. He put the pips carefully on one side of his plate. There were four.

I didn't tell him that I had an admirer. His name was Ed Cutler, which I never shortened to Ed. He was a temporary waiter at the Cowboy Saloon, and lived in a caravan behind a silo, which was why he smelt of manure. He had black greasy hair and tinsel eyes. He walked home with me across the fields, and proclaimed his love for me from the centre of nettle patches, or halfway over hedges.

Ed Cutler's hobby was herbal medicine. His pockets rattled with small glass bottles, and he was always stuffing weeds into his pockets to take home for his experiments. He tried to persuade me to drink tincture of oregano, and rubbed my temples with the juices of passion flowers, which made them throb. The waitresses gulped the stuff as if it was gin, but I was playing hard to get and politely refused. This approach seemed to make Ed Cutler arduous and operatic.

Ed Cutler didn't see himself as a waiter, and wanted to build a teepee and live in the Welsh mountains, and for me to go with him, and sometimes when he was being particularly charming, waggling his thin hips, and step dancing around me in my chef's outfit, while steaks burnt on the grill, I nearly said yes.

But although I was flattered, and eager to lose my virginity, his kisses made me feel like I was being attacked by a pecking bird, and when he embraced me on the corner of my street, his lips were thin against my cheeks, mouth and neck. It was like being bitten. Unfortunately this always reminded me of swans. He bought me presents; flimsy jewels and decorated eggs. He asked me to stay the night in his caravan, but I didn't fancy the sheets, which were grey nylon.

Ed Cutler invited me to go with him to the cinema. I agreed weakly. I had persuaded myself that he was good looking although I had to half close my eyes to see it. The other waitresses were much kinder now I was hooked up with Ed Cutler. They winked at me whenever he walked past. I had joined an invisible girl's club. My neck was covered in cloudy red blotches.

Before I went out with him I applied some lipstick to my pale mouth, and as I was standing there, trying to be feminine, I sensed someone standing behind me.

It was an unpleasant moment. Jean's reflection in the mirror was pale and lopsided. She had just got out of bed and her hair was sticking up.

'I see you're going out!'

'That's right,' I answered, stiffly.

'Well, it's all right for some.'

Her martyrish smell filled the room.

I stormed out of the house.

I met Ed Cutler on a corner. He was wearing a denim shirt and tapping his foot on the pavement, anxiously. He had washed his hair. I was wearing a coat of no particular style. Underneath the coat I was dressed in a blue caftan and a pair of knitted socks. He told me that I looked like an Indian squaw.

We went to see *The Exorcist*. The cinema was so old that a piece of ceiling plaster fell on my head when I sat down. It was due to be demolished. A furtive usherette sold us a couple of gummy ice creams. Ed Cutler urged me to remove my coat, and then snuggled up to me, his hand resting casually on my bony knee.

The cinema was full. A large man eating boiled sweets was rummaging about on the other side of me. He swallowed the sweets whole. In front of me was a curly redhead who trumpeted loud whispers into her friend's ear.

Ed Cutler's hand was shaking.

The film started. Ed Cutler reached into the folds of my breasts, but I was already too frightened for heavy petting. I grabbed his hand and sucked it nervously. He appeared to find this oddly pleasurable and breathed heavily. He grasped my other hand and plumped it squarely on his audacious belt buckle. It slithered downwards which encouraged Ed Cutler to chortle with excitement. He undid his zip enthusiastically. A few herbal remedies dropped out of his trouser pockets and he shook them away with exasperation. I fiddled lethargically in his pants. It was like putting my hand into a bowl of warm bananas.

The man with the sweets started to whimper. I thought he must be frightened.

Throughout the film Ed Cutler wriggled under the palm of my hand, and awkwardly flapped his fingers up and down the blue caves of my caftan in an attempt to caress my inner thighs. I was so confused by the film, and by my own libido, that I clamped my knees together, trapping Ed Cutler's hand between my legs. He squeaked and then gave up, got up noisily and stumbled to the men's toilet for some minutes. For the last half hour of the film everything was peaceful, apart from the last growls of the devil on the screen; the large man stopped swallowing sweets, and the redhead curled down into her seat and appeared to be fast asleep.

By the time the film had finished I was so anxious that I had chewed Ed Cutler's thumb to a pulp. There was a puddle of sweat under my chair. The large man didn't move, and was staring at the screen with wide eyes. The redhead was roaring with tenacious laughter that got stuck in my hair. I stood up giddily.

Ed Cutler was winking at the redhead. My own head was swivelling around and there was a nauseous voice somewhere in me. I leant down to find my velvet bag among the clutter of ice cream wrappers and nasty thoughts that were lurking on the cinema floor. I knocked the large man on the elbow and he slumped forward. I screamed.

Everyone stared at me. The redhead giggled. Ed Cutler prodded the man's coat and he fell back. He was quite dead. His eyes were boiled sweets.

It took a long time for anything to happen. We grouped together, Ed Cutler, the redhead and me, looking at the corpse. The usherettes leapt about athletically behind us hysterically fluttering their hands, but our inner circle was suddenly quiet and meditative. I noticed the curves of the man's ears, the beautiful shape of his nostrils, the gradual greying of his hair, the knot of his tie, the peculiar life that still lived in his face.

When the ambulance men scuttled in we awoke and walked together to the foyer. The redhead told us her name was Alice, and I felt as if I had known her all my life. She was an aromatherapist.

Ed Cutler affectionately squeezed my cheek, and we parted sadly. After that he never asked me to the cinema, or anywhere else for that matter, although he treated me carefully, as if I was a Christmas tree whose needles might fall off if I was shaken.

Soon after our date the Cowboy Saloon went bankrupt and all the cows cheered and had an all-night party in the fields. Ed Cutler enrolled on a needlework course, in readiness for making his teepee, and I became a vegetarian.

Later I discovered that Ed Cutler and Alice married, in a wedding held in a field by the side of a motorway. They had six children, all of whom they named after herbs. I know this because I read about them in the newspaper, as the entire family had lived up a tree protesting against the building of the Newbury bypass. All because of a boiled sweet going down the wrong way.

Note To Myself

Now can you see why I need privacy? I am bad luck. There is
something inside me that creates calamity. Wherever I go things
fall apart. I am a leaking vessel with a virus, soon to be flung back
out in the world. I should be put in a special lead box, or isolated
in a high tower. It was ridiculous to think that anyone would ever
want to look after me. Gwenny must be crazy.

I wonder if Jean is dead?

The Disappearance

Oona, the boat, and my father disappeared. He set sail and did not return.

We left the door open for him at night, and even lit the fire in the high parlour, but he did not appear. His shadow festered over his desk. Lifeboats trailed the oceans scanning the oily sea for flares and calling for him through megaphones.

Jean was perplexed. Her rotting mast had gone. She roamed the old house in a fret looking for clues. We rifled the drawers of his desk searching for billets-doux, or signs of intention, infidelity, vice or even maps that might be overthumbed in certain places, but all we found was blotting paper and name tags.

We didn't know what to do, so we had to speak.

At first this was very difficult; like learning a foreign language. I had to alter my whole body vocabulary, my routes around the house, my view of myself and my world. What I found very odd was that Jean was genuinely upset, and I didn't know why. It seemed to me that all she wanted was to be alone with her music and silk underwear, but now George had gone she appeared to miss him. Christ, they hadn't slept together since the Night of the Horse.

Gradually and imperceptibly she began to alter his image. His stature became grandeur, his peculiar silence was dignity, his knotting was artistry.

On the day he was pronounced officially missing, I came across Jean feverishly tracing his signature onto a cheque. She had lost weight.

She glared at me and shoved the cheque book into a drawer.

I said (with difficulty), 'What are you doing Mother?' (I called her mother as it seemed the most formal way to approach her.)

'He paid for everything,' she spluttered. 'I didn't even have a bank account. That was why I married him.'

'Does that mean we have no money?' I asked politely.

Jean didn't answer. In her eyes I saw wartime shadows of allotment fences and ration books. The days of the dishwasher were finally over.

Then she put on an old pair of yachting trousers and some Wellington boots and trudged out of the house. The other respectable houses in the street huddled closer together and gossiped about my mother's downfall. She had stopped combing her hair and it fell in greasy lanks around her face.

I followed her. She wound her way to the graveyard and leaned idly on a Victorian gravestone, biting her nails. She was talking to herself. Later she wandered home and lay motionless on the floor in the kitchen.

Mabel came to stay and tried to be jolly, but Jean had shrunk to the size of a mollusc, and clung to the legs of tables afraid that she too might be carried off by the tide.

Mabel boiled milk and stirred spoonfuls of honey into it, and mashed potatoes in an effort to make Jean feel secure. She raised her thick eyebrows at me and shook her head.

Jean rambled, in spasms, telling us that all the money had gone. That George had spent it all. She had searched every bank account and found every one to be in the red. All that remained was a collection of expensive crocodile skin handbags.

'I only wanted security!' she moaned, and Mabel clucked her tongue.

'I went to buy a pot of mustard, on account,' she confessed, 'and they refused me!' She looked at me then. 'And it's all her fault!' she spat.

At this she began to holler.

Mabel scooped her up and put her to bed. I could hear her sobbing all night. I was superfluous. I went to George's study and unknotted some lengths of rope.

Signs of poverty started to dampen the doormats. I had no ingredients left to cook with; Frank couldn't pay his subscription to the Holy Order of Orange Energy. I owed Mr Berry, who subsequently ran out of tea bags and parrot food. We floundered from debt to crisis. The telephone was cut off. Some of the furniture was sold, leaving toothless spaces in the house that weren't there before. Jean pulled herself together, but her eyes had changed colour and her teeth were dirty. She had occasional rages when I was often the target. She told me I was cold and ungrateful. Neither of her children treated her properly, she shrieked. I picked her words out of my clothes as if they were shards of glass and put them carefully in the bin.

I was going through a mostly silent Mao Tse Tung phase, and wore cloth caps and cotton tunics, and Chinese slippers. I moved around the house without making a sound. Jean thought I was like an evil spider.

Sometimes, though, she played the piano and sang wartime songs with Mabel, and they recklessly put the heater on and forgot about the bill. (I often went and sat in the room after they had gone, to feel its steamy warmth. One time I wrote my name on the misted window.) Jean sang so heartily that she lost her voice for days afterwards. Mabel jiggled behind her, turning the music, joining in the choruses.

It's a long long way to Tipperary.

I was very lonely. The door was always shut.

After such sessions Jean often vowed that she would find a job, and discussed the subject fervently with Mabel, listing professions that she might try, ranging from shop girl to brain surgeon. Jean struggled to see herself in each role. I found it hard to imagine her working. She was not consistent enough.

After Jean discovered a building society account with a small amount of money in it, the phone was reconnected. It rang loudly. I picked it up, suspiciously.

It was Aunt Margaret, my father's cousin, who having lived frugally all her life was quite rich, and seeking a home for her final years. Without discussing it with Jean I agreed instantly. She was to live in the high parlour on the ground floor. We were to be her carers. In return she would support us.

Catastrophe

Gwenny had gone home to feed her cat. I wobbled to work. On the way out of the flat I could see three large plastic bags propped up against the back wall. Above them a shadow lurked; a cloud of something festering. I averted my eyes. It could be anything; a bad dream, the ghost of a rat. Who could be sure? I studied the ground which was covered with earth worms, wriggling painfully towards distant flower beds.

I shut my ears as I walked past the hospital, afraid that wails from Ward One Hundred might reach me, or that the matron might wrench herself from the television and forcibly put me back in the women's ward. As I limped past a group of student nurses I heard humming, and looked carefully at the tarmac, afraid that they might have transformed themselves into bees.

I had bitten the flesh of my inner mouth to shreds by the time I reached the institute. It was all I could do to breathe.

As I tiptoed through the monumental doors I thought I smelt unfamiliar uniforms. I quelled this uneasy idea and proceeded methodically to the basement, where at least I still had a chair, and a couple of ancient mud pots to date. Loudspeakers were calling my name, but I ignored them, in case I had imagined them, or in case I was not who I thought I was.

I scurried on. I was aware of the presence of Theobald somewhere behind me, and the albatross above my head. Then I was forced to stop. A large policeman had landed before me, blocking my path. I froze and looked up into his square denim face.

'You are, I assume, Miss Gertrude Hardcastle?'

I didn't answer, just in case it was a trick. I smiled instead.

'Please answer yes or no!' he commanded.

'Yes.' I spoke carefully. The Head Curator was nodding his head behind the owl collection.

'What have I done?' I asked, feeling suddenly nauseous. I was afraid that the policeman might start giving me advice.

'Can you come with us please. We want to ask you some questions.'

It occurred to me that during my stay in hospital I may have missed my interview, so I might not even have a job. I glanced enquiringly at the Head Curator. He avoided my eye and muttered to the policeman.

'Miss Hardcastle's been off. She was in a car accident. She hasn't been very well.'

'We have to question everyone,' the policeman countered.

'What about?' I asked bleakly. 'I'm a very busy person.' I don't know why I said this as I wasn't. Dimly, I recalled that being busy was something professional people said all the time.

'I'm a very highly qualified professional,' I continued meaninglessly.

'We know Gert,' crooned the Head Curator. 'It's only routine.'

'What?'

'Are you denying all knowledge of the crime?' barked the policeman.

'What crime?'

'She doesn't know anything!' squeaked Theobald from the balcony above us, rustling painfully in a new suit.

'Come with me!' said the policeman, and we walked slowly back through the anatomy section, then up the stairs past Space and the Universe to the Head Curator's office. I didn't like it up there, and the sight of all the stars and planets made me see black holes.

'If you don't mind,' the policeman said to Theobald and the Head Curator when we reached the door, 'I would like to see Miss Hardcastle alone.'

He steered me through the door, then turned back.

'We'll need to trace the girl who worked in the cafeteria.'

Eva. She would be standing in the town centre holding a questionnaire, speaking into the glazed eyes of passers-by on the subject of interest free credit, and how to seal yourself into your house for ever.

'I'll phone her,' the Head Curator said quickly as the door closed.

I sat down opposite the policeman. His face was grim.

'Is someone dead?' I enquired.

'Last night the mummified body of an Egyptian princess was taken from this building. From our enquiries we know that you and... er... Eva were quite attached to this mummy, and often visited the part of the museum where she was encased. I would like to know your whereabouts last night.'

He sat with his pencil poised, waiting for me to speak.

Tears started bubbling up in my eyes. Everything I wanted or loved disappeared, drifted away, lost substance. I couldn't bear it any more. I just couldn't. It was the last straw. The policeman was embarrassed. He had expected me to be nonplussed, not deranged with grief.

'I'm sorry,' I spluttered.

'Could you answer the question,' he went on coldly.

I managed to say, 'In bed,' which he wrote down.

'Were you alone?'

'No, I had a friend with me.'

I had been hanging on to Gwenny telling her the story of my childhood in tidal waves.

'You deny any knowledge of the crime then?'

'Where would I put her?' I sobbed hopelessly.

'That's what we need to find out.' He snapped his notebook shut.

'You can go... but I haven't finished with you yet.' I lurched out of the door and into Theobald's thin arms.

He patted my back and consoled me. 'Never mind,' he cooed. 'She's been dead for thousands of years.'

A Good Spirit

The day Aunt Margaret arrived I made a cake in the shape of a book, as books were Margaret's trade. Jean and I pretended to be friends. We waited outside the front door, watching her step down from a black car, driven by some invisible driver who purred off without showing his face. Aunt Margaret swayed on the pavement before Jean ran to hold her up. She was wearing a shapeless black crepe dress with a large brooch dangling from her breast. Her skin was mottled and fleshy. She reached for Jean with a hearty wave and staggered into the tremulous house.

'Home!' she boomed, frightening the foundations. 'How delightful!'

Everything Margaret uttered was filled with praise. She complimented the table, the plates, the window-sills, my nose and my mother's necklace before plumping herself down and wiping her eyes.

'I am so, so sorry!' she moaned, looking at George's empty chair.

'He was never a careful boy,' she added thoughtfully. 'His feet were very large. His mother knitted his socks for him. That was a great mistake. He thought he was special.'

Frank, who had been loitering by the stairs, wearing a see-through gown, wisped upstairs before she got into full throttle.

'Who was that girl?' asked Margaret vaguely, and when we told her it was Frank she sniffed and yelled 'HA!' as if she had swotted a fly.

She spoke in a sing-song voice, that soared and dipped. She peeked at George's old parlour, which was now almost full of her bed, and exclaimed with delight.

Jean was serving up lamb chops made from grated nuts with instant mashed potato and mint sauce, which I had cooked. Aunt Margaret's eyes glittered, and then she demanded that we say grace, and intoned in a loud voice that we suffered and gave thanks for everything. This lasted several minutes and, by the time she had finished, the dinner was nearly cold.

When Margaret saw my cake she roared with enthusiasm.

'My Lord!' she exclaimed. 'How gifted you are!'

After dinner Aunt Margaret demanded that Jean and I look at her family portrait. We sat awkwardly in a line on the sofa, looking down at a sepia family with straight backs glaring at a trembling photographer. Margaret was seated with her three sisters on a hard sofa. Behind them five brothers arched their spines in tight Bakelite jackets. Either side, their parents, who were Scottish mountains, with glacier hairstyles, loomed, looking harsh and brooding.

Margaret began to cry. Jean went to find some brandy.

'We were a wonderful family!' wailed Margaret, clinging to my cheesecloth shirt. 'Wonderful!'

'Where are they now?' I mumbled casually.

Margaret ignored my question.

'Do you watch television?' she questioned hotly.

'Yeah, sometimes,'

'We used to read Latin and Greek, for amusement.'

'Oh.'

'We adored each other.'

I nodded. Margaret wiped her nose on my sleeve.

'You see, Gert, when the war came everything changed. These boys...' and her hands shook and she raised them above her head in a hopeless gesture, 'all died.'

'Dead?' I echoed, hopelessly.

'And for what?' Margaret lurched to her feet. A misguided tourist was pressing his nose flat against the window. He looked like a frog. Margaret shouted at him and he dipped away.

'We sent them parcels. We wrote poetry for them. We were left behind, like cliffs.'

Jean reappeared with three glasses of brandy. She was making a cooing, shushing sound with her lips. Together we ushered Margaret back to her seat. She gulped the brandy down in one mouthful. I handed her mine.

'The letters they wrote were tragic,' she babbled. 'Telegrams came. What were we to do? We were ruined. The grief! It was a mountain with no peak. We charged on, angrily. This sister, Eleanor, she was a pilot, and Emily here was the captain of a ship.'

Jean gazed at the row of sisters, fascinated. She looked down woefully at her smooth hands.

Margaret was happy again now, and laughing. 'And, me, I

taught poor, illiterate children to read books.' She slumped back happily, drinking Jean's brandy.

'I've even been to tea with the Queen,' she gurgled, her eyes beginning to close.

'Margaret has had streets named after her,' murmured Jean as we transported her large pillowesque body to the bed.

'Streets, and children. Thank you for having me,' she added, childishly.

This was a conversation that we had most nights. It became a kind of chant. The portrait was hung on George's wall, replacing a weather chart. Late at night I heard Margaret speaking to it softly, and I wondered what she made of us, living as we did, like islands in a house with too many doors.

Mr Berry

As I grew up Mr Berry went downhill. For three years we had sat together formally and politely reading our set books and drinking tea together. I had even passed exams. Milton the parrot had aged and had white feathers appearing round his eyes, making him seem owlish. With all the upheaval concerning the disappearance of my father, and the instalment of Aunt Margaret, I had forgotten Mr Berry. Visits to his house had been brief hours of serenity among chaos. Now Margaret was settled I had started to notice him more. Then, for the first time, I met him outside the house. He was sitting on a bench in a public park, not far from the men's conveniences, and he looked horribly lonely. I sat down beside him. His breath smelt of liquor and fear.

As I joined him he murmured something I couldn't catch, then fell sideways, onto my lap. I stared down at his tousled head. I knew he would hate himself for this lapse of emotion. A flock of tenors waddled past on their way to chapel; their white surplices pulling them along. Mr Berry was sniffing. He pulled himself upright and wiped his eyes.

'Sorry Gert,' he stuttered. Then, 'You're lucky, being female, your voice will never break.'

I felt an immediate sense of inadequacy.

Then he got up, like an old codger, and together we stumbled round the cloister, while the choirboys sang in Latin. We stared at the epitaphs on gravestones. It was raining. I was afraid to leave him alone, although he kept straggling away from me. It was quite dark when I finally said good night. Everything was louder and more important than usual. I could even hear the trout swimming down the river.

The next Thursday he opened the door in his dirty dressing gown, with his face unshaven, and my tuition gone from his thoughts. He slumped down into a wooden chair. I could smell the sour excrement of Milton rotting in his unclean cage. The milk had gone off too. Every surface in the house was littered with cigarette ends and empty bottles.

I made him a foul cup of coffee and lost my temper.

'Look,' I told him, 'I've got my education to consider. What's the matter with you?'

He sighed helplessly.

I did the washing up then, which was scummy and unpleasant. I opened the windows which made Mr Berry crouch in the corner of the room as if I was letting the devil in. I put a heap of empty bottles out for the dustman. Then I even washed the kitchen floor and wiped the table. Still he gaped at me with misery and confusion.

I don't know why I was so fond of Mr Berry. He was a wreck.

On the way out I saw a newspaper torn in shreds lying in the hall. A headline remained – 'Man Apprehended With Minor In Layby. The boy in question cannot be named...' I picked up what was left of the sheet and scrumpled it into a hard ball. On the way home I threw it at a swan who hissed back bitterly in moral indignation.

The Post

Dear Ms Hardcastle

We are sorry to have to tell you that you have not been successful in your application for the post of New Archivist at the Archaeological Institute.

We enjoyed meeting you, and wish you luck elsewhere. Please invoice us for any travel expenses you may have incurred.

Yours sincerely

A Working Life

Aunt Margaret wasn't over-generous with the cash, and we all had to work for a living, apart from Frank who had stopped doing anything but meditating. I became a stacker in an electronics factory, and an artist's model. Jean was working in a clothes shop, selling silk handkerchiefs and embroidered bras. She loitered about all day listening to blues music and ignoring the customers. She was knitting Aunt Margaret a whimsical shawl from cobwebby wool, in dusty colours. It was so beautiful that people asked if they could buy it, and Jean was dreaming of a price so high that we could buy back the armchairs and the dining table.

The electronics factory was a great random shed filled with sharp floating specks of metal that glistened in rays of sunlight shining through holes in the roof. There were thousands and thousands of boxes filled with intricate parts; washers, screws and wires like worms. We counted out numbers of these unnameable bits and labelled them. I didn't know what they would become. Perhaps I have touched the insides of submarines, car radios and hoovers. The factory smelt of armpits and cigarettes. There was a round stained clock above our heads whose hands never moved.

Tea break was announced by a wailing hooter and an awesome silence as all the fingers stopped working and the workers queued in a long line for a mug of sweet frothy tea. Our throats were choked up with metallic dust, and I was resented by the big women for being on a temporary contract. They looked as if they might chop me up and put me in bags. Their arms were big enough to pick up the factory en masse and throw it into the Southern sea. I lost patience with this counting of minuscule nuts and bolts and became slapdash; grabbing handfuls of them and chucking them, willy nilly, into boxes and writing 'one thousand small parts' on the top.

Standing naked beside a one-bar electric fire was a more lucrative profession, although my hamstrings were heavy with the effort. I was misled at first, thinking that I was posing for portraiture, not life. An art lecturer with a beard of scree told me to take my clothes off. The room was packed with eighteen-year-old youths wearing purple sweaters, and fey young women with beads in their noses. I undressed with unusual difficulty. When I emerged from behind a scanty screen I was sure I could hear cackling. The inept lecturer handled me like a Barbie doll with double-jointed limbs, letting his hands dwell on my upper legs and at the bottom of my back. He left me standing as if I was embracing a pillar, but there was no pillar. Soon the art room was filled with the scraping of charcoal and lead and measuring of my loins from a distance. When there was a coffee break I was often stuck and had to be oiled.

After the session was over some of the young men hung around and made me a cup of coffee. They continued to eye me as if I was still naked. Barefoot, I strolled around the forest of easels, looking at images of great jutting bellies and sacking breasts. My ankles were depicted as huge stumps. Most drawings were from the neck down, but some rare interpretations of my face showed vast mouths and oblong noses. One artist had concentrated on my pubic hair which filled an entire sheet of paper. He made it look verminous. He was one of the ones who made me coffee. His name was Kevin. He said he had a motorbike and would take me to the woods. I was more interested in Heather who had drawn me as a rearing horse.

On payday I had four five-pound notes folded neatly in my velvet purse. My calves were aching from a crouched, naked pose. My hands were pitted with scars from the electronics factory.

I walked beside the foamy river, conjugating the Latin verb to love. *Amo Amas Amat.* A deep pink light infused everything. There was a scent of roses in the air, and the townsfolk were sitting peaceably on their patios listening to the water spilling along. I stopped to roll a cigarette, watching a swift skimming and darting over the river. In the graveyard the bones were sleeping and for once there were no bells.

In this dusky heaven I relaxed for some time, watching the sky turn azure blue and the river darken to meridian green.

An old man pushing an ancient pram came towards me. He was wrapped up in a festoon of rags and blankets. As he came closer I saw that moss grew on the back of his ancient coat, and newspaper stuck out from the inside of his boots. He was wearing a top hat. Every few minutes he stopped and studied the ground intensely, and then took a small plastic dustpan and brush from the carcass of his pram and diligently swept the pavement. When he came closer I decided to slip away under the shadow of a willow tree, and to head for home.

As I walked away I was sure the man was calling me, but when I turned he was merely speaking to the sky which was now dark velvet blue with angelic stars.

I was strangely disturbed by this incident, and that night I dreamt that I was lying in the pram, and that the tramp was Jean.

Gwenny

Gwenny was back in my flat, making toast. I was sitting in the armchair holding the letter from the museum, feeling like a snail that had lost its shell. There was nothing left to do but drink, and no-one to drink with apart from Gwenny with her clear eyes and hot laugh. That day I had been out searching for the mummy. I had wandered around the city skips, hoping to find her royal toes sticking out of the piles of builders' debris. I went to a street that was heavy with gun smoke and motorbike fumes and wandered in and out of long thin shops with old garnished men who sat sucking gum and drinking tea from tin mugs. I told them I would pay good money. They didn't answer. I stumbled through wastelands of scrap cars, and down back alleys where sodden dolls lay broken on the cobbles and half-eaten prams were carcasses waiting for vultures. Alsations threatened me from the other side of walls laced with glass. I stopped a gang of children in a street. They had saucers for eyes and hollow cheeks. Behind them in doorways tiny Indian girls in bright saris stared at me as if I was a social worker. I asked them if they had ever been to the municipal museum. They shook their heads, and gazed at me open mouthed.

'I've lost something very important!' I wailed.

'What's that? Is it your cat?'

'No.'

'What then?' blurted another with a long mouth and a small jacket.

'Do you know what a mummy is?' I whispered.

'You've lost your mummy?'

They laughed then, like baby birds, and then scattered, running in all directions, leaving me feeling lonelier than I have ever felt before.

Gwenny looked at me as if I was a broken piece of furniture that she was about to mend. My body was heavy with whiskey. I looked at her and shrugged. She rolled up her sleeves and opened the window wide, so that a confetti of scraps of paper swirled around the room and light streamed in defiantly.

'Why don't we get out of here?' said Gwenny suddenly. 'You and me.'

The Debt

I was having a short back and sides at the barber's. The room was powder blue and smelt of surgical spirit and old men's whiskers. A row of men were looking at me as if I was a dangerous type of profligate weed that was growing unchecked through the flower beds of Britain. I was wearing one of George's dinner suits, which was so large it made me look as if I worked in the circus. The barber was grumbling and wielding his whirring blade with ill-temper. He said I'd be better off having a perm at Veronica's salon over the road. He had short plump fingers and a bald head. He spat on his metal comb. Above the basins was a pornographic calendar showing a young woman with breasts as big as footballs. Her tongue lolled out as if she was thirsty. The barber whizzed dangerously close to my ear. The tiled floor was covered with my hippy hair. A boy with an angelic face was sweeping up the curls. He winked at my reflection in the glass, and patted his own close shave as if we were comrades.

'Shorter!' I ordered firmly when the barber grudgingly held a mirror up to the back of my head. He growled and attacked me again with his fine scissors, while outside a bishop's wife with a coiffure the height of an ornamental bush pointed me out to her lean friend who was dressed in a white trouser suit. I pulled a face at them, imitating the lewd look of the girl in the calendar, and they shuddered and moved away.

That's when the tramp in the top hat appeared, pressing his face against the barber's window. He parked his pram firmly on the pavement and walked into the barber's shop. The other customers held their noses and grimaced.

The tramp removed his hat and bowed to the assembled clients. Some blackened cinders dropped out of his matted grey hair. He mumbled greetings with lavish sweeps of his fingerless gloves. His presence seemed to fill the small busy room.

The barber glanced up, then washed his hands and dried them on a clean towel, with a harassed expression.

'I would like a shave,' announced the tramp in a refined Scottish voice. There was something familiar about him.

'I'm sorry, we're busy,' cut the barber, stroking his shining pate, not looking. The tramp shrugged. The barber was rubbing gel into my sleek new hairdo, chuntering on about ne'er-do-wells and the state of the streets.

The tramp peeled off his coat.

Underneath he was much smaller.

'Looks like you could do with a haircut,' commented the cherubic boy with the broom.

The tramp nodded sadly.

'I said I'm busy,' snorted the barber, brushing me down

roughly.

'I could cut his hair,' said the boy. 'If that's all right with you Mr Fan.'

The barber looked up at the bulging breasts, as if asking for inspiration.

'Go on then,' he sighed wearily. 'He's not qualified,' he added mercilessly to the tramp, who was sitting down on the red leather chair, and allowing the beautiful boy to tuck a towel around his neck.

The tramp blinked understandingly. I watched the boy take a large pair of scissors and begin to cut away the thicket of hair that obscured the tramp's face. The barber handed me my coat.

That's when I realized who it was.

I walked quietly up to the boy who was whistling happily and cutting hair as if he was a prince hacking down a thorny forest.

Henry met my eyes in the mirror and smiled politely. She didn't recognize me.

'We've met.'

'Ah,' agreed Henry, frowning.

'In Glasgow. You were on your way to Muck.'

'I see,' she murmured, as the boy tenderly brushed away the stray hairs that had fallen over her blue eyes.

'How are you?' I asked. The row of untrimmed men were feeling threatened. They started pulling up their socks and tightening their ties.

'Still looking,' Henry smiled at me.

'Do you know the facts of life?' she asked. 'Yes, thanks,' I answered. Then I handed her a five-pound note. She was perplexed, and turned it over and over.

'You've got lovely bone structure sir,' chirped the boy cheerily.

'From my mother,' sighed Henry, leaning back and closing her startling eyes. 'My daughter has the same bones. You would like her.'

'Goodbye then.' I patted her earthy shoulder. She opened one eye.

'Goodbye laddy,' she said politely.

I left her then. The boy made a swift movement with his head that meant that he knew she was a woman, but would keep quiet for the sake of peace in the already perturbed barber's shop.

I thanked him and left, and walked home ignoring the rude chants of schoolboys, and the fat tuts of young women in skirts, feeling trustworthy at last.

Frank

'Gert?'

The voice is internal. Frank.

'Oh it's you.'

'Where have you been?'

'Drunk.'

'She's right, your friend, I think you should leave.'

'What?'

'Get away from that place.'

'How?'

'Just go. Write to Jean.'

'I haven't finished thinking.'

'Don't leave it too long.'

'Frank?'

'Yes.'

'I wish you were here.'

'Sorry Gert.'
'Will I ever see you?'
'No, I don't think so.'
'I see.'

Frank Comes Down From The Attic

Heather from the art college came round to see me, one evening when Aunt Margaret was being visited by a grown-up child she once saved. I opened the door. The tourists smiled encouragingly as I let her in.

'Come in.' I was pleased. She had red rusty hair and carried a portfolio.

The sitting room was a little embarrassing. It was half empty, and I couldn't work out where we should sit, as there was only one chair. I turned on the gas heater and sat on the floor while Heather towered above me in the armchair.

Heather was wearing striped tights and a cardigan with no buttons.

She was a Lesbian Separatist.

I asked her what one was and she explained, and I decided, on the spot, that I too would be one, which involved rejecting the penis and going to a women's group with Heather. I would have gone to a nunnery with her if she had asked me.

When I asked what would happen at the group, Heather described a kind of discussion, which I was not so keen on. I would have preferred an orgy.

When she went she kissed me twice in a foreign way.

I was slightly perplexed. Would being a Lesbian Separatist make me even more separate than I already was? I was scared that I might fall off the edge altogether. I repressed these fears and pinned a badge to my T-shirt with S.C.U.M embossed upon it, and clumped downstairs to wash Aunt Margaret's dentures out.

Something was happening to Jean. She had discarded her mollusc shell and emerged in a velvet blue gown that hung loosely from her thin body. She had also finished Aunt Margaret's shawl. It was so large that my Aunt could wind it round her shoulders three times. When she wore it she was so warm that she also had to have a fan, in case she boiled. Aunt Margaret told me that the shawl was made of Jean's discarded grievances. Around Margaret's shoulders these became trivial and fell away in the form of sweat.

Despite the fact that I was now a Lesbian Separatist I still continued to rely on Mr Berry for my education. We never alluded to the incident with the whiskey, and pretended it had never happened. I was squeezing Mr Berry dry of knowledge. It was incredibly trying. I would put books before him, pointing to the place from which we should begin. Often there was a long and bleak silence while he looked blankly at the text before him, then up at me hopelessly. Then, as if he was an unreliable car that had just been jump-started he began to splutter, and I wrote down every word he said, thirstily. I told him what to set me for homework, and I even got hold of the last year's exam papers and forced him to go through the questions one by one.

When he ran out of information he would stagger to the kitchen to make a cup of instant coffee. He had long forgotten wholefood and herbal tea. Even then I followed him with my notepad and made him debate wearily with me while he spooned stale Marvel milk into the cups.

Sometimes he forgot his inner torment and let go, and then he would wave his arms about and become enthusiastic, but a word like LOVE could send him plummeting back into misery, and unfortunately English literature is studded with references to the word.

His only work was teaching me, and he couldn't even do that properly. I was his sole employer, and everything he earnt came from my hard work. The rest was social security cheques. I didn't think Mr Berry understood how hard it was to stand naked all afternoon, or to assemble fragments of dishwashers without losing heart.

I had become a martyr, but no-one seemed to notice.

I was so busy working, understanding *Hamlet* and cajoling Aunt Margaret that I had forgotten Frank.

When he eventually came downstairs it was with a vengeance.

I couldn't help thinking that Heather was right about men. They caused a lot of trouble and needed constant bailing out or their emotions would fester and become dangerous.

And I couldn't stop thinking about George, and his endless knots, which we accepted as part of his personality. If only I could have taught him the cha-cha-cha, then perhaps we would have been closer. Heather wouldn't refer to her father. She said he was a perpetrator of patriarchy, but secretly I thought of my own father as less of a monster, and more of a tangle.

Frank didn't even have a knotting system to keep himself in place.

He had been in the attic for years now, praying to a photograph of a man in a dress.

When he appeared I was watching a programme about juvenile delinquents on television and wishing I had more time to be a juvenile delinquent again.

Although I didn't look at Frank his face was reflected on the screen, and I noticed that his eyes were wide as quarries. I turned round. His robe was tattered, and smeared with something brown. He was carrying a newspaper and a pebble. He put the pebble on the television and looked at me meaningfully. Then he showed me the newspaper. It was a tabloid, and it was creased and dirty, as if it had been in a dustbin.

'Read it!' he squawked.

I turned off the television.

The headline in front of me read PLANE CRASH KILLS HUNDREDS.

'Oh dear,' I murmured.

'I did that,' announced Frank. 'By mistake.'

Then he dissolved into tears. I waited until he stopped sniffing.

'Of course you didn't,' I answered rationally.

'Do you see?' asked Frank.

'See what?'

'What I see?'

'Obviously not,' I answered firmly.

Frank put a pebble on my shoe, then whispered, 'It's all right now, it won't happen again.'

'What are you talking about Frank?'

He sank down cross-legged on the floor. The brown marks were burns.

'What's happened to your robe?'

'The leaves around the window keep burning me. Will you come and see?'

Unwillingly I trooped up the narrow stairs. I hadn't made the journey for over a year; not since, as a last resort, we'd searched the house looking for George. Aunt Margaret was shouting orders from her rug. I was unaccountably and overwhelmingly depressed. Frank was breathing heavily. I wondered if he ever slept. I could see the bones in his face through his skin.

The attic was not the Zen temple I expected, but more like a room under siege. Most of the furniture had been pushed against the door, and we had to climb over chairs to reach the centre of the room. There were pieces of guru's face torn up all over the floor, and two candles were flickering in insubstantial candlesticks. The bed was a cat's cradle of ripped sheets and there were boxes of matches everywhere, and pebbles placed in enigmatic patterns all over the floor. Frank pointed to the window and I saw that the clematis leaves were blackened and scorched. He was frightened. He whimpered, then pressed another pebble into my hand. 'Hold this, it helps,' he whined.

'What happened Frank?' I asked dutifully, holding the stone to my breast.

'She came in and distracted me, that's why the plane crashed.'

'Who?'

'A woman. She wants something. She set fire to the leaves. She's here now.'

I could smell that tang of ink and bad breath. I shuddered.

'Can you sort it out Gert? I just don't think I can manage any more.'

'Yes, of course Frank,' I said quite gently, leading him downstairs. I blew out the candles and propelled him in front of me. The journey took hours. Frank was continually stopping and chanting and putting pebbles on bookshelves and under carpets.

In the kitchen I gave him a cup of tea, but his mouth was clamped tight with terror. I noticed how thin he was and how his skin was quite yellow.

I phoned Jean, who was staying with Mabel. Down the line I could hear music and laughter.

'You'll have to come home,' I sobbed, 'Frank's dying.'

I wrapped him in a blanket then, and we stayed together being twins waiting for Jean. Aunt Margaret was nearly hysterical with demands, but I didn't go to her. There was rum in her voice, and she was instructing the spirits of a thousand illiterate children to come and find us.

We were all deluded. All crazy. It was a menagerie.

After a few hours Jean ran in with an expression of guilt and rage.

She saw us both sitting there like refugees and became motherly for the first time in years. She took our temperatures, even though I told her I wasn't ill, just prematurely aged.

Last Days

It was just me and Jean now, and Aunt Margaret, who was not so much a person as an unruly spirit. Frank was in an institution. We went to see him every afternoon, and tried to distract him with insignificant chatter. He had joined a chess club and never got dressed. His body had a fleshy, heavy look, as if it was filled with toffee. He said the drugs they gave him were nice, but his eyes said the opposite. We took him chocolates and trashy novels. He didn't hear stars galloping any more, and a pebble was just something you found on a garden path. The other patients looked after him. They called him the Professor, which made him seem older than he really was, but he did look old. He telephoned us a lot. We listened.

Jean and I listened a lot. We ate tinned soup and crackers. We played Scrabble. It was oddly pleasant. We were abandoned by men. The house had begun to menstruate.

Upstairs I could still hear footsteps, so I didn't go there. We were in a state of limbo. The doctors didn't know if Frank would get better or not.

It was during this period of waiting that something happened which shocked me deeply. I was walking wearily from one job to another, worrying about Lesbian Separatism, and if it was really my bag, and Frank, and Mr Berry, and everything. Heather had given me piles of pamphlets full of spelling mistakes printed on Gestetners. She was a bit pushy, Heather, and secretly I thought all the political stuff was ruining her art. All she painted now was naked women scrunched into uncomfortable boxes with torn magazines pasted over their mouths. I just wished she'd cheer up and paint something jolly.

I was thinking about all this when I walked past the open door of a bar called the Broken Doll. A putrid waft of fumes gathered in a cloud on the pavement, and there, in the centre of it, falling from the bar door was the pale woman who I had once met with the artist after I tied Eileen to a tree. She crouched on the pavement. Her face was bleak with terror. The artist appeared like a tree struck by lightning above her and started kicking her round the head. She was screaming and wailing like a siren, and his mouth was clenched into a misshapen nail, twisted with ugly glee.

People from the bar were gathering round, screeching like men at a cockfight. She was a prawn, turned in on herself in a curl on the ground. The other drunks pulled the artist backwards in a lurch. Some of them were laughing. It was a dance I had never seen before, but one which was familiar, even ritualistic. Her tears were repetitive. She was like the girl with red shoes that couldn't stop dancing. I watched a woman in a grey T-shirt

299

scrape her up and hobble away with her. This, I thought, must never happen to me.

Cameron

We were visiting Frank, sitting in a Victorian glass house in regulation deck-chairs and sipping thick tea from thin cups. Frank was struggling with his identity, and taking his spectacles on and off. Other relatives sat in shocked clumps, having conversations that were designed to impart sanity. They were talking about the price of socks and the sweet natures of most dogs. In the corner, alone, there was a gnarled black man, smoking a long pipe and humming to himself. He looked up and waggled his grey head at Frank who saluted him, then blushed and put another cube of sugar into his teacup.

A male nurse with dreadlocks appeared with a trolley full of pills, and the patients stirred and widened their eyes. One by one they went up to the trolley and accepted a small plastic phial containing the day's tranquillizers. The black man didn't move. He held out his long fingers and waited for the boy to come to him.

Jean fanned herself with a napkin and remarked upon the healthiness of the rhododendrons.

Outside on the lawn a Chinese woman was dancing. We watched her hold an invisible ball above her head. A doctor, standing in the shade of a malevolent shrub stared at her, then took a Polaroid photograph. I was suddenly aware of being watched. Above me a video camera whirred and coyly turned its head to one side.

Frank suddenly left the table, distracted, and walked out of the conservatory with his hands in their old praying position. I followed him nervously. We walked past a juicy rose bush that was heavy with bees. Frank stopped and stared at it. I stopped too, and together we watched a bee descend into the labia of a rose and suck. Frank whispered, 'You'd like it here.'

Above us, through an open window, a girl's voice screamed, 'I'm coming undone.'

Frank didn't appear to hear her. 'Gert,' he said, his grave face wincing.

'Yes,' I answered politely.

'You wanted to ask me something?'

I remembered the holiday when I followed Frank everywhere.

'I'm sorry,' he said dutifully. 'I'm sorry about twisting your arm.'

I examined his face. It was like mine, but inside out.

'Don't worry about that.'

'I am attached to a piece of floss,' Frank went on airily. 'It only stretches this far.'

'Have you tried walking further?' I enquired, sensibly.

'Yes.' Frank shook his head and turned back.

'What happened?' I murmured.

'I got stung. By a bee!' Frank burst into peals of laughter. The asylum raised its eyebrows, and I realized Frank was in here for a long time.

When we got back to the conservatory Jean had fallen in love. She was with the black man, who was holding her hands and singing 'Blue Moon' into her stormy eyes. She giggled.

'This is Cameron. I am trying to persuade him to join us for tea tomorrow,' she told us carelessly. 'He plays the trumpet. He says he might, if he's not busy.'

Cameron made a trumpet sound with his lips.

'Why are you here?' I blurted, worried.

'I just forgot to sleep,' he intoned in a high-pitched voice. 'Just forgot. Lost my trumpet in a cloud of smoke. Fell out of a moving ship. Too many songs going round in my head. Trumpets. Waves. Women.'

Jean laughed indulgently.

Frank shuddered and said he needed to get back to a dream.

Jean shook hands with Cameron.

We walked together to the airy foyer with its milky statues of naked horses.

'What do you want with him?'

Jean pouted.

'Haven't we got enough to worry about,' I protested. 'He's under surveillance. He could be a murderer.'

Frank whispered, 'He plays flat notes in his sleep.'

Jean shrugged.

'Maybe not tomorrow,' she trilled. 'But someday!'

It sounded like the chorus of a sentimental song.

Ascension

With trepidation I was lured to a meeting of the Lesbian Separatists, with wine and cheese. They met in a living room of a house that had morbid velvet curtains and three vivid sofas. They were all wearing round spectacles, and most of them were at universities studying anthropology. When I smiled they didn't smile back. They were discussing something very important which made them angry and hot. They pushed their hair back from their foreheads and shouted. Most of it was about foreign countries and political parties. One woman, called Heidi, ran from the room in tears when they turned on her like dogs, snarling. At the head of the meeting a big woman called Ariadne held the notes. Heather squirmed at her feet like an ornamental dog.

They asked me if I had Come Out. I answered, 'Well, I'm here aren't I?' and they sighed together in a long sulky breath, exchanging furtive sneers.

After a while the words were clarinets and I couldn't hold on to the meaning of what they were saying. It was oppressive. I wanted to admire someone, but found it hard to find a recipient. Heather wouldn't even look at me; she only had eyes for Ariadne. I grabbed a wine bottle and drank the whole bottle silently. Suddenly the group was looking at me, waiting for me to say something. I realized with a horrible lurch that we were each supposed to say how we felt.

Heather probed, 'How do you feel Gert?'

'Like a box of chocolates,' I answered, and nobody laughed.

'You have to Come Out,' commanded Ariadne adamantly. 'We must all Come Out.'

'Where?' I slurred.

'To our parents, for a start,' quipped Heather.

Then I got it. We must confess.

I tried to tell them that I hadn't slept with a woman yet, so it seemed a little premature, but their beady eyes were fixed on me and I was, I realized, the anthropological specimen of the night.

'My father's gone,' I confessed pathetically.

'Your mother then!' Ariadne shouted.

'OK then!' I agreed, wanting to end the discussion.

'I'll come with you,' rallied Heather, 'to give you support.'

'That's all right. It's not necessary. My brother's in a mental hospital, you see.' I picked up the bottle and let the last drips fall into my mouth.

'You were supposed to share that wine,' bleated someone accusingly.

'It is necessary,' Heather went on, picking up on Ariadne's tone. 'You can't wriggle out of it. I've done it.'

'Well done,' I groaned.

'What happened?' enquired Heidi, who still had red ditches down her cheeks.

'They hate me, of course,' snapped Heather. 'And my Art.'

Ariadne patted her on the head and Heather wagged her tail.

The problem was I couldn't work out what they wanted. It was just too difficult.

Ariadne boomed, 'Tomorrow then!'

I got up, and stumbled drunkenly. They were all looking at me as if I was somehow traitorous. I didn't understand what I had done to make them so hostile.

'What's wrong with now?' I roared, rising to the bait, and deciding to hoist them with their own petard.

'I'm not sure you're in the right state; you're drunk,' demurred Heather.

'I'm as right as I'll ever be,' I screeched, frightening some of the thinner members.

'I'm game!' yelled Ariadne.

'Yes, yes,' shouted a medley of degree students, rising to their feet like a choir.

For the first time I was part of a movement and filled with a sense of righteousness and euphoria. Everyone was smiling at me now. Even the windows had more respect than at first, and the sofas had become quite insignificant. I was reminded of Miss Reedcake, my old sports mistress, and running, and girls' schools, and daisy petals.

'Come on!' I ranted at the top of my teenage voice.

Behind me a stampede of desert boots jumped up and I sped out of the door followed by five or six women with faces like torches. As we cantered out of the house our eyes shone like headlights before us, so fixed were we on our mission. It was only as we jogged around the last corner, and headed towards my front door that I began to have doubts.

But this entourage was a runaway train that wouldn't stop until it reached my door.

Jean was sitting with Aunt Margaret, who temporarily believed she was a river and swirled beautifully between great white cotton sheets. She looked up with a Victorian smile at the line of anthropologists before her.

'How nice,' she whispered. 'Gert's brought some girlfriends round. Jean, why don't you get some chairs.'

The hot women were suddenly silenced at the sight of Aunt Margaret, who towered above them spiritually and mentally in the guise of a waterfall.

'I like girls!' she rumbled. 'Girls are good swimmers on the whole!'

Jean returned with the chairs, and we gathered around the bed dutifully.

'She's weak,' muttered Jean. 'She's ebbing. And Frank's rung eight times.'

The group was quiet now, and all that could be heard was their pants after the exhausting run. Margaret started speaking, believing she was standing at a pulpit, and told the story of her life. I was completely done for, and rested my head on the candlewick bed cover and instantly fell asleep.

When I came round Aunt Margaret was tinkling away happily to herself. It occurred to me that all her grief was running away down the mountainside, and when it was all gone she would die singing. The women had gone. Jean was fast asleep on the other side of the bed. It was as if we were resting on imaginary banks.

Margaret opened one eye blearily.

'Your friends stayed for some hours. I told them everything. I think they enjoyed themselves. They said you wanted to tell me something.'

'Oh that.'

'Ha ha,' Margaret babbled, then burped.

'I'm a Lesbian Separatist.' It sounded like something in a jar.

'At least you're healthy,' Margaret muttered.

For a moment then she opened her eyes and was frighteningly lucid.

'Speaking of which,' she said authoritatively.

'What?' I asked, frightened, expecting a lordly telling off.

'There's a dead poet in this house. I've seen her several times and managed to converse with her about many things; poetry of course, and corsets. Very interesting the way they used to make them. Very uncomfortable. Anyway, as I said, she's been hanging around, doing nothing, something which always causes trouble. It's all to do with this business.'

'Business?' I echoed weakly.

'What you just said. What was it, lesbian soup?'

'What?' I was genuinely confused.

'Seems she never got a chance to be herself. Fell in the soup and never got out of it. Died before it was declared and so on. Says she knows you. She said to say she's sorry about the trouble she's caused. She festered, that's all. I'm taking her with me.'

'Where?' I asked dimly.

'Paradise!' hooted Margaret. 'Where else?'

'I thought your friends were lovely girls,' Margaret said sweetly. 'That poet said she liked the look of the spidery one. Ariadne. Said she might visit.'

And then she hummed for a while.

'It's called Coming Out,' I said softly.

'Ah. Like cherry blossom,' tinkled Aunt Margaret. Then she took off her old silver ring and gave it to me, curling my fingers around it with her old hand, as if it was a secret.

I must be the only person in the world who came out before I even came in.

'If I were you,' Aunt Margaret advised, 'I wouldn't tell Jean.'

At that moment Aunt Margaret dried up and began to sing.

A Death In The House

Jean was quiet as a nun. Aunt Margaret was buried in a temple in Highgate Cemetery. She ascended to heaven at the age of one hundred and two. Her body was soft as a butterfly and she was covered with fine silver hairs. Her obituaries were numerous, and her funeral was crowded with old and passionate women and dusty ministers who wiped their tears with grey handkerchiefs and sang like seagulls. We still had visitors coming to see the room where she spent her last days. I hoped it put Harriet's nose out of joint. The visitors touched the bed and crossed themselves, and I was beginning to wonder if we were in the presence of a saint.

I ran round to Mr Berry's house waving a piece of paper. I had passed all my exams. He was building a house of cards that toppled over when I blew through the door. He laughed and his whole face creaked with the effort. We put on a waltz and danced around the floor together, and I understood that the exams were for him as much as me. I was Mr Berry's achievement. Together we had seen to my education.

I also realized that I loved Mr Berry. I loved him because he was so weak.

After we were through with dancing we looked through lists of universities and planned my future. I wanted to do Oriental Studies. I wanted to get away from everything Southern, and move on to other worlds where roofs were domes and there were no boys in gowns. I asked Mr Berry if he would like to walk around some campuses with me, saying the word 'campuses' several times; it was part of my new dictionary.

Then he said to me quietly, 'I'm going home.'

'Where?' I asked.

'To Ireland,' he said. 'You were my life's work! There's nothing for me here.'

And I could see that there wasn't.

That was the last time I saw Mr Berry. He was standing at the door, and I realized that he was still in his dressing gown, and his waving hand was shaking.

At the corner I turned. He was still there. A line from *Paradise Lost* burst into my mouth and I whispered it, not knowing why, '*Dovelike sats't brooding on the vast abyss*'.

I can forget that endless piece now. Thank God, I thought.

Jean

Every week Jean visited the trumpet player at the leafy asylum. They drank tea, hummed tunes, and clicked their fingers. They looked into each other's eyes, swaying and egging the other on. The trumpet player wore dapper jackets, and Jean put on her red shoes. Their fingers danced together on the wooden table in the conservatory.

Jean asked him the nature of his madness, and he told her how he got played out on cruise liners. Night and day he played the trumpet, until it was glued to his lips, and his fingers couldn't stop moving. He told Jean this, and then he burst into tears for three weeks, until his face went soft, like treacle toffee.

Then Jean bought him a new trumpet and he took it out of the box as if he had given birth to a new child. The doctors hovered behind them nervously, as if the music might whirl him away. He played one long blue note, and smiled. At the end of the visit Jean put the trumpet back in its case and carried it home. She spent the evenings polishing it with a lavender rag.

He was writing a trumpet solo for my mother, and one day, Jean said, he would come and live with her, but there was no hurry. Take each day as it comes, she said. I'm free, she told him. I've got nobody left but you.

Gwenny's Question

Gwenny and I were going to Paris. Gwenny was leaning over a desk looking into the nervous eyes of a boy with a career in tourism ahead of him. She was questioning him wildly about timetables, boats, trains and planes. He was so confused by her that the computer had seized up. She was tapping her nails impatiently on a glossy picture in a brochure of the Eiffel Tower.

'Which airport?' he asked politely,

'I don't know!' muttered Gwenny.

'When would you like to fly?'

'Actually, I think I'd rather get the train,' I murmured feebly.

I started idly leafing through brochures. I looked at the pictures of swimming pools and cocktails of obligatory sunsets. I liked listening to Gwenny. She was so unpredictable. She was leaning across the desk now, prodding the computer keys. It clicked, and suddenly whirred into action.

I left her to it, and gazed out of the window.

That's when I saw Eva. She was standing in the middle of the pedestrian precinct, with people rushing past her, holding a clipboard. Her face was set in an expression of surrender. Her beauty seemed to have fallen away from her like leaves from a tree. It was awful. I nudged Gwenny, but she was too absorbed in the business of tickets, and when I turned back Eva was gone.

'Come on, get a move on!' Gwenny was haranguing the boy again, who feverishly passed her two train tickets, and sat back exhausted.

Later, Gwenny and I went and sat in a misty café, clasping mugs of hot chocolate, trying to remember our school French. Just as I was lost in the middle of a disintegrating sentence describing who I was, Gwenny interrupted me, and grabbed one of my hands which I had been waving about in a Parisian manner.

'I've been wanting to ask you something,' said Gwenny. Gwenny was rarely so serious.

'What?' I asked anxiously.

'Just tell me. Why don't you speak to your mother?'

The Last Train

The day before I left home in autumn, when the river was a mush of brown leaves, Frank was allowed home for the weekend. He sat staring at the television as if it was a wild animal. Jean was clearing out cupboards; an activity she had applied herself to with venom ever since Margaret's death. I was tiptoeing around Frank, worrying about what would happen after I left.

He didn't seem depressed. In fact he was calm and wide eyed, like a tired child. He had started to smoke, and beside him an ashtray was filled with half-finished tab ends. When he didn't smoke he chewed gum. It seemed like his mouth was never still.

At about ten o'clock we escorted him to bed, turning back the covers and tucking him firmly between the sheets. He closed his eyes straight away. The front door was locked. I don't know how he managed to open it.

He must have lain in bed for some hours, listening to the rain outside, and the trains rushing by. I imagine him struggling out of bed, and trembling as he fumbled his way to the door, still dressed in his institutional pyjamas, his mouth moving in a neverending prayer.

The street would have been a long winding corridor, longer than our first journey to the Furthest Nursery. Maybe he was aware of my dreams as I slept. It must have taken him a long time to reach the railway line, past the closed eyes of shops and the birds sleeping in rows on the ledges, as it was nearly dawn when he got there and the sun was a weak pink ball rising on the horizon. He stood on the bridge, looking down, waiting for the first train to scream up the line, hell-bent for London, hearing its scream in the distance, clenching his fists.

What was I dreaming of that night? Why didn't I wake up?

Frank waited until the express train thundered over the viaduct and into the tunnel, and just as the sparks flew from the rails, and the noise was so thunderous that he forgot everything, he hurled himself forward and was broken instantly into a thousand tiny pieces that flew into the air and broke the speed of the great engine, nearly causing the train to de-rail.

Harry

And now I was leaving again.

As I was packing I could see Harry waving at me from outside. He was trying to say something with his irregular mouth. I opened the door and he beckoned me out.

'Look,' he crowed, pointing victoriously at the dustbins.

The rubbish had gone. The alley was scrubbed and clean.

'Are you responsible?' I asked him.

'You could say that,' answered Harry. 'I pulled strings.'

Then he leant very close to me, so that I could feel the electric bristle of his chin against my ear.

'Guess who's staying at my house?' he whispered.

He was grinning like a child who had just found fifty pence in a gutter. I shook my head.

'I've got Her,' he announced proudly.

'Who?' I gasped, although I knew immediately who he was

talking about.

'She's at home on the sofa. I'm going to look after her. I got a book out of the library. On preservation.'

'Well done Harry,' I said, and kissed him.

The Letter

Jean sometimes felt she was trying to drink an ocean with a bent teaspoon. Living in a bedsit on her own was not as bad as she had envisaged, and she had experienced some good times with Cameron. He had taught her to be loose again, for one thing, and he had shown her how to own nothing. She had no idea what to do next, now that he had gone. Lately she thought about me most of the time. She wrote many letters, but I never wrote back. The space between us was full of grief. Then on the last day of her tenancy she came downstairs to discover a letter, the paper calloused, the ink faded, smelling of old men's furniture. It had obviously travelled, being thumbmarked and heavy with the breath of foreign postmen. She picked it up. There was no-one in the house. Their two rooms on the fourth floor were open wounds. A bag of miscellaneous string was the only item left in the bedroom. She took the letter to the communal kitchen, holding it in front of her, as if it was a promise. There was a kind of buzzing in her left ear, as if a blade of grass vibrated somewhere beyond her eardrum. As she tore it open my front door key fell into her hand.

The letter was from me. When I wrote it I was on a train with Gwenny on my way to Paris. Gwenny was asleep, snuggled into the corner of the carriage with a contented expression on her face. Outside there was nothing but rocks and dust. A man with stormy edges was telling me the story of his life. He was only six when I interrupted him.

'Excuse me,' I said, 'I must write a letter. Do you have any paper?'

And he turned out to be a paper merchant with suitcases filled with paper, papyrus, root paper, paper made from crushed beetles, moist paper, blotting, thin parchment, petal notelets, envelopes made from industrial waste, fried and boiled paper. He displayed his wares on the train seat and I picked a strange mottled shade of handmade parchment which was the most expensive of the range.

And then I wrote to Jean.

Dear Mum,

I'm really sorry that I haven't been in touch before. I had some trouble at work, and to cut a long story short, I lost my job. I'm going away for a short while with my friend Gwenny, who I'm sure you will like. Please stay in my flat while I'm gone. I paid the rent for the next couple of months. When I get back I would like to talk to you about Frank. I hope you enjoy living in my flat. I cleaned it up before I left, and there's no rubbish there now. My friend

Harry may call on you to check that you are all right.
   With love
      Your daughter Gert

'Gert?'

'Is that you Frank?'

'Yes, it's me. I'm glad you wrote to her. It wasn't her fault.'

'No. I just couldn't find the words, that's all.'

'I'm not going to call you any more. I'm going to sleep.'

'I thought you might say that.'

'It's just you kept on waking me up.'

'You never did like to be disturbed.'

'Don't get me wrong. I'm glad you called.'

'So am I.'

'You did it Gert.'

'Did what?'

'You grew up.'

By the same author

Novels and Short Stories

The Taxi Drivers Daughter
Bloodlines

Poetry

Indelible, Miraculous
The Poetry Cure (edited with Cynthia Fuller)
Apology for Absence
Sudden Collapses in Public Places
Sauce
Modern Goddess
Small Beauties

Plays

The Taxi Drivers Daughter (Novel Adaption by Live Theatre)
Manifesto for a New City (Northern Stage)
Eating the Elephant and Other Plays (New Writing North)
Cold Calling (Methuen Plays, Live Theatre Anthology)
Attachments (Live Theatre)
The Last Post (Live Theatre/Durham Elements Group)
Doughnuts Like Fanny's (Quondam Theatre Company & Sandra Hunt)
Personal Belongings (Live Theatre, Edinburgh Festival)
Venetia Love Goes Netting (Live Theatre)

The Night Tom Jones Came to Barrow (The Ashton Group, Barrow)
Eating the Elephant (The Ashton Group, Barrow)
The Women Who Painted Ships (BBC Radio 4, Live Theatre)
Black Diamonds (Quondam Theatre Company)
Head of Steel (Quondam Theatre Company)
Rafferty's Café (Quondam Theatre Company)
The Cure (The Crucible Theatre, Sheffield)
Mother of Invention (Northumberland Youth Theatre)
Gone with the Lettuce (Northumberland Youth Theatre)
Growing Pains (Tyne & Wear Theatre in Education)

Radio Plays and TV

The Waiting Room (BBC Radio 4)
The Street (BBC Radio 4 Live Broadcast)
Appointments (BBC Radio 4 Women's Hour)
Cold Calling (Tyne Tees TV/Live Theatre)
Posties (BBC Radio 4 Women's Hour)
The Black Path (Radio Three)
'Vermin' (BBC Tyne Online)
Sealife (BBC Radio 4 Philosophers/Think Tank)
Scraping the Sky (BBC Radio 4 Five Monologues)
Home Truths (BBC Radio 4 Write Out Loud)
She Hadda Fly (BBC Radio 4)
Snapping (BBC Radio 4 Write Out Loud)

Julia Darling

www.juliadarling.co.uk